P9-BUI-599

MURDER BY GRAVITY

A QUILTED MYSTERY

MURDER BY GRAVITY

THE COFFIN QUILT

BARBARA GRAHAM

FIVE STAR

A part of Gale, Cengage Learning

GALE
CENGAGE Learning®

Farmington Hills, Mich • San Francisco • New York • Waterville, Maine
Meriden, Conn • Mason, Ohio • Chicago

GALE
CENGAGE Learning®

LIBRARY OF CONGRESS CATALOGING-IN-PUBLICATION DATA

Graham, Barbara, 1948–
    Murder by gravity : the coffin quilt / Barbara Graham. — First edition.
      pages ; cm. — (A quilted mystery)
      ISBN 978-1-4328-2947-6 (hardcover) — ISBN 1-4328-2947-5 (hardcover)
    — ISBN 978-1-4328-2944-5 (ebook) — ISBN 1-4328-2944-0 (ebook)
      1. Sheriffs—Fiction. 2. Police—Tennessee—Fiction. 3. Quilting—Fiction.
    4. Tennessee—Fiction. I. Title.
    PS3607.R336M855 2014
    813'.6—dc23   2014027425

First Edition. First Printing: December 2014
Find us on Facebook– https://www.facebook.com/FiveStarCengage
Visit our website– http://www.gale.cengage.com/fivestar/
Contact Five Star™ Publishing at FiveStar@cengage.com

To the rescuers—of people, animals, and places

ACKNOWLEDGMENTS

I need to thank so many people for their assistance and patience during the writing of this book. It can't be altogether entertaining to listen to my whining about the mystery quilt or the characters not doing exactly what I ask them to do. It seems little to ask of imaginary friends that they behave at least as well as my real ones, but they don't.

Thanks to my husband, Dennis, who is willing to let me stab him in the back.

Thanks to my best friend, Michelle Quick, who is willing to test my mystery quilts even though she doesn't like them.

Thanks to my dogs, Max and Grace, who have heard the story in progress almost every morning during our walk at the lakes and still want to go there.

Thanks to my editor, Alice Duncan, who must wonder about the way my mind works.

THE COFFIN QUILT
A MYSTERY QUILT BY THEO ABERNATHY
FIRST BODY OF CLUES

Finished size is 72″ × 48″, which makes a long lap quilt. All fabric requirements are generous and based on standard widths of approximately 40 inches. The instructions assume familiarity with basic quilt construction techniques and the use of an accurate 1/4″ seam throughout.

Remember this is *your quilt*, not mine. If you yearn to use calicos, or jungle prints, or baby fabrics—go for it. No one is entitled to criticize your choices. When people show me the quilts they have made from my patterns, I am often blown away by their creative choices and find myself wishing I had done it like that. Have fun!

This quilt can be done in any color palette. For a more muted look, use varying shades of one color. The fabrics (A) and (D) should have the strongest contrast to the other colors.

Fabric requirements:

Fabric (A) is the main or theme fabric. Select a print on an uncluttered background or a solid (uncluttered in the sense that the motifs are not tiny and pressed against each other). 2 yards.

Fabric (B) accent color, reads as solid, goes well with a color in print (A). 2 yards.

Fabric (C) another print sharing colors from (A). 1 yard.

Fabric (D) a strong accent color—is much lighter or darker than fabric (A) or is a definite change of color and reads as solid. 2/3 yard.

Cutting instructions. Be sure to label each cut with color designation and size:

From fabric (A) Cut:

4 strips 4 1/2″ by LOF (length of fabric)
4 strips 2 1/2″ by LOF
1 strip 2 5/8″ by LOF—cut into 16 squares 2 5/8″
3 strips 2″ by LOF

From fabric (B) Cut:
4 strips 2 1/2″ by LOF
3 strips 2″ by LOF
7 squares 7 1/4″
14 squares 4″
28 squares 3 1/2″
14 squares 3″

From fabric (C) Cut:
16 squares 4″
28 squares 3 7/8″

From fabric (D) Cut:
4 squares 4 1/2″
32 squares 3 1/2″
14 squares 3″
16 squares 2 5/8″
4 squares 2 1/2″

CHAPTER ONE

The cold awakened Theo Abernathy. Hoping for warmth, she tried to snuggle closer to her oversized husband. Tony could usually heat the world, but he wasn't in their bed. His side was still warm so she moved into his spot and pulled the quilts higher around her ears, hoping it wasn't time to be up. Being married to the sheriff of Tennessee's smallest county meant never being quite sure where he was, when he left, or when he'd be back if he was called out in the night. If one of the children cried she heard it immediately; when his cell phone rang, she usually slept through it. She'd gotten plenty of practice ignoring calls during the first four years he'd been sheriff.

Her eyelids lifted slightly. Pale light seeped between the edges of the curtains, making a vertical line of white between the expanses of dark red and gold striped fabric. White? Ignoring the cold, Theo crawled out of the bed and scurried to the window to check. Snow before Halloween? Opening the curtains, she stared at the fairyland created by snow covering the trees and grass of the park across the street. They had been warned about a storm approaching, but when she went to bed, it was rain driven by howling winds. She guessed this newest weather change and Tony's disappearance were connected.

The boys trotted into the room, excitement in their eyes.

"Will they cancel school? I hope not." Chris looked disappointed. "We're supposed to have a party."

Theo knew he had worked hard on his Halloween costume

11

and was eager to show it off at the school. She had helped him cut head and arm holes in a cardboard box. The rest, the decorating, was all his work. He was going as a television—showing cartoons. Theo had to laugh. "It's still days before the party. The snow will melt."

"Where's Dad?" Jamie climbed onto the bed and pretended to look under the covers.

Theo knew Jamie would be thrilled to have school canceled. She guessed Jamie was already anticipating a snowball fight in the park. His plan for a Halloween costume wasn't much different from his usual clothes. Jamie planned to add a numbered football jersey and a helmet and magically morph into his current favorite player.

"Even if they cancel school for today, your party isn't until Halloween. There's still plenty of time for the weather to clear up." Theo, not knowing the answer to anything they'd asked, heard the twin girls fussing in their cribs.

The day was getting off to a rip-roaring start. She sincerely hoped school would not be canceled. If it was, she would have to take the boys to her quilt shop with her, and they would be bored within fifteen minutes. Entertaining two active children and two babies did not allow her to get much work done, and the new quilt pattern had to go to the printer today, tomorrow at the latest, so it would be available for the winter shoppers. Deadlines were not flexible. Mothers had to be.

"Please let this day be normal," Theo whispered out loud, and then laughed, having amused herself. She didn't know what normal looked like. Between her work, her family, her husband's work, and his extended family, they hadn't had more than a handful of days they might be able to call "normal" since they had moved back to Silersville, Tennessee, from Chicago.

★　★　★　★　★

Snowflakes drifted past his office window, surprising Sheriff Tony Abernathy. The forecast was rarely quite so accurate. Snow this early in the season was rare and unexpected. As long as it melted on the roads instead of freezing, it shouldn't cause too much trouble. Nothing seemed to bring out the "stupid" in the county residents like a half an inch of snow. There would likely be a heavier snowfall in the higher elevations. The Smoky Mountains with a coating of frost or snow could rival any Christmas card for sheer beauty.

The edge of a massive storm had brought them cold, driving rain that quickly turned to ice, and this snow was accurately predicted to follow. This autumn had been unusually warm, but now that was yesterday's news. If this storm continued to grow as predicted, there were bound to be power outages and a multitude of traffic accidents, plus his small department had many frail and elderly citizens to check on.

Silently thanking his secretary/assistant, Ruth Ann, for setting up a community listing of people in need—the elderly and impoverished—Tony hoped the system was working. He knew Ruth Ann couldn't have everyone on her radar, but probably most were. Up in the ageless Smoky Mountains, there were still roadless pockets of homes, ones filled with independent, but endangered, people. Even places where the mail carrier still arrived on a mule.

Tony's study of the beauty of nature ended abruptly when he spotted his deputy, Wade Claybough, standing in his office doorway. Normally Wade was good-looking enough to stop traffic, at least when women were driving. Today the younger man looked like he'd been locked in a room with a hungry lion. "What happened to you?"

Wade staggered into the room and fell, more than sat, onto a chair. "It's a dangerous world out there."

Tony's hand automatically reached for the telephone. "I'd better make sure the road crew is prepared."

Waving off the suggestion with one hand, Wade said, "It's not the roads, it's the crowd gathered to watch the football team and the cheerleaders winding through the town. This is just for homecoming. I can't wait for the Halloween parade."

Before Wade could say more, Rex Satterfield, the wizard on the dispatch desk, interrupted. "Sheriff, there is a multi-car pileup out on the highway, near Ruby's. Sheila and Mike are working another couple of accidents. Can you and Wade check this out?"

Minutes later, Tony stared at the cluster of vehicles blocking the road. Ice on the pavement seemed the obvious cause of the accident. Front bumpers tangled with door panels. The rear of a pickup dangled over a ditch. The assorted drivers stood together in a clump, chatting and pointing at something he couldn't see. A couple waved him over. They were smiling despite the fact that their back bumper was resting in a weedy ditch and the front bumper was aimed almost directly at the sky.

"When we tried to stop, there was no traction and we just slid off the road."

Cautiously making his way across the road, Tony soon understood. He was doing more ice skating than walking. He notified Rex to call out the sand truck while looking to see what damage there was and maybe learn what was making the drivers so cheerful.

The star of the show was a puppy. Standing on the slick pavement, homely enough to be totally endearing, was a mixture of collie and maybe bulldog. It had short bowed legs, a squashed face, and long hair. Thankfully, a round green rabies tag dangled from a leather collar. Tony knew it would have the owner's phone number on the back and make it easy to find the puppy's home. It ambled toward Tony with an odd rolling gait and sat on his left foot. He'd swear the puppy laughed when Tony lifted it into his Blazer instead of standing still and being its personal furniture. "Don't get comfortable. I'll take you home when I get this clog cleared up."

By the time the tow truck arrived and the road was cleared again, and he'd filled out enough paperwork to satisfy everyone, especially the insurance companies, the puppy had fallen asleep on the passenger seat. It snored and it drooled on the faux leather. Now Tony had a moment to check for an address or phone number on the tag, hidden under the heavy fur. The puppy's name was Sammy.

He dialed Sammy's number on his cell phone and a woman answered. When he identified himself and described his furry passenger, the woman laughed, a sound of great relief.

"Oh, thank you, thank you for rescuing her. Can I come get her?" The owner chattered on. "I don't know how she escaped."

Tony understood. He'd spent some time looking for his own dog on occasion. In her youth, Daisy had been an escape artist. "She's asleep in my car. If you give me your address, I can deliver."

Moments later, Tony pulled into a short driveway belonging to a modest home. The falling snow blowing around the side of the house was stacking mostly in the yard next door. The front door opened and a young woman with purple hair popped outside in her slippers, without a jacket. She did carry a leash. "Where's my naughty girl?"

Now wide awake on the front seat, Sammy began barking, wagging, and wetting all at the same time. The woman flushed with embarrassment and offered to get a towel.

"It's okay." Tony lifted the dog to the sidewalk and held onto her until the clasp on the leash clicked onto the collar ring. "I have what I need to clean it up. It won't take me but a moment." He waved the pair toward the house and pulled out the industrial tub of wipes he kept in the Blazer. It was far from the worst clean-up job he'd done in his vehicle this month. Hauling drunks was the worst.

"I found a hole under the fence." Sammy's owner kept a tight grip on the dog's leash but stayed near the Blazer. "That's how she got out." The woman frowned at the puppy. "No more digging."

The puppy's response was a noncommittal swipe of a tongue. No promise was made.

Tony climbed back into the Blazer. Before he could turn the key, Rex radioed to see if Tony could help with some frozen pipes. Every deputy, every firefighter, and every other person on the community volunteer list was already tied up. Tony agreed immediately.

The drive was short, and he was greeted by the elderly couple standing in their open doorway waiting for him. At least they were warmly dressed, in heavy coats, boots, and hats and gloves. The house was frigid inside. "Thank you for coming, Sheriff."

Tony nodded and went to work. His initial check of the cold water produced nothing. "If you think it might get this cold again, and now that winter's on the way that's very possible, you might leave the water running a bit." He turned the hot water handle and water trickled out. It was tepid. "Well, that's a good sign. The pipes aren't completely useless."

The couple nodded like toddlers. "Our son usually comes to turn on the heat, but he had to go to Nashville."

Tony was so relieved that they normally had assistance that he didn't mind slithering around in the half-frozen mud in their crawl space in order to light the pilot light. Smelling something a bit off made him look past the furnace. Puffed up like a balloon, a dead possum sharing the same space made him momentarily yearn to be sitting behind his desk. He had acres of paperwork he could be enjoying instead of this. He dragged the corpse out with him. Heating it would only make the stench worse. "Once the heat starts working its magic and the hot water melts some of the ice, your pipes should open up just fine."

Tony hadn't had breakfast and now his stomach was grumbling and gurgling complaints. The best solution he could come up with was having a big slice of apple pie at Ruby's café. He'd be able to work on his notes, eat, and catch up on local news. He hoped Blossom Flowers, the plus-size baking queen, wasn't letting her upcoming wedding keep her from the kitchen. She was the closest thing to a groupie he'd had, or ever expected to have. He was in luck.

Blossom waddled from the kitchen, delivering his prize in person. "I'm glad you got here when you did."

Tony couldn't help himself from asking, "What's the problem?"

"Oh, there's no problem. Yet." Blossom giggled, setting more than just her chins in motion. "I'm not baking again until after me and Kenny get back from our honeymoon."

Tony could hardly protest. She was entitled to some time off following the nuptials. He hoped it was a short trip.

CHAPTER TWO

"Uh, Sheriff?"

It was the hesitation in the question that fully caught Tony's attention. Looking up from his notebook, Tony was struck by the man's neatness. Standing before him in Ruby's Café was a middle-aged man wearing pressed jeans—with a crease, no less—polished loafers, and a bright orange Hawaiian shirt under a suede jacket. Not the usual attire worn by his county's residents, especially not on a snowy day. The oddly familiar face didn't immediately come with a name. "Yes?"

"I tracked you down." The man moved closer to Tony's table.

Tony found the phrasing interesting. More intriguing were the beads of perspiration on the man's forehead, and his flushed cheeks. The café was far from being too warm. His visitor was breathing hard. "What's the emergency?" Tony was halfway out of his chair when his visitor waved him down.

"No emergency." The man gasped and swallowed hard. He managed a half smile. "It's not like they are going to get any deader."

"More dead," Tony corrected silently. He tried to pretend the meaning of the words had not disturbed him. "Have a seat."

As the man settled into the chair across from him, Tony pushed his empty coffee mug to one side and turned to a clean page in his notebook. He noted the date and time. "Let's start with your name."

That did bring a jovial grin to his visitor's face. "Chuck Wilson. I guess we've both changed a bit since elementary school."

Tony laughed. "I had hair back then." The name put everything into place. Chuck and he had been good friends in fourth and fifth grade. They hadn't had a fight; as they grew older they just didn't share the same interests. Tony was all about sports and Chuck had his nose in books.

The café door opened and Wade walked in. The handsome deputy greeted everyone with a smile and made his way to Tony's table.

"Have a seat." Tony waited until Wade complied. "Mr. Wilson is about to tell us about our next new job for today. I trust it will be more exciting than traffic accidents and lighting pilot lights." He omitted the possum episode.

Wade's eyebrows lifted. "Sounds interesting." He pantomimed drinking coffee to Pinkie Millsaps, the morning cook who was doing double-duty as waitress. Two more mugs of steaming black coffee arrived in seconds.

While waiting for the coffee, Chuck Wilson had been carefully breathing, gradually calming himself so he could speak. "The wife and I recently moved back to Tennessee from Minnesota. Better winters and lower taxes." His smile widened. "Plus, we're closer to our families. My mom's in a care home in Knoxville and Sherrill's originally from Pigeon Forge."

Tony didn't interrupt. There was something innately competent and organized about the man, and clearly he was shaken.

"We're renting a small place for the moment, but we'll move out of the old house and into a bigger newer house after the current owner gets a few things fixed." Chuck started breathing hard again and paused to wipe the sweat from his face. His shaking hands made the task harder. "My wife's afraid of spiders, so she sent me down into the old root cellar. I'm the gofer who's supposed to clean it out so she can store, you know, roots I guess."

Wade suggested the man drink some water. The glass had been in front of Chuck for a while but he hadn't seemed to notice it.

Chuck used both hands to lift the glass and still the water sloshed over the rim but he managed to swallow some. "I've got this big orange cat who thinks it is fun to wrap himself around my neck like a fur collar and ride around everywhere I go."

At that departure from their topic, Tony's mouth opened, but, before he could say anything, Chuck continued.

"So we're down in the root cellar, the cat and me, and I'm kinda hunched over, when suddenly the cat leaps from my neck and runs through a space down there. It looked like a big mouse hole to me. The cat won't come out and I'm waving the flashlight around and slapping the wall and suddenly pieces are falling off and I find out it's some kind of a false wall. I pulled a board loose and there's my cat s-sitting on b-bones." He paused, heaving for breath again. "Bones. There's bones. Human bones."

Tony didn't ask why he was so sure. Human skeletons were pretty distinctive. "Did it smell bad?"

"N-no. At least I didn't notice it." Chuck managed a few more gulps of water. "I was so shocked to see a skull, I didn't notice much else."

Tony guessed the bones had been down there a long time. "Why didn't you just call me?" Tony looked around the café. "Why come here?"

Chuck sat silent, wide-eyed. "I, uh . . ."

"Okay, let's try this question." Tony thought "shock" was the correct answer to his previous question. "Where is the house?"

"Oh, I didn't tell you, did I? I live just across the road and up a little." Chuck finally seemed a bit less panicky. "One of your deputies, a girl, visits my neighbor sometimes. As you're going up the hill, his house is to the right, mine is to the left and down a bit."

"The old house?" Tony could visualize the row of newer homes and the much older home that had been there forever.

"Yes." Chuck smiled. "A very old house."

"I know that house," Wade said. "My best friend in the first grade lived in there. His name was Billy Bob Buchanan."

"Mr. Buchanan is my landlord." Chuck seemed a little puzzled. "I thought his name was William."

Wade nodded. "Oh yes, he's officially William Robert, but he was always Billy Bob when we were in school."

Tony let the name game flow around him thinking it was funny how today's conversation seemed to connect so many people from the past. The mundane name story would distract Chuck, and maybe he wouldn't stroke out on them. Once he settled down, he'd most likely slap himself in the forehead for not being able to process Bobby being familiar for Robert. Tony pulled a couple of antacids from his shirt pocket and chewed them slowly.

It wasn't the first time someone had found human bones around here. This section of East Tennessee had several old settlements even before the town was founded. Many souls had passed on and many more had been born. Gardens had been planted over unmarked graves. But this situation was new to him.

Bones inside a root cellar. What were the odds of the house being built on top of an old burial ground? Remote to none. Some group or another would have mentioned it by now or passed around a petition for preservation. Plus, putting bodies in a root cellar was not the same as burying them.

Tony decided it was too late to quit his job. If this situation had come up in the summer, he could have either not run for reelection or he could have come out in support of his idiot opponent. Matt Barney made dirt look smart. So now, Tony had almost four more years left to serve. On top of the wacky weather and buried bones, Halloween was almost here. Oh, goody, a skeleton for Halloween. What kind of horror stories would arise from this? One thing the citizens of Park County had plenty of, was imagination.

"Let's go over and have a look, shall we?" Tony rose to his feet. Wade and Chuck jumped up to follow him.

It took them maybe five minutes to get to the house. Most of that time was waiting for traffic on the highway to clear so they could cross it.

Chuck led the way down the rickety ladder into the root cellar. As he had described it, the space was small. Twentieth-century shelving leaning against one wall was empty except for a few canning jars filled with green beans, at least that's what they appeared to be through the thick coating of dust. The three men standing took up all the floor space in the main area. Two of them had to press against the wall to let the third one bend over and peer into the tiny chamber containing the bones.

Being careful not to touch anything, Tony was folded in half as he studied the bones. To him, it looked like at least three complete skeletons neatly lined up side by side. Two were smaller than the third one. He thought maybe there was a fourth one, but he couldn't be sure without disturbing the others. Shards of rotten fabric were strewn about, but the bones themselves seemed undisturbed. His immediate impression was of nonviolent death. He saw no apparent damage like bullet holes in the skulls or shattered limbs. The bodies had most certainly not been thrown into the cellar and landed in this position.

"We'll leave them here for now," Tony decided after some consideration. "Wade, why don't you take some photographs and I'll call and see if the TBI is interested in antiques." Not for the first time, Tony was thankful the Tennessee Bureau of Investigation was prepared to lend a hand to the investigations in smaller counties. His county, Park County, was the smallest geographically, but not in either staff or crime. "And, after you get your photographs, Wade, let's go chat with your old friend Billy Bob."

Tony shook hands with Chuck and promised to stay in touch.

On her way to her quilt shop, Theo remembered she had promised to stop by the county dump and check on her friend Katti Marmot. The Russian mail-order bride was almost due to deliver her first child. When Theo had been pregnant with the twins and confined to a wheelchair, Katti had been her assistant and the women had bonded. Theo was anxious to see what Katti had decided to do about decorating the nursery. Katti professed not to know the gender of the new little Marmot and the mother's passion for all things pink had created a lot of community interest in her nursery decorations.

Katti was happy to see her. "You had two." She patted her own huge belly. "How you sleep?"

"I didn't sleep." Theo had brought the twins inside with her and released them near Katti. The girls immediately smiled and reached for Katti, who cooed and blew kisses at them. "How can I help you?"

Katti ignored the question. "Come see baby Valentine's nest."

Whether the baby would actually be named Valentine remained to be seen. The parents-to-be had referred to their unborn offspring as Valentine from the beginning.

Since the day he'd decided to find a mail-order bride, garbage guru Claude Marmot had added onto his tiny house, twice. Using scraps of this and rescued pieces of that, he had tripled the space. It was still small. A tiny alcove created by the bedroom addition had now become the nursery.

The walls in the nursery alcove were painted a joyous pink. Not a timid pale pink but one requiring more than a single coat to bring it to its full depth. Katti had called it "Valentine Rose."

Theo, something of a color expert, called it "dark flamingo."

Frilly white tieback curtains covered the window, splitting over a roll-down shade. The shade itself was pale pink, but it had been carefully hand-painted with white bunnies, green grass and trees, and a pair of brilliant blue birds. The nearby cradle glistened with glossy white paint. Theo couldn't guess what its original purpose had been. It might have begun as anything from a lobster trap to an antique nail barrel, but now it was a perfect cradle hanging in a stand made from a tree branch. "It's beautiful, Katti." And it was.

"See the blanket." Katti's smile was luminous as she fluffed the cradle's contents. "My Valentine thanks you."

Theo laughed. It had taken very little time for her to make the small blanket of lusciously soft plush fabric. It was napped like thick velvet but softer. Theo had put pink plaid on one side and mint green on the other. Predictably, the pink side was facing up.

CHAPTER THREE

Tony and Wade found William Robert Buchanan, aka Billy Bob, without difficulty. He had moved away from Silersville but not too far. He was now Professor William Buchanan at Maryville College. According to the plaque on the wall next to his office door, his field was psychology.

"Come in, come in," Wade's friend enthusiastically greeted them. "I just love to learn how people think. We're like seashells and snowflakes, you know, no two are exactly the same. Not even identical twins."

Tony sat back and let Wade and Billy Bob chat and reminisce for a bit and then slipped in a question. "Do you own your parents' old house in Silersville now?"

"Oh, no." Billy Bob relaxed in his professorial leather chair and steepled his fingers. "I'm only the landlord. When my folks moved to coastal Georgia, they appointed me their agent."

"How long ago?" said Wade.

"Oh, gosh, it's been maybe five years now. They didn't want to sell the house, in case living in Georgia didn't work out and they decided they wanted to move back." Billy Bob rolled his eyes like a teenager. "Now they think selling it will be the best plan. I'm just the middleman and feel a bit like a Ping-Pong ball."

Tony worked the timeline out in his head. The Buchanans had moved away about a year before he was elected sheriff the first time. Tony guessed he'd be chatting with their former sheriff, Harvey Winston, before long. The old man's mind was still sharp and his memory for people had always been outstanding. "You don't want the family home for yourself?"

"Not really. I thought about it a lot." Billy Bob's shoulders rose and fell. "It's not a huge drive from here so we could commute, but there's miles of stairs in the house and my wife's already talking about having her hips replaced. She's barely thirty but she already has this terrible arthritis, and the fewer stairs she has to climb, the happier she is."

"And the rest of your family, they're good with selling the old place?" Wade asked. "I mean, they do know what you're planning?"

Billy Bob's grin widened. "You mean because I'm trying to sell a house that's been in the family for over a hundred and fifty years and comes with a ghost?"

Tony nodded.

"Yes. It *is* hard. I love the old place, but I don't want to live there and I'm the last of my immediate family line." He laced his fingers together and rested them on his desk. As he leaned forward, all trace of humor vanished from his face. "I've thought long and hard about this and talked with my folks until we are all sick to death of the subject. We want to see the house owned by people who love it. People who will plant flowers in the window boxes each spring and mow the yard. And paint. Gallons of paint. You know what it is like with these old houses. Maintenance is a nightmare."

Tony did know. He loved his wife's old family house. In fact, it was the oldest brick home in the county, and her family had lived there for generations. Now he and Theo had added a new addition to it and had destroyed its historical purity. One of the topics raised by his opponent during the August election had been the new addition. The historical preservationists group was headed for them with torches and shovels, but luckily his opponent was worse than a cartoon figure or Tony might have lost his job. "I do know."

"So, what do we do about the skeletons down there?" Billy Bob had been totally surprised when they'd described the situation. "I had no idea there was a false wall, but then, it was mostly my mom and grandmother who used the space."

"Your new renter was certainly upset by the discovery." Tony met Billy Bob's steady gaze.

"No kidding. That's quite an understatement. Did you know they called me and cancelled the lease before you arrived today?" Billy Bob shook his head. "I was shocked, you know, just when you think you can guess what people will do or say, they just blow you away."

Tony found it surprising as well. It wasn't like they had found something grisly and nasty in the bedroom closet. He said, "I've called the TBI. We're supposed to collect the remains and the surrounding dirt and anything else down there that might tell us who these people are, or were, and how they came to be dead and not even actually buried in the root cellar."

"And then?"

"Since this is not a crime scene, we're to ship it all to some anthropologists." The Tennessee Bureau of Investigation supplied forensic assistance to the local sheriff's departments. Tony had taken a fair amount of ribbing in the past, with TBI people calling Park County the murder capital of Tennessee, but he couldn't fault the work they did. All those man-hours and state of the art equipment were invaluable. Without them, his forensics would be radically different. He might be able to solve some of his cases without their help, but any halfway competent defense attorney would have a field day with them.

Billy Bob leaned forward. "I can remember my grandmother climbing up and down this old ladder into the lowest area. The ladder didn't look like it could support two June bugs, but

Gram liked to keep her jars of beans and jam down there. I went most of the way down once; it was dark and narrow and then kind of opened up, and there were a couple of shelves. It was cool down there, but it creeped me out. I kept expecting some giant mutant bugs or rats to attack us."

"Anything else you might recall from the past that might have been connected to the old house or the cellar?" Tony looked at his notes. "You mentioned a ghost."

"I always thought the place had a ghost, but it was in the house, not the cellar."

"Rattling chains in the dark?" Tony was surprised. The man did not seem like a believer in the supernatural. "Screams in the night?"

"No." Billy Bob closed his eyes, almost like he was listening to the past. "It was rather benevolent. Like old family members checking on the new ones, keeping watch. Whispers." He grinned. "No screams, moans, or chains."

Tony wasn't sure if he believed in ghosts. "Did they visit often?"

Billy Bob's eyes opened and he blinked against the sudden light. "No. There were just times when they dropped by for a visit. Except for when my mom was so sick with pneumonia, they came every night during that episode. Keeping a vigil, I guess. They didn't come back for a long time once she recovered."

Wade said, "But you didn't live there full-time when you were a child, did you?"

"No." Billy Bob shrugged. "Our family had a different house. After my grandparents passed away, then we moved in there. But even when I was younger, I probably slept as many nights in that house as I did our own."

★　★　★　★　★

In the wide and complicated world of annoyances, petty to major, Theo thought getting a grocery cart with a wonky wheel raced to the top of the list once it was too late to exchange it. The twins filled up most of the basket, leaving the seat and the underneath shelf for delicate grocery items like eggs. The girls couldn't damage cans. Theo chatted with them and laughed, even as she stacked tuna and soup cans around their chubby legs.

As Theo struggled to turn the increasingly awkward cart down the next aisle, she barely tapped a display of Halloween treats with one corner of the cart. In seconds, the entire cardboard tower filled with popcorn balls—dyed orange to look like jack-o'-lanterns—flipped onto its side. The cellophane wrappers kept the treats clean, but they managed to roll, awkwardly, an amazing distance down one aisle and toward the checkout area.

Children, including hers, were shrieking and clapping. Ones not confined to a cart either picked the balls up or kicked them like soccer balls until a parent stopped them. Theo watched as an older couple was laughing too hard to pick up the popcorn balls at their feet. She thought, as much entertainment as she had brought to the assembled shoppers and staff, that maybe she should take a bow. It was chaos, and yet during the height of the confusion, Theo suddenly felt a breath of warm air waft across the back of her neck, like someone had deliberately breathed on her skin. The sensation was paradoxically chilling.

Theo shivered and turned to see who was behind her. No one. At least, no one who seemed close enough to blow on her neck. She couldn't identify the source, and the movement of the air had stopped. Gone as though it never happened. Theo glanced back at the shopping cart. A folded piece of yellow paper rested on the top of her eggs and bread. It had not been there seconds earlier. Simple curiosity made her open it.

"There's a private investigator posing as a victim of domestic violence. Trust no one." The note was unsigned.

The grocery store was neither large nor crowded. Even so, Theo couldn't guess which shopper had delivered the message and didn't try to determine the identity. Theo absolutely understood what the meaning of the message was and why it was delivered to her.

Theo quickly pulled her cell phone from her purse and, with shaking fingers, pushed the buttons to make a call. As she waited for the call to be answered, she noticed a woman slowly walking past her, carefully steering her cart to avoid the scattered popcorn balls and the people cleaning them up. Theo had seen the woman before, but they had not actually met. Had this woman delivered the message?

Her call was connected and Theo spoke without preamble, "I just received an anonymous note claiming there's a spy. Keep an eye out." She pressed the "call end" button and continued to watch the woman and the cart. Trying to think about six things at one time clogged her brain for a moment, and then suddenly she really focused on what she was seeing. Surprised, she spoke out loud. "There's a knife sticking out of that woman's back."

Theo hurried after the woman, the increase in cart speed making the girls scream with delight, especially as the wonky wheel made a straight line impossible to steer. Theo almost crashed the cart into another display. "Ma'am?" No response, so Theo tried calling out to her again, louder. "Ma'am?"

Stopping to gaze at Theo, a look of confusion and inquiry crossed the woman's tired face. "Are you talking to me?"

Theo's head was bobbing up and down. "How can I help you? Are you all right?"

"Absolutely. And yourself?" Lovely but sad, large dark eyes met Theo's and the woman smiled politely. She looked decades younger when she smiled.

Theo blurted out, "Yes, but I don't have a knife stuck in *my* back." Even as the words tumbled from her lips Theo regretted her unfortunate tendency to let her thoughts spill uncensored from her lips. Surely she could have phrased it better, or at least not all but shouted at the poor woman.

"What are you saying?" The woman turned her head from side to side as if trying to see down her own back. She must have finally seen the handle protruding from her heavy sweater. "Oh, my." She swayed on her feet, clinging to the cart handle, obviously dizzy.

Theo knew she couldn't support the shopper's full weight but helped the woman slide down until she sat on the floor before pressing the "emergency call" button on her phone. What would she do without her cell phone? She used it often, but was not chained to it.

"Theo?" Rex was working the dispatch desk. "What's the emergency?"

"I'm fine." Theo also thought caller ID was a wonderful invention in this situation. "I'm at Food City, in the aisle with canned soups, and there's a woman here who has obviously been stabbed in the back. The knife's still embedded in it, but she's unconscious now."

"Please stay on the phone." Rex's voice was quiet but authoritative.

Obligingly, Theo kept her phone pressed to one ear. Seconds later, Rex returned to her call.

"Okay, Theo, the ambulance is on the way and so is Mike," Rex said. "Please stay there until they arrive."

"Don't worry, I'll wait." It didn't take long. One advantage of living in such a small community was that it didn't take very long to get from one side of it to the other. The clinic and ambulance bay were only a few blocks from the store.

Still, by the time the ambulance crew made it into the grocery store with their gurney, a small crowd of curious onlookers had jostled until everyone who wanted to watch was close enough to do so. There was no small talk between the paramedics and anyone else. Instead, they focused on the unconscious woman. After checking her condition, they talked quietly to each other briefly, and then into their radios before they carefully placed her on the gurney. They kept her on her side and packed her like crystal, making sure she couldn't roll and push against the knife. No one touched the knife.

Deputy Mike Ott made his way through the little crowd to Theo's side. He smiled. "I'm sure you don't seek out these situations."

"I know." Theo gave a little laugh and a shrug. "It's a gift."

"Want to tell me what you saw in here or we could go outside or—?" Mike herded her and the girls away from the crowd watching the paramedics.

"Here. Let's get it done quickly. You're busy and I still need a few more grocery items." Theo didn't give Mike time to finish his question. "There really isn't much to tell. I was just doing my shopping and noticed there was a knife sticking out of the woman's back and I asked her if she needed help or something along those lines. If you want to know what I think, I don't think she had a clue the knife was there until I mentioned it."

Mike's expression changed from professional curiosity to amazement. "How could she not know?"

"Beats me, but she didn't." Theo shivered a bit; the shock and adrenalin of the episode were fading and now she felt chilled. "As soon as I pointed it out to her, she became faint and then collapsed."

"Do you know her?"

"Not by name. I think she is new in town, and she always looks sad whenever I do see her."

"So you don't know her name or who, if anyone, is a relative?" Mike frowned as he worked on his notes.

"No." Theo couldn't imagine a sadder situation. A potentially serious injury and no family. At least not one they knew about. "You'll have to ask someone else."

CHAPTER FOUR

Tony stood on the sidewalk outside Theo's quilt shop. He was momentarily distracted from his curiosity about his wife's whereabouts by a citizen, Nem, the egg man, who stopped him on the sidewalk. Theo didn't usually take a long time to run her errands, so Tony assumed she'd return in a few minutes. In the meantime, he was forced to bend over at the waist in order to hear what one of his favorite "old guys" was saying. The elderly gentleman was regaling him with a story of an autumn blizzard that had hit when the old man was a boy. Tony wouldn't be surprised if the man's recollection of the depth of the snow was adjusted to fit the length of his legs at the time, but maybe not.

From the corner of his eye, Tony watched as the unmistakable figure of a chunky woman, Bathsheba Cartwright, definitely not his tiny wife, charged in their direction. Trapped. Tony wouldn't just walk away in the middle of the old man's story, and he doubted this woman would shy away from interrupting them. He couldn't quite suppress a groan.

The old guy peered around, checking to see what Tony was watching. No explanation was necessary. "She's coming at us like a runaway train. Uh-oh, she's almost here. We could go inside."

Tony thought the old guy's expression hid nothing. The elderly man and the middle-aged woman had clearly collided somewhere. Whatever their history was, he surmised it had not ended on a high note. They made it two steps closer to the quilt-shop door.

"Oh, Sheriff!" The woman, Bathsheba, sounded relieved to have caught them. "Nem." She barely acknowledged the elderly man's presence and quickly turned to concentrate her intense gaze on Tony, dismissing Nem. "We need to talk. We have important plans to make, you and I."

"Pardon me?" Tony studied her face. Excitement, not fear, lit her dark eyes. "Plans?"

"Certainly. I can't have you and that gorgeous Wade Claybough stepping into my investigation. The sooner I can get started, the sooner order will be restored." Bathsheba paused, her breath depleted, and inhaled through her gaping mouth. "Don't worry, there's nothing for you to do in this investigation. I'll handle the whole thing."

Tony didn't know what she was talking about but knew he wouldn't like it, whatever it was. He leaned closer, staring into her eyes. "Don't get involved."

"Nonsense." She patted his shoulder. "I've already begun."

He watched with some curiosity as the much shorter woman managed to look down her nose at him. Given that he was quite a bit taller than she was, he found it intriguing but not enough to amuse him. Not even his mother patted his shoulder like that. "Stay out of my department's business."

"Nonsense. I have every reason to volunteer." Digging through her voluminous purse, Bathsheba didn't look up and actually laughed at his words. "I see it on television every day. Citizens like me helping the clearly incompetent police get to the bottom of crime. You should be thrilled I'm here to help you."

"Incompetent? Help me?" Tony blinked, hoping he would quickly awaken from this nightmare. "Television?"

Nem, the egg man, the elderly gentleman he'd been chatting with, suddenly burst into wild laughter. Wobbling, the senior citizen almost stepped off the curb and would have fallen into the street if Tony hadn't quickly reached out a hand, grasped the old guy's elbow, and hauled him back onto the sidewalk. Still chuckling, the old man whispered. "She thinks she's Miss Marple."

"Not even Agatha Christie would send Miss Marple into this county." Tony frowned again at the woman. "Are you writing a book by chance?"

"I intend to." She appeared to be confiding in him as she brandished a notebook and pen she'd retrieved from the voluminous bag. "As soon as I solve this first case, I'll dictate the whole story to my secretary. I'll be much too busy with personal appearances to type the whole thing myself."

Momentarily distracted by the picture she painted, Tony repeated, "Your secretary?"

"Oh, yes, I'm sure the publishers will supply one." She blinked. "I can't be expected to actually write it all down myself. Silly man."

Tony was reminded of the book he was working on himself. It took enormous amounts of time and energy, but he continued to plow forward. He had neither a secretary nor a contract, and none of the professional authors he'd met professed to having such assistance. If there was a secretary, it was the author who paid the salary. "I'll say this again. Stay out of my department's business." The ringing of his cell phone gave him a good excuse to turn his back to the woman and walk away.

"Yes, Rex?"

"Sir, your wife just called to report a woman with a knife stuck in her back at Food City. I sent Mike over. I imagine they might still be there."

Tony found his wife in an aisle of Food City, surrounded by chaos. She was talking to Mike Ott and moved the shopping cart continuously to keep the twins occupied. "Theo, honey."

"No." Theo glanced at him and shook her head vigorously, the movement flinging a golden curl over one eye. She swept it back into place. "Don't 'Theo, honey' me like I am somehow responsible for this."

The force of her anger was a surprise, he guessed, even to herself. "What happened?"

"I did not stab that woman. It is not my fault."

"I never thought it was." Tony backed away a few inches, checking the woman on the stretcher, now being pushed toward the front of the store by the paramedics. They handed him the woman's purse. He guessed something else was really upsetting Theo. "Do you know this woman?"

"Not her name, but I've seen her around town a little, usually here shopping for food." She watched Tony glance around, studying the faces of the curious. To her, in spite of the variety of shapes, ages, and colors, their expressions looked similar—curiosity mixed with shock and concern.

"Sheriff, look at this." One of the paramedics pointed to the knife in the woman's back.

Tony leaned forward and Theo did as well. He snapped a couple of pictures with his cell phone. The handle of the knife protruded from her, but the blade was buried all the way in to the guard.

"Yikes." Theo backed away. "I hadn't really looked before."

"There is almost no sign of bleeding." The lead paramedic squinted, looking up at Tony. "What's really weird is the blood has already dried against the blade and it looks like it formed a seal, so it's been in there for a while."

"It's a good thing you're leaving it in." Tony waved them on their way.

"I am. We'll transport her to the clinic and let the doctors decide the next move." The two paramedics quickly wheeled their patient toward the door. The sea of spectators parted to let them pass. Tony said, "We'll check the store's security recording but I'm guessing from your description, she arrived with the knife in place already." He opened the woman's purse and pulled out her ID, an expired Kentucky driver's license and a handful of cash. "Either she's driving around without a license or she lives close enough to walk here."

"That looks like a lot of cash." Theo leaned closer. "Unless it's all ones."

Tony flipped through it, counting. "Forty-eight dollars. One five and the rest is ones." He made a notation in his notebook and then sealed the cash in an evidence bag he extracted from one of his pockets. "If the motive was robbery, it was unsuccessful. Unless she started out with more."

Tony sat in Ruby's Café trying to concentrate on his notes when a couple of voices intruded. The booth he occupied was turning into his office away from his official office. He needed food, lots of food, to keep up with the demands of the day.

"I don't like to talk behind my boss's back." Tony couldn't see the woman's face. She sat with her back to him.

"But?" Her male companion was middle-aged and looked bored. Tony thought he looked familiar but couldn't place him.

"Well, don't you think it's a bit peculiar for a married man to be shopping for engagement rings on the Internet?" The woman's voice dropped. "I saw him."

"Couldn't it just be a gift for his wife?"

"His wife already wears a rock. What's she going to do with another one, 'n' besides," the woman exhaled heavily. "I've heard him whispering to someone on the phone at the same time that I've been talking with his wife. They both work within ten feet of me."

Overhearing this conversation, Tony thought, "Not my business." It wasn't the first time Tony wished he could unhear something unpleasant about the people around him. Couldn't they be more considerate?

"Well, it's not my business either, but I can't help what I hear." The woman's voice was increasingly strident.

"Twice in one day, Sheriff?" Pinkie Millsaps collected the menu. "What'll it be?"

Tony placed his food order with Pinkie, wondering if it would turn out to be a late lunch or early dinner. A bowl of hot stew and fluffy biscuits sounded like a good way to get warm again. So far today he'd dealt with accidents, a lost dog, frozen pipes, and several vehicles needing help starting. A stabbing in the grocery store. Not to mention several skeletons. The TBI didn't need to come but Vince, who had helped Tony's department before, wanted to come observe. Simple curiosity. He would arrive when he could.

Most of the other incidents had been easily taken care of, or postponed, except the stabbing. The old couple with the frozen pipes had neither the money to pay for a plumber nor the foresight to leave the water running just a bit. Warmer now and with water for washing and drinking, their situation had improved. He did add their names to Ruth Ann's master list of people in the community who needed to be checked on when the weather turned against them, in case their son was away. It would be easier to drop by and check on them than to fix the problem when they were swamped.

Mike Ott slid into the seat opposite him. Tony had thought his deputy looked tired when he'd seen him only minutes earlier in Food City; he looked even worse now. The new father worked long hours and, as Tony knew only too well, a new baby and a good night's sleep were not generally words used in combination.

Mike stared into Tony's coffee cup before looking up, his lips curved into a smile. "Do you ever get used to having your family involved in episodes?"

"Episodes? That's an interesting word. What's up?" Tony grinned. "That is, besides you, Ruby, and Mary Olivia?" Tony didn't have the heart to tease the exhausted father by using the beautiful baby girl's initials—MOO. The family had received a number of cow-themed gifts.

His own initials, MAA for Marc Antony Abernathy, had garnered him any number of unwanted, unappreciated, and not terribly creative nicknames. It had not created in him the desire to inflict such things on other people, and certainly not on perfectly innocent babies.

Mike's red-rimmed eyes spoke volumes.

"Look on the bright side." Tony grinned. "At least Mary Olivia is not twins." It hadn't been that long since his two youngest children began sleeping through the night. For months the two baby girls had taken turns being awake, almost like they felt a duty to deprive their parents of as much sleep as possible.

Mike blinked, but his eyes didn't seem to focus on anything. "I don't know how you've survived four children. It's harder than it looks."

"Well, for starters, they have never all four cried at the same time," Tony said. "And, to be fair, Theo is the one left with the mob when I get called out. She's tiny but tough. I'm not sure I would have survived if we reversed the roles."

"Well, sir, I've never associated you with the word 'delicate,' but I'll agree with your assessment of your wife." He took a mug of coffee offered to him. "She is tough. And calm in an emergency."

"Sheriff?" Rex said. "I've got a report that someone has found Boston's dog."

"Without Boston?" Tony could tell his lunch break was over.

Time to get back to the chaos of work.

"Yessir. I thought you'd want to know." Rex's normally eerily calm voice sounded worried.

"Thank you." Most of what Tony knew about newcomer Boston Quist was that he was a veteran who settled in their county but remained a homeless man. All efforts to assist him with finding housing had failed. Not that there wasn't any housing; Boston just said he couldn't stand sleeping inside a building where he couldn't see the sky and wouldn't move into any place they'd found for him. Boston was apparently harmless, and his dog was vaccinated, licensed, and Boston's constant companion. Tony had frequently encountered the pair in the park across the street from his own house. He'd seen them, each wearing a pack, down by the creek, and at various places around town, including dining on the back deck at Ruby's Café. Only at Food City did Boston leave his dog outside and alone. Finding the dog without the man was cause for concern. "Where was the dog?"

"Out on Mulberry Lane, near one of those new homes." Rex paused. "The call was made by Mrs. Dixon, you know, the veterinarian's wife. The house number is twelve fifteen."

"I'll check into it. Have Wade meet me there."

Minutes later, Tony headed toward Mulberry Lane. It was a short road, just outside of town, and there were only six houses on it. His department checked the area regularly, as a matter of course with patrols, but the residents were quiet and he'd never needed to be in any of the houses. House number twelve fifteen was a large gray stone house on a several acre lot. Well-manicured grass and old trees and flowerbeds, now dormant, spoke of constant care. He parked on the driveway and climbed out. Inside a fenced yard directly behind the house, four dogs of varying sizes and breeds welcomed his arrival with a symphony of barking and tail wagging.

Wade was already there, parked to the side and waiting for him. "What's up?"

"Mrs. Dixon called to report finding Boston's dog."

Wade pressed his lips together and glanced away but not before Tony saw the flash of concern cross his face. "But not Boston?"

Tony knew that Wade, even more than himself and his other deputies, checked on Boston, making sure he was eating and taking his medications. Tony had been in the Navy, Wade the Marines, and Boston was Army. The gist of it was they were all military veterans. Any or all of them could have ended up like Boston.

Mrs. Dixon, a forty-something woman with prematurely gray hair, trotted around the corner of the house and waved for them to join her. The dog, not one of the pack in the yard but carefully tied to a tree near the side of a shed, was a Belgian Malinois. A full bowl of water was set next to the tree. The dog was apparently healthy, except for an old, healed injury to one paw, and clearly well-fed and cared for. His intelligent face bore an anxious expression, but he allowed the woman to pet him.

Tony thought people who said dogs had no expressions or feelings were stupid. This dog was intelligent—and worried.

Mrs. Dixon studied Tony and Wade. "Have you seen Boston?"

"No, at least not today." Tony held a hand out to the dog, who sniffed it and stepped back. They'd encountered each other many times but had never been formally introduced. "What's his name?"

"Mouse."

"Not an accurate name, is it?" Tony knew the dog was smart, protective, and very well-trained. Professionally. As if realizing they were there to help, Mouse now stood quietly watching them all with intelligent, large dark eyes.

Mrs. Dixon smiled, but the worry didn't leave her face.

"Boston often sleeps back here." She turned and led them all in the direction she had come from.

"How did you meet him?" Wade moved to Tony's far side.

"At first, we met at the park. We talked about dogs because he had Mouse and I had a couple of my dogs with me. Later, I found him sleeping here one morning." Mrs. Dixon stopped near a small shed. "It was raining, and he was under the overhang." She smiled at the memory. "In spite of his name, Mouse has a very impressive growl."

Tony tried to place when he'd first become aware of the pair. "How long ago was this?"

"Maybe four, five months." Mrs. Dixon shrugged. "We offered him the guesthouse in exchange for yard chores." She pointed to a small structure. "I think he stores some of his things in there, but I don't think he has ever slept inside. He does use it for a mailing address."

"Let's have a look." Tony led Wade away and left Mouse with Mrs. Dixon.

"Why would he leave his dog?" Keeping his voice low, Wade glanced back at the duo.

"He wouldn't. At least not without a very good reason." Tony felt positive of that. Mouse was Boston's friend, family, and responsibility. He didn't have any facts, but he was pretty sure Mouse was a war veteran too. "Use your radio. Have everyone looking for Boston."

Wade complied. "There's a place I've often seen Boston, but he always had Mouse with him."

"What if we just turn Mouse loose? Don't you think the dog would find him for us?" Tony watched the dog pacing on his tether. He looked like a parent waiting for an overdue teenager.

Wade considered the question. "I think he'd take off like a shot. He might find Boston, but I doubt we could keep up with him, and he's sure not going to listen to any command either of us might give him."

"We don't need to lose both of them." Tony talked to dispatch. "Just let me know if someone spots Boston. Call it a wellness check."

CHAPTER FIVE

Tony noticed Deputy Sheila Teffeteller yawning as she filled out her endless paperwork. Reports, citations, and descriptions had to be detailed and accurate or the lawyer for the defense would tear the case apart. His only female deputy wrote the most lucid, organized reports he'd ever read. Once he had suggested she give the male deputies a workshop on the subject, which she had respectfully and adamantly refused to do. He couldn't blame her. It would be hard work and unlikely to produce the desired result.

"Sleep seems to be in short supply in our department this week." Tony frowned, seeing nearly as much fatigue on her face as he'd seen on Mike's. "What's keeping you up?"

"Nothing particular." Sheila blinked. "It's the season. Now that fall has arrived, I feel like Baby, wanting to eat continuously so I can pack on the extra pounds and hibernate."

Now that she mentioned it, Baby, the black bear, had looked a little heavier the most recent time Tony had encountered her with her human companions—not owners, for she was too wild—Roscoe and Veronica. The romance between Roscoe Morris, an odd job man, and Veronica, a college professor, seemed to be continuing happily, despite their educational differences. Baby had quickly adjusted to her new home, the woods behind the "log cabin" the couple had purchased. The cabin was in fact a two-story structure, quite large, and was built on fifty acres of land bordering the national park.

Roscoe and the professor's small wedding ceremony had taken place on the back deck, overlooking the woods. Baby was dressed formally for the event, which meant a white satin bow had been tied around her neck. At the end of the ceremony, Veronica and Roscoe had launched a paper bag filled with rice, confetti, and birdseed with their medieval-style trebuchet. When the paper bag struck the intended target, a packing crate painted white for the occasion, the bag burst, sending the contents flying.

A cheer from the observers celebrated the hit. The groom kissed the bride and received an even louder cheer.

A few of the other members of the couple's vegetable warfare group had traveled long distances with cannons and medieval devices designed to fling edibles and gave the happy couple a twenty-one vegetable salute. Squash, pumpkins, and a few apples spattered the packing crate. Applause, whistles, and shouts accompanied each strike.

Cheering loudest had been a flock of birds, lined up on a split-rail fence, waiting for their chance to nibble on the tasty bits of food.

Tony thought it was the most unique and entertaining wedding he'd ever attended, and reminded him it had been awhile since he'd seen any of the Morris family. It also reminded him that Boston had attended the Morris wedding. He'd been one of several veterans driven out to the house by Arthur Jones.

"I saw two of them boys headed into the woods above the Nest. It looked like a fight was brewing," Arthur Jones said, when Tony asked if he'd seen Boston recently. The man was the local, and unofficial, veterans' program director. "I was surprised not to see Mouse with him."

Minutes later, Tony headed up into the hills, toward the now abandoned, small, poorly constructed housing development once called the Shady Nest. He hoped to end an argument before someone got hurt. Too much anger and not enough work could create some powerful arguments. Or worse.

The sound of fists hitting flesh and bone was one Tony could recognize anywhere. The cause was obvious. Two men, down by the creek, were locked in hand-to-hand combat. This was no simple bar fight. These were well-trained veterans. Neither showed any signs of surrender. One of them was Boston. The other had a familiar face but was not a man Tony could immediately identify. After each blow, there was a grunt or moan or just the whooshing sound of air leaving lungs. Neither man was talking.

Tony ran as fast as he could, but it was slow-going trying to run through the underbrush and snow. When he reached the space between two old-growth trees, he saw the two reasonably fit young men, both with hand-to-hand combat training, pummeling each other. The snow had been churned into mud.

Tony recognized Boston's opponent. He was one of Sheila's ragtag cousins, definitely a Teffeteller, but Tony didn't know his first name. Tony was not in the mood to fight and guessed if he stepped in, they'd both turn on him. Still, their combat was too vicious to ignore. If this kept up, someone would be killed or maimed. Tony pulled out his pistol and yelled, "Sheriff. Stop." He might as well have whispered. He fired once, into the ground.

Two angry faces turned toward him but neither released his opponent.

"Let go." Tony stood his ground but now aimed his pistol at the combatants. He talked into his radio, keeping Rex apprised.

Luckily, the two men finally showed some sense and took a step away from each other. Their expressions made it clear the fight was not over. Panting from exertion, they stared at Tony, looking like they'd enjoy taking on another person. He did not lower his gun. Two against one. Weirder things had happened than two combatants becoming allies against a common foe.

"What's this about?" Tony didn't take his eyes off the pair, but saw another vehicle pull up. Wade. Reinforcements.

Both combatants watched Wade exit the car and climb toward them. Breathing heavily, the pair stared at him. After a moment, their eyes cleared a bit, and they seemed to realize where they were again. Tony said, "Tell me what's going on."

Defiant, Boston shook his head, but after a few moments, his fisted hands gradually opened.

Teffeteller kicked at the snow near his feet. "He took my cake." The whisper carried through the frigid air.

"Excuse me?" Tony didn't see any sign of food. "What cake?"

"Over at the free lunch." Teffeteller sniffled. "It was the last piece of chocolate cake."

"Heaven help us," Tony murmured and holstered his gun. "Where's the cake now?"

Boston said, "Isn't one. The loser of this fight has to move away so the other one gets the next piece. We came up here so my dog didn't get hurt."

Tony said, "Boston, you come with me. You"—he pointed to the Teffeteller man—"stay here with Wade."

Boston followed Tony's instructions, but anger etched his face into even harsher lines than usual.

"You abandoned your dog." Tony assumed the dog was more important than life to this man, and he felt gravely concerned by Boston's actions. They moved some distance from the others.

Something like fear flashed across Boston's face. "Is he okay?"

"Yes. But he's worried, and so is Mrs. Dixon. She says you never leave Mouse, not ever."

Boston nodded. He flexed his hands wide and balled them into fists. "I couldn't risk him being hurt during the fight. He'd want to protect me."

"What's this really about?"

Boston shook his head.

"You want to spend some time in my jail, without Mouse?" Tony didn't like threatening the man, but he needed to make his point. "He'd be well-cared for. Mrs. Dixon likes him and he seems to like her."

"No." Boston surrendered. "Not that. Mouse needs me like I need him."

It was what Tony was counting on. "What about the fight?"

"It's stupid."

Tony felt positive the man was telling the truth. Boiled down, most of these scuffles were stupid, fighting over the winning or losing of a card game, the affections of some girl who didn't like either of them, the results of a football game. "I don't care. Tell me."

"It really *was* about cake." Boston didn't look up. "There was only one piece left and we both wanted it."

"And while you were arguing over it," Tony guessed. "Someone else got it."

Boston's head snapped up. "Yep. We thought we'd settle ownership of the next slice out here." He stared into Tony's eyes, breathing hard. "Fighting felt pretty good for a while. Cleansing, you know, but I'm done now."

"Okay." Tony heaved a sigh of relief. "I'll take you back to the Dixon's but there had better not be a next time." Boston nodded.

He would have Sheila talk to her relative.

"Who would have guessed?" Tony stared at the neat row of containers. Under the watchful eye of Vince, from the TBI, Tony and Wade had excavated a lot of the root cellar at the old Buchanan house and found four skeletons in one small area. With the exception of a few small wrist bones obviously missing from

49

the upper skeleton, they appeared to be complete. They filled jars with dirt under the skeletons.

"Sheriff, I've made a few statements in the past about your crime statistics, but this is off the chart." Vince from the TBI stared at the hole they'd dug. He was there because of simple curiosity. "Never would I have dreamed of this."

Tony wouldn't have, either. Park County had seemed like the quietest, dullest place imaginable when he'd been a boy. Granted, his attention was on school and sports, so it would have taken something dramatic to attract him. Even his school boy crush on a girl named Leslie could not compete with a baseball.

"I don't suppose you want to take a guess at how long those bones have been down there," Tony said.

"You're right about that." Vince fiddled with his pen and shifted to slouch in another position. "I will tell you that it's obvious that at one time, someone knew they existed."

"Why?" Tony believed it too, but was curious about Vince's theory.

"Well, mostly because I don't believe those four dead people built the false wall. And because they weren't buried deep and any number of critters would probably have gotten involved if the hatch or whatever you want to call the upper-level door wasn't latched. Do you catch my meaning?"

Tony did. The bones would have been scattered and gnawed by wild animals, and many, if not most, destroyed. "They wouldn't have been neatly stacked either."

"You want to know what I think?" Vince stared at the small space.

Tony most certainly did. "Tell me." Tony held his breath, hoping it wouldn't mean more work.

"If these turn out to be old, *old* bones, like they initially appear to be, they could date from the Civil War era. How many fugitives or slaves passed through this part of the state?"

"Only God would know the answer to that question. Hundreds, at the minimum." Tony hesitated. "This was a crossroad back then. Slaves, free men, deserters from both sides, escaped prisoners of war. Some men were heading north while some traveled south. Families migrated west."

Vince nodded. "Tennessee was a split state. This end sided more with the North, and the western end with the South. Family loyalties were divided. About the only thing everyone in the state agreed on was there was too much bloodshed and it looked like the war would never end."

"Sheriff?" Doc Nash wasted no time getting right to the point. "Your grocery store stabbing victim is ready to talk."

Tony wasted no time getting Wade and heading to the clinic.

"Doc Nash is dealing with an emergency. Come this way," Nurse Foxx whispered as she led them down the hall. "Physically she'll be fine. It's a miracle. The knife missed every vital organ and blood vessel. Emotionally, I don't know. Something she said made it sound like her daughter-in-law was the one who stabbed her."

Family disputes were Tony's least favorite things to become involved in. There was not enough time or privacy to ask "Foxxy," as she was called, anything else. She held the curtain back, and led the two men into the cubicle. The clinic had several beds, but there were only curtains separating them. It was not a hospital, but occasionally a patient spent the night here.

Tony sat on a chair placed near the head of the bed and smiled at the woman stretched out on her left side on the narrow bed. An IV dripped fluids into her right arm and a monitor kept track of her blood pressure and heartbeat. "You certainly look like you're feeling better than you did the last time we met."

Puzzlement pulled her eyebrows together and made the woman's face crinkle. "We've met?"

Tony gave a little shrug. "Well, we weren't exactly introduced and to be fair, you *were* unconscious at the time. I'm Sheriff Abernathy and this is my deputy, Wade Claybough. How are you feeling?"

"Much better." A faint smile accompanied her response. "Can I leave now?"

Tony shifted on the chair, placed where she would not have to strain to see his face. He waved his notepad and pen. "Would you at least tell us your name? The term 'unknown female' is imprecise. I prefer my report have somewhat better details than that."

"Maybelle Ruth." The hint of a smile removed ten years from her estimated age. "No relation to the "The Babe."

Tony smiled at the woman. "And where do you live, Mrs. Ruth?"

"Maybelle," she insisted and gave him a local address. "It's my son's place."

"I hope you're enjoying your visit." Half expecting her to contradict his assumption, he waved at the medical equipment. "Except for being stabbed in the back, and now, of course, chatting with me."

Her head did not move. She did not blink as she stared into his eyes. "I want to leave now."

"I think you need to wait for the doctor to give the word." Tony pulled the chair closer to the bed and leaned slightly forward, getting closer to her eye level. "Will you please tell us what happened?"

"Nothing happened." Her eyes fluttered closed. "I'm fine. I want to go home."

"Assault with a deadly weapon is not something I can ignore." Tony was surprised she wouldn't talk, unless . . . His stomach soured. Sometimes family violence victims would pretend nothing had happened. This phenomenon was not confined to marital disagreements. All ages and all genders were potential victims.

Maybelle's spine straightened and her eyes opened, only to glare at him. "There was no assault. I did it to myself."

"Okay, how'd you stab yourself? Show me." Tony wanted her to get mad and quit being someone's doormat. "Here, you can show me with this." He handed her a small flashlight from his belt.

Maybelle made a couple of feeble attempts to demonstrate but failed. She didn't change her story, but it gave Tony some fingerprints to compare to the ones on the knife. The weapon removed from her back was already locked up in the law enforcement center. Doc Nash had a fair amount of experience with the chain of custody and handling of evidence. Between Theo having seen the knife embedded in Maybelle's back and the doctor who removed it, Tony didn't think he'd need the victim's cooperation to hand the case over to Archie Campbell, their prosecutor.

"It was an accident. A silly accident." Maybelle flapped her hand in obvious surrender. "I stepped back to get out of the way; the kitchen is so tiny, there just wasn't room for all of us, and I backed into the knife my son was holding."

"Seriously?" Wade's eyebrows rose and his pen lifted from his notebook. "That's the story you're going with?"

"You don't have to say a word." Tony frowned again, thinking it was the dumbest story he'd heard in ages. "I think in this case, the fingerprints will be enough for a conviction." He was good and sick and tired of people being bullied, beaten, and keeping silent. "No one has the right to do this."

"Oh, no, you can't." Even though the woman lay on her side, packed like fine china to keep pressure off of her wound, she attempted to sit up but ended up sprawled across the bed, her eyes pleading and filled with tears. "You must believe me, it's not what you think. I want to leave. Now." Her words were barely audible over the sound of labored breathing. They turned into gasps for air.

As the poor woman thrashed about on the narrow bed, Tony rang for the nurse. To him, it looked like she was trying to remove the tube delivering oxygen into her nose and the IV line into her arm at the same time. Total panic. The monitor tracking her heart rate and blood pressure flashed what he assumed were emergency readings. It was not the time to ask more questions.

Nurse Foxx came into the cubicle in seconds and he and Wade left, sent away with little more information than they'd arrived with. Now they knew she was protecting someone.

CHAPTER SIX

When Tony stepped out of his office, late in the afternoon, he found Ruth Ann behind her desk and her husband, Walter, sitting with their most avid confessor, Orvan Lundy. It was too late for Tony to step back into his office and pretend to be out. Plus, after the frantic morning and the wild beginning of the afternoon, he was swamped with paperwork. He thought maybe hearing one of Orvan's tall tales might perk up the day.

"Making a confession?" Tony expected this situation to follow their normal pattern. The old man would confess to some crime, even if it was nonexistent, and Tony would learn more about what was really happening under the quiet surface of the county. "Did you do something I should know about?"

"No sir, I ain't done nothin' wrong. You know I'm a good man. My doing wrong would be like sanding against my grain." Orvan's faded blue eyes filled with tears. "How can you think I ever did wrong?"

"Let's just say I have an overactive imagination." Tony wasn't about to launch into a description of every crime he believed the old sinner had committed. Maybe not recently, but Tony was reasonably sure Orvan had killed more than one person. Being reasonably sure would not hold up in court, even if Tony could supply the names of the victims. He settled the discussion by ignoring the melodrama. "What can I do for you?"

Ignoring Tony, Orvan focused his rheumy eyes on Ruth Ann and smiled. "My angel."

As if seeing Orvan for the first time in years, instead of having his skinny frame parked near her desk, Ruth Ann batted her eyes and waggled her fingers in a greeting. "Mr. Lundy."

Walter nudged Orvan, pushing him slightly closer to Tony. "Quit staring at my wife and tell the sheriff what you heard."

"A haint." Orvan slipped his trembling hands under the buckles holding his overalls on, almost as if he was protecting his fingers from something. Something trying to steal his hands. "It were terrible, terrible, I thought they was a-comin' to collect me."

"Did you see the haint?" Ruth Ann left her desk and all teasing behind, and she came to stand next to her husband. Her question, though, was aimed at Orvan.

"No, my angel. I jest heer'd it. The cries of the dead." Orvan started shivering and shaking so hard that Tony and Walter carefully pressed him onto a nearby chair before he collapsed on the floor.

Tony looked to Walter. "Did you hear it, whatever *it* was?"

Walter didn't answer right away. He rolled his shoulders and closed his eyes. "Maybe. I wasn't with Orvan at the time. I was taking my morning walk, but I heard something strange this morning too. It was a high wailing cry, but I couldn't tell where it was coming from or if it was a bird or was human. If I hadn't heard it myself"—Walter stared into Tony's face—"I'd have said Orvan was crazy or drunk. Possibly both."

Tony pulled out his notepad. Recently much recovered from near death, Walter was married to Tony's secretary/assistant/lawyer and expert office organizer. Tony occasionally had nightmares about Ruth Ann leaving. Ruth Ann had recently begun a new county assistance program matching volunteers with people in need, and she had teamed her husband up with the most cantankerous man in the county. Orvan Lundy was old and tough as leather but he was spry and frequently misinterpreted real events. He was also rapturous in his adoration of Ruth Ann.

Orvan sat next to the much larger man, seemingly content for the moment to let someone else do the talking.

"Tell me, Walter, what exactly did you hear?" Tony was curious, not concerned. He hadn't heard anything peculiar himself and knew sounds heard up in the mountains were often hard to locate.

"At first, it sounded like an airplane, you know, a small one. Private." Walter paused and glanced down at the floor and up again. He shook his head like he didn't believe what he'd heard. "Then, like I said, there was this one drawn-out endless scream that covered the sound of the airplane."

"Banshees," Orvan mumbled, almost inaudibly. "They was banshees. Nothin' else makes such a sound."

Tony studied Orvan's face. Eating regularly made him much stronger now. It looked like he was almost back to his normal irritating self. "Banshees? Okay. But what kind of sound do they make?"

"It was kind of a high shriek," Walter broke in. "Maybe a long wail would describe it better."

"What time was this?" Tony made a few notes to himself.

Walter thought for a moment. "I walked after breakfast. When I arrived this morning, it was maybe nine, nine thirty. Orvan was fussing about the new time coming."

"New time?"

Brilliant white teeth flashed. The grin on Walter's chocolate face grew wider. "Orvan's not pleased about our going off daylight savings time."

Tony could imagine the fun conversation the subject of such an event could stir up with the grouchy old man. Orvan was about the most contrary, argumentative citizen in the county and would dispute the color of the sky just to keep from agreeing with anyone.

Orvan broke in, his gnarled, callused hands waving, "It give me chills."

"The time change?" Tony decided to be purposely dense to see how close to his normal behavior the old man achieved.

"I cain't see how you keep this job." Orvan's face became one giant frown line. "You ain't smart enough to grow dirt."

Walter's grin confirmed Tony's assessment. The old guy was back to normal.

Surprised by the depth of his relief, Tony smiled back. "Okay, Orvan, so why do you think it was a banshee? We haven't had many of those lately."

Orvan squinted at Tony, a hint of suspicion on his face. "I heerd one years ago. Just before my old granny passed away. Like to made every hair on my head stand on end." He paused, staring at Tony's bald scalp.

Tony waited for Orvan to ask a rude question, but he didn't. "So, Walter, you heard an airplane and a scream?"

"Yes. First the plane, then the scream, and then silence." Walter spoke softly. "I might not have paid any attention to the plane if something didn't scream, long and drawn-out."

"That makes no sense."

"On that we agree."

"Could you tell what direction it came from?"

"Somewhere maybe east or southeast. Until the scream, it was just another small plane motor passing overhead. Nothing to attract any attention at all. And to be honest, I didn't even hear the scream very well."

"Why did you wait so long to come in?"

"Sounded stupid." Walter gave a half shrug. "Still does. I'm not convinced it wasn't some critter caught by a predator, but Orvan and I talked it over and thought we'd check with you. You know, in case you knew what it was or had other reports."

Tony thought the rather mild expression on Walter's face was a lie. The man had heard something. And whatever that something had been, Walter had found it very disturbing. And still did.

"Just a minute, I'll ask what similar calls there might have been." Tony headed for the dispatch desk. Rex did not seem surprised to see him and already had a list prepared. Tony stared at the list. "Why?"

"While they were waiting, Walter told me part of the story and I thought you'd be curious."

"What did other people hear?" Tony got the question out but before Rex could answer it, he had to respond to a 911 call. Someone needed an ambulance, a call easily dealt with.

Rex returned his attention to Tony. "I got several calls, none from people in town, asking if there was any need for them to be concerned. Quite a few asked if someone was trapping wild hogs. They'd all heard a scream of some kind but didn't know the source."

Tony wouldn't be surprised if someone had tired of the wild hogs trampling through their property. They were mean, dangerous, and no permit was needed to shoot one.

"You'll enjoy this one though," Rex played a recording made that morning. In it, Rex's voice remained calm, and spoke clearly and briskly. The caller, a woman, was not calm or clear. She spoke in a high-pitched tone, her words running together. "I heard a terrible scream."

Rex finally broke in, having listened long enough to get the gist of her story. "Where are you?"

"At my house."

"What's your address?"

"I don't think that's any of your business. I don't give out my address. Really! How dumb do you think I am?"

A glance at Rex's expression sent Tony back to his office.

Neither of them would benefit from anger or amusement.

Tony suggested the wild pig story to Walter and Orvan. The old man shook his head.

"Those pigs can produce a mighty scream when they're agitated." Walter nodded but didn't look convinced. "I guess it could have been a hog in a trap."

Maybe half an hour later, Rex called Tony. "About the scream, it's been totally quiet out here for a little while and it's given me time to think. A few people called right away to ask about the sounds, but others have waited and given it some thought and then called, just to make sure we knew about it. But right now, I've got a different kind of caller on the line with news about the event. I think you should talk to this guy."

"Put him through." Tony felt like this could be the longest day in his life.

"I just did." The ringing phone interrupted them.

"Uh, Sheriff, like I told the guy who answered the phone, I had a bit of an accident over on your side of the mountains."

Before Tony could ask more or process Rex's connecting the caller to his office telephone before he was asked to, the deep voice rumbled on.

"The guy fell out of my airplane—honest to God, he just climbed right out of his seat and fell out. There was nothing I could do to stop him. I couldn't land up there with trees all around and rocks and the creek under me."

"My side of the mountain? Seriously? Is this some kind of a joke?" As soon as Orvan and his entourage had vanished, Tony had started working on the budget figures, knowing he'd need to be exact with his facts and figures at the upcoming town meeting. If he couldn't explain where every last dollar in his department budget went, the fickle citizens of Park County might decide to recall the August election and vote in his opponent. That would be bad for him and for the county. Tony doubted his opponent could operate a light switch, much less handle the myriad duties of the office. He'd be responsible for everything from courtroom security to the jail to policing the county.

His focus was divided until three words in the telephone statement finally caught his full attention. "Fell out" and "airplane."

"Sheriff, you there?"

"Yes, yes, let's start over. I missed a lot of your statement." Tony pushed aside his files and opened his notebook to a fresh page. "What's your name?"

"Gentry Frazier. That's Frazier with a 'zee.' "

"And where are you now?"

"Asheville, North Carolina."

"When did this happen?" Tony glanced at his watch. It was three thirty. There would still be daylight for a while.

"Oh, maybe an hour, hour and a half ago. Might have been a little longer."

"Where?" Tony thought the confused time frame was odd. Why didn't the pilot know when the event occurred?

"We were just outside the national park and flying over your county. There's a tiny bald surrounded by some old-growth trees, really dense stuff. I'm guessing only God can get in there—didn't see a road anywhere close."

Tony knew the spot. The bald in question, one of the mysteries of the Appalachian Mountains, was known as a grassy bald. The naturally treeless area covered with thick grasses and encircled by ancient oaks was on a ridge, near a cliff and a stream. He thought Frazier's assessment of accessibility was spot-on. "How did someone fall out of your plane?"

"Yessir. It was crazy. My client and me, we were looking for a special fishing spot he knew and all the sudden he's climbing out of the plane, until he was almost completely stretched out on the wing and he's shouting for me to land, but Sheriff, I swear there's no place to land up there. Too many trees and too many rocks."

The sounds coming through the phone now were quick breaths, as if Frazier was running. "I looked for a place to set down but never saw a good spot at all. My client was hanging onto his fishing gear more than the plane. Once he climbed out onto the wing, he jumped. I mean it. He got his feet under him and jumped off."

"While he was opening the door, you couldn't grab him by the belt?" Without seeing the airplane, Tony had no real hope of visualizing the situation.

Frazier wheezed. "There's no door. I fly an antique biplane. You just climb in and sit down."

With that information, Tony could picture the general layout of the plane. He had seen quite a few of those old planes. The pilot usually sat behind the passenger, a situation that made no sense to him, but he knew zilch about designing, or flying, an airplane.

"I took a picture of the area where he landed, with my phone, if it will help. Do y'all have Internet over there on your side of the mountains?"

"Yes." Tony stared at the phone, semi-stunned by the question. "The stone tablet days ended for us at least two weeks ago." If Tony wasn't so concerned to hear of a missing man, he might have said more; instead he gave the pilot his email address and then asked his own question. "What's the man's name and address?"

Frazier said, "Name's Franklin Cashdollar. Hold on while I get the address for you."

There were sounds of papers being shifted around, but Tony was only vaguely aware of them. He recognized the name and he knew, albeit slightly, the man. Franklin was Silersville's mayor's brother. The phrase didn't trip off his tongue, but it was the way the man was cataloged in Tony's brain. It also meant that Franklin was Carl Lee Cashdollar's father. Tony really did not like being the bearer of bad news, especially to a friend, and Carl Lee was a friend. Death notification was a part of his job Tony dreaded.

The pilot rattled off a North Carolina address and gave Tony a warning. "It's a really, really swank area. If you call, you'll probably have to deal with a butler or secretary."

"Thanks for the heads up." Tony made a few more notes before glancing up at the computer screen. The promised photograph had arrived. Tony clicked on the file and up popped an aerial view of about the most treacherous, remote, rugged spot in the county. On his back, spread-eagle on the snow, lay a man in a dark jacket and pants. He was wearing what looked like an antique flight helmet, the soft kind with attached round-lensed goggles. Tony zoomed in and could see more details. One gloved hand still clutched a fishing pole. "I'm looking at the photograph now. Any chance he survived?"

"Oh, man, I don't think so." Frazier cleared his throat. "I flew as low as I could, looking for him, and although I circled around after I found him and was able to take the picture, I never saw anything move. Not so much as a twitch. If he didn't die on impact, he's probably gone now."

Tony wrote down all of Gentry Frazier's contact information, including the registration number on the airplane's wing.

CHAPTER SEVEN

Tony lifted the binoculars to his eyes. It was amazing that so many huge trees managed to grow in such a desolate place and then mysteriously stop, leaving an open area. On the other hand, no one would ever come up here to cut a tree when so many grew in friendlier areas. This terrain was rock, crevices, and fallen logs. Only the smallest bit of open sky was directly over the body.

It didn't require an expert or a genius to deduce that the body had arrived in the clearing after the snow. It lay flat on its back, arms extended and legs spread, like someone making a snow angel. It did not have the spreading and closings of the arms and legs to complete the angel picture, but the impact of the body landing had formed a crater in the snow. The snow surrounding the body was undisturbed, as was the corpse. Mostly. From this distance it appeared to be a man, dressed in ordinary, outdoor clothing, boots, and a jacket. An old-fashioned flying helmet covered the hair and ears. Dead. Eyes open, staring up into the sunlight.

Tony knew it wouldn't be long before the major carrion crew would be swooping in to investigate and clean up—birds and beasts looking for a meal.

"I can only think of one way to achieve this." Tony hoped someone would have a better suggestion. "He fell from the sky. It has to be Franklin. Surely there can't be more than one lost skydiver."

When his deputy turned to answer, Wade's eyes were invisible behind the dark lenses of his sunglasses. "What's he holding?"

"That has to be a fishing pole. The pilot said he carried his fishing gear when he left the plane." Tony was intrigued as well. "Start taking your pictures. I want to see if we can get closer." There was no reason to believe this was foul play, but Tony couldn't come up with a way to explain this situation any other way. People didn't just fall out of the sky. He called Rex in dispatch. "Call out Doc Nash."

They had left the Blazer at the end of the road and started walking, picking their way closer, trying to avoid falling on ice or loose rocks. They managed to travel maybe half a mile in slow motion. During that time, they watched three different small planes pass overhead.

Tony was surprised. "I didn't realize how many of those fly over in a day but I guess it's almost every time you look up during tourist season."

Behind him, Wade's voice caught his attention. "You know the doctor is *not* going to find this amusing. The man hates snow."

Tony did know, but he had no choice. Mother Nature prevented his walking much closer to the body. "We'll have to borrow the mules."

Wade frowned. "Can't we use ATVs?"

"Nope." Tony handed Wade the binoculars. "Unless you can see a way. All I see is a possible deer track we can follow. That's some hostile landscape."

Wade studied the terrain for a few moments but didn't disagree.

Tony sighed. He hated everything about this situation. "I'll get Sheila to come up here and keep the predators at bay. She can use her rifle to frighten away as many critters as she likes. I sure don't want any of them messing with the body."

"Too late." Wade frowned. "It looks like something has been here; something small snacked on the face." He adjusted the focus. "And you're right; he's definitely holding a fishing pole."

"Seriously?" Tony reclaimed the binoculars. Sure enough, the dead man clutched a fishing pole in one hand. If Tony was any judge, the man had hoped to protect it during the fall. It made Tony think their corpse had been alive during the descent. "I thought it was a joke."

Wade tried to walk closer to the clearing but stopped almost immediately and shook his head. "The rocks around here are super slick. Nothing like a little ice. I guess the mules win."

In his mind, Tony kept hearing Orvan's description of a scream. Tony imagined that if it was he, himself, who was falling far and fast, off a cliff or out of an airplane, he would be screaming like Theo on a roller coaster. But Orvan and Walter heard their screamer in the morning. Had there been two?

Tony stared at the mule with little enthusiasm for the upcoming ride. He and the oversized animal had a history. It wasn't confrontational, and neither one of them was likely to resort to violence. They simply agreed to disagree. Tony had limited experience riding horses or mules, and this one was not interested in being training material.

Man and mule both sighed, recognizing the inevitability of their awkward partnership. Tony placed his left foot in the stirrup and heaved his body upward, landing heavily on the saddle. The mule shifted his weight, taking several tiny steps backwards and stopped.

Wade's mule was about the same size as Tony's but Doc Nash straddled a much smaller animal, his medical bag attached to the saddle horn with a length of orange plastic cord. Their guide rode ahead, leading a riderless mule with a metal basket strapped to its back. Tony was almost positive there would be no living person to carry back.

"How far are we going?" Doc Nash pulled his jacket close around his neck. An orange stocking cap decorated with a big white T was pulled down to the upper edge of his glasses and over his ears. He still looked cold.

Wade pulled his sunglasses forward, almost to the end of his nose, and met the doctor's inquiring gaze. "If we had wings, it's only a few miles. On land, this is going to take a while."

The doctor's voice was almost a whine. "Can't we borrow a helicopter?"

Wade's grin exposed beautiful even teeth. Tony thought his brother Tiberius, the dentist, would approve of the obvious care Wade took of them.

"The clearing is not large enough for one to land, so no, unless you want to jump out or slide down a rope ladder." Wade continued, "I haven't done it for a while, but I bet it's not a skill we're apt to forget."

Tony nodded. He'd done it too, but more than ten years ago at the most recent. This was not something he thought of as a "do or die trying" situation. One of them would have to carry the doctor down on their back. "No way." His words were in agreement with Wade and his decision. "The sooner we go, the sooner we'll be back."

Heading away from the trailhead where their guide had parked the oversized stock trailer, they were soon traveling single file, taking care not to get too close to the rear of the mule in front of them. It was an effective way to eliminate conversation and have the peace and quiet to think.

Tony's thoughts, though, were anything but peaceful. The early snow covered the ground, making it extra treacherous. A stumble over a branch could send mule and man crashing off the trail. He was so busy watching for hidden dangers on the ground, he didn't see the low-hanging branch. Whap! It slapped him in the face. The scratches didn't feel deep but the cold air made them sting.

He did not relish the idea of breaking bad news, but it would be worse to report inaccurate bad news. What if this was not the mayor's brother? Or, if by some miracle the man was still alive, a premature report of his death would be pointless and cruel.

They had moved out of cellular phone service, but carried a pair of working satellite phones. Darkness would be their worst enemy. They had food and a tent and sleeping bags but hoped they wouldn't need them. Just ride in, collect the body, and leave. But life was rarely simple, and Mother Nature had spoiled any number of well-made plans in the past.

In the end, they made it to the body with daylight to spare. The body lay face-up on the snowy ground, gloveless hands clasping the fishing pole. The heavy jacket was at odds with the bare, pale bluish fingers. The old-fashioned flight helmet with its attached goggles gave him an eerie alien appearance. There were animal footprints in the snow near him but no human prints. Tony saw no sign the man had moved at all after landing, and found himself releasing the breath he'd held. At least the man had not suffered long after landing, assuming he was not dead in the air.

Wade's camera clicked incessantly, making a record of the scene, the body, and the doctor's actions.

It was definitely Franklin Cashdollar, unless he had a secret twin. Tony knew the man well enough to identify the body, and all of the identification in the man's wallet confirmed it. Franklin's brother, Silersville mayor Calvin Cashdollar, was the local undertaker. They'd get Calvin's opinion later, but there was no reason to hurry.

Doc Nash grumbled and groused, checking the liver temperature, and examining the general condition of the body. "Let's load him up." He offered no other information, but Tony would describe his expression as guarded. Doc Nash was good at secrets and also a world-class poker player.

And so they prepared for the return trip. Working together, they strapped the body onto the litter and adjusted the weight, balancing it for the mule. After Wade took another hundred photographs, their grisly parade returned to the road. It wasn't quite seven in the evening when they got back to town. Tony was grateful they had not gone off daylight savings time yet.

Minutes after dismounting from the mule and climbing into the Blazer Tony had left at the trailhead, he and Wade received another call. No rest for the weary, but some days were like that. No one else was available to follow up.

Still dressed in their heavy clothes, Tony and Wade stared at the man sitting on the front steps of a house about a mile from town.

Blood oozed from a gash on the man's left cheek and dripped unheeded onto the front of what Tony thought of as a "not clean this century" T-shirt.

On the ground nearby, surrounded by several unhappy-looking paramedics, lay a woman in old, dirty, ragged clothes. The paramedics blocked his view of the woman's face, but he could see a lot of blood covering her chest and arms. "What happened?"

The man pressed a shaking, and filthy, hand to his bleeding facial wound. He finally released a long breath and looked into Tony's eyes. The bloodshot eyes looked confused. "She told me to shoot her."

"So you did?"

"Yessir." He sniffled. "She does not like it when I don't do as she says."

Tony felt a combination of concern for his grievously injured citizen and irritation at humans in general. "Start from the beginning."

"Is she gonna be okay?" The man tried to look past Tony to the body on the ground. "She said to shoot her, I did, I went inside, and she stayed outside." He wiped his blood-covered hand on the side of his pants. "I came out to see if she was hungry an' if she wanted a sandwich and thought she was lookin' mighty poorly so I called nine-one-one."

"You didn't call for help right away? Right after you shot her?" Tony glanced up from his notepad. "Why not?"

"I asked her did she need a doctor and she didn't say yes. Just plain mule stubborn as ever."

Tony wondered who was responsible for these people. They seemed to have no clue about life and death.

"She still ain't said a word." His face wore an expression of confusion mixed with surprise.

"No," Tony agreed. "What about you? What happened to your face?" When there was no reply, Tony tried again. "The bleeding."

Their genius wiped some of the blood from his face with one dirty hand, studied it briefly, and then wiped it on his pants. "She broke a beer bottle on my head."

Tony thought the man might have deserved it, but there were always two sides to these events. It was not as easy to break a bottle as it appeared in the movies. "You carry a gun?"

"Damn right. It's always with me." The moment the words passed his lips it seemed to shake something in his brain. "I mean, yeah, 'course. How else was I supposed to shoot her? I have a gun, not that I carry it all the time." He patted his hip.

Tony agreed that his question was stupid. After the day he'd had, stupid was the best he could do. "I'll need to take it for a while."

The man quietly handed Tony a well-aged revolver. It wasn't any cleaner than the owner. Tony slowly shook his head as he wrote down the information on the evidence bag.

Tony drove away, following the ambulance down the driveway. He glanced at Wade. "Get cleaned up and eat something. We'll make some local calls, and then I'll let you drive us to North Carolina." Tony hoped a shower and some food would rejuvenate his brain. The unhappy task of notifying Franklin Cashdollar's relatives of his death was not going to be quick or easy.

Wade opened his mouth, as if to ask a question, then closed it.

"You want to know why I don't just have the North Carolina cops break the news?" At Wade's answering nod, Tony said, "Not only is he the father of a friend but that man's body landed in our county. If there is something wonky, I want to be part of the investigation."

"Shouldn't we check his fingerprints, you know, just to be sure?"

Although he was sure about the man's identity, Tony agreed. "Yes. Let's have every dot in place and every 'T' crossed."

It took them only minutes to stop by the clinic where Doc Nash had stashed the body. A quick fingerprint and they were gone. Wade's comparison took very little time also. Hanging on Tony's office wall was a project he'd done a few years earlier. Carefully framed behind glass were the fingerprints of four Cashdollar men. Although there were some differences, of course, Calvin, Franklin, Carl Lee and the patriarch, Roosevelt Cashdollar, shared a distinctive family swirl.

CHAPTER EIGHT

Theo leaned against the door frame and took a deep breath. The unexpected snow had created turmoil all day. It had also created a busier than usual day in her shop. Even though it was not quite Halloween, suddenly every quilter she knew seemed ready to make Christmas quilts, placemats, or insulated things to keep baked potatoes warm. Theo needed the business. She was exhausted. A glance around her office/workroom did nothing to relieve her fatigue. Guilt, yes; it added to her mother's guilt.

She had sent the boys upstairs to her office when they arrived after school. They had promised to come get her when the twins awakened from their naps. Looking around, she was surprised to see them all awake.

Chris and Jamie had created a nest for the twins. Chairs were turned on their sides, cushions protected them from sharp edges, and a couple of bolts of brand-new fabrics were partially undone. Even from her spot near the door, she could identify pizza sauce on the now-unsellable fabric. She didn't know whether to scream, cry, or laugh. Four small, happy, dirty faces watched her.

Exhausted, Theo realized there was no place for her to sit. "Where's my chair?"

Chris pointed to a portion of their barricade. "We couldn't just let them loose in here. They move fast."

"Mom okay?" Jamie coached the baby in his arms. "Say,

72

Lizzie sorry."

To Lizzie's credit, she babbled something. Theo was just as happy the girl's early words would not be a lie. Lizzie's fingers spread wide and a large spool of thread tumbled to the floor. The ensuing unhappy cry exposed all of her tiny pearl teeth.

Clutched in Chris's arms, Kara giggled and poked her finger into her older brother's nose. Chris gently pulled her hand away. "You were gone for a long time." Chris looked way too serious for his age. He was tall for a ten-year-old and Theo was small for a woman. It put their faces at almost the same height. Theo thought she detected disapproval in his expression. "There was some pizza in the fridge and we reheated it. They were hungry."

Theo glanced at her watch and gasped. She had been downstairs for two hours without checking on her children. No wonder Chris was giving her a sad look. "I'm sorry. I had no idea. You know the monitor was turned on. You could have called me up at any time."

Jamie laughed. "We had fun."

Chris joined in. "Yeah, we did."

Theo was so relieved that all of the kids were fine and happy and forgiving, she offered them hot dogs and potato chips for dinner. As long as she wasn't being a good mom, she might as well add another junk-food meal into the equation. "Your dad is super busy, so we'll eat early and not wait for him."

It was almost seven thirty in the evening when Tony parked the Blazer in front of the mansion, just out of town, belonging to Mayor Calvin Cashdollar and his wife, known locally as Queen Doreen. Wade pulled in right behind him and cut the lights and engine on his vehicle.

They had discussed the order of announcements—should they tell the brother or the son first? They decided on the brother. Tony guessed the mayor/undertaker might have already heard rumors from his sources.

The expansive front porch seemed a bit less welcoming than usual now that it was covered with snow. No one appeared to have climbed these steps since the storm began. Why would they bother to shovel them, if no one was expected? The family cars would be in the garage, attached to the back of the house. Even Blossom's sister, Pansy Flowers Millsaps, who worked for the couple, would most likely come into the house through a different door and leave the same way.

Tony pressed the button next to the door and listened to an eight-note chime. A few moments passed before the front door opened. Queen Doreen stood behind the full-length glass of the storm door.

"Sheriff?" Doreen's expression went from curious to concern as she spotted Wade, standing in a shadow. "Wade? Has something happened?"

Tony nodded. "Is Calvin at home?"

"Yes, do come in." The mayor's wife stepped back into the foyer, allowing them access. "You can hang your jackets there." She pointed to a row of clothes hooks at the top of a finely crafted, cherry wood storage unit.

As Tony removed his jacket, and carefully wiped his snowy boots on the rug designated for the job, he realized he'd never seen Doreen without her trademark high heels. She was almost as short as Theo, and tonight she was dressed in a gray sweatshirt and sweatpants and pink bunny slippers. Without her city clothes, Doreen looked younger and more approachable than he'd ever seen her.

Calvin appeared around the corner, chewing something. "Sheriff?"

"I'm sorry to interrupt your dinner." Tony's stomach rumbled. He'd lost track of time. He had no idea when he'd last eaten anything. "I don't have good news."

"Do you want to sit?"

"Let's do." Tony doubted the mortician would faint at the idea his brother had died, but he wasn't prepared to deliver bad news in a hallway.

Calvin led him and Wade to a small sitting area.

"In fact, I'm afraid I have bad news." That was about as bald a statement as his own head.

Startled, Calvin glanced at his wife and back to Tony. "What is it?"

"Your brother, Franklin, was found dead earlier today." Tony watched the mayor, carefully looking for his reaction. There wasn't much to see.

"I see. Well . . ." Calvin blinked. "Thank you for telling me. Did he kill himself?"

The mayor displayed as little emotion as if he'd heard about a stranger's death. Tony felt shock. Suicide was not usually the first suggestion of a family being notified of a death. "Why would you ask that?"

"I don't really know. I guess I just wouldn't expect Franklin to die of pneumonia or anything else us mere mortals would succumb to." Calvin studied the floor for several long moments, then met Tony's gaze. "I envied his courage. He jumped out of airplanes, led men into battle, and rode the Dragon's Tail on a motorcycle, safely, in bad weather, in record time. Three things I would never consider doing."

"He's never seemed quite human," Doreen added. "Do let us know when the service is scheduled."

Moments later, Tony and Wade found themselves standing on the front porch and the door was closing behind them. It was the fastest departure after a death notification that Tony had ever experienced.

Wade blinked, apparently stunned. "Well, I guess we can go

tell Carl Lee, now."

Tony had nothing to say. He walked down the steps and climbed into the Blazer. In moments, he was headed back to town and on to break the news to the deceased's son.

Maybe it was because Franklin's brother had been so unimpressed by the man's death, it wasn't shocking when his son was not much more bereaved, at least not on the outside. To his credit, at least, Carl Lee asked what had happened.

"We aren't at all sure. The reports are conflicted, but evidently he fell out of an airplane, or, more exactly, off the wing. He was not wearing a parachute." Tony felt stupid just saying something so dumb.

"That's absolutely, totally ridiculous," Carl Lee murmured. "My father's probably made more parachute jumps than any other man his age. He's an ex-paratrooper; the man could pack a parachute in his sleep. Whatever else he did or didn't do, he always took care of his equipment." Carl Lee looked into Tony's eyes. "Someone probably pushed him."

Tony thought he heard the words, "I don't blame them." Wade was focused on his notepad and didn't appear to have heard the statement. Imagination was not an asset in this case. "Anyone specific you'd nominate for the job?"

Carl Lee sighed and sank back into the sofa cushions. "I have no idea. We haven't spent much time together in the past twenty-five years."

"He lives over in the Asheville area?" Tony made a note of his question. He hated reading an answer later and not being able to recall the exact question.

"And you're busy trying to come up with mileage. It's about seventy-five miles, maybe a hundred if you take the scenic route." Carl Lee rubbed the bridge of his nose. "My wife and I have gone over a few times since he retired and moved there."

"Retired from . . . ?"

"Sorry, I assumed you knew. He went to West Point and made the Army his career. He moved to the Asheville area after he retired. His wife has property over there."

Tony guessed "his wife" was not Carl Lee's mother but needed to know for sure. "Your mother?"

"No. My mother died when I was ten. This is his third wife, Laura Dill Cashdollar. She's got something very attractive to my father."

"And that is?" Wade asked.

"Money. Lots of it." Carl Lee sighed. "All my life, I wanted his approval. I guess I just quit trying."

"Thanks, Carl Lee. We'll go over to Asheville and break the news to his widow." Tony and Wade were almost out the door when Carl Lee spoke again.

"I suppose I should tell you . . ." Carl Lee's voice was barely audible, and his eyes had filled with tears. "I had breakfast with him this morning. In Asheville."

Tony felt a wave of disappointment. He liked Carl Lee, and the idea the man had been keeping potentially important information from him did not sit well. "Why not tell me right away?"

Carl Lee lifted one hand and let it fall. "I'm not sure. Maybe it was the idea that I had to have seen him very close to the time he died. We weren't close, but I didn't wish him dead."

"What about suicide? If you saw him such a short time before he died, what was his mood? Did he sound like he was maybe wrapping up loose ends, saying goodbye?"

"Not at all." Carl Lee relaxed a bit. "He had his usual hearty breakfast. We talked a bit about him and his wife coming here for Thanksgiving, but he seemed to think it was unlikely. His wife is a very social woman and often throws big charity events, and he thought there was something planned for Thanksgiving as well. Given the status of our relationship, it was odd that he brought up seeing us again in the next ten years . . ." Carl Lee's voice trailed to a stop.

Tony thought the sorrow in Carl Lee's eyes was older than this most recent tragedy. "How long before today was the last time you saw him?" Even as irritated as his own mother made him, he couldn't quite visualize seeing her only once a year. Especially since she only lived a mile from his house.

"He and Laura came through around last Christmas, dropped some presents off, but didn't stay more than an hour." Carl Lee did the math. "That's about ten months ago."

Tony considered the relationship. It probably wasn't as unusual as it felt to him now that he lived so close to his mother. Not everyone had a parent and siblings popping in and out at will. Four and a half years earlier, when he and Theo were living in Chicago, their own visits with his mom had probably been separated by about six months. Theo's parents had died when she was a baby and the "old people" who raised her, her grandparents, had seemed old enough to be her great-grandparents. They had died while Theo was still in college. She had no siblings and not many cousins, so family events were not at all like those he grew up with. "Did you sense any undercurrents in their marriage?"

"You mean like he feared for his life?" Carl Lee stared into his face.

Tony sat back in his seat. He had not been thinking along those lines, but he'd follow Carl Lee's lead. "Not exactly fear, but anything he was disturbed about?"

"I did think maybe life with Laura was not perfect." Carl Lee laughed softly at his own statement. "But then, I would say no one's life, married or single, is actually perfect." He smiled at his wife. "My life is much happier since I married Jill, but still, it's not perfect."

Tony couldn't argue with Carl Lee's thinking. His own life

was not perfect. He had a wonderful wife and children, but none of them was perfect. Nor was he. Anyone who claimed to have a perfect life, or a perfect family, was probably dangerously delusional. "But your father's life?"

"My father's marriage track record is not without problems. He divorced his second wife, Joyce, after five years. I was never quite sure why he married her, and I was a bit surprised it lasted as long as it did." Carl Lee studied his long fingers. "I always sort of believed he married her so I'd have a mother, or at least a live-in housekeeper when I was a teenager. No one ever said anything that might verify or refute my idea."

Tony was curious, not suspicious. "Where does Joyce live now?"

A ray of light illuminated Carl Lee's bright blue eyes. "North Carolina, not far from Asheville. She moved there after my dad married Laura. Their last home together was in Virginia, not far from Washington, D.C."

"She followed him." It wasn't a question. Tony did a mental distance calculation; it was neither close nor terribly far between Asheville and Washington D.C. "Do you know how Laura, wife number three, and your father, first met?"

"I believe it was at some function in D.C. My father attended any number of parties given for highly placed politicians and diplomats." He squeezed his big hands together, making the bones in his long fingers gleam through the skin. "Those kinds of events often attract people with money as well as people who want to meet the rich."

Tony jotted down some notes, including Carl Lee's appearance and attitude. "Do you suppose your father has a girlfriend, or is maybe cheating on wife number three?"

"No. I don't think so. I think he found what he wanted with Laura. Money and prestige." Carl Lee's voice lowered. "In truth, Laura's all right, and I liked Joyce well enough. I do think she deserved better than she got."

"You do have their current addresses?"

"Yes, I'll get both of them for you. Anything else?"

Tony checked his list of things he'd wanted to ask. "Did you meet your father somewhere for breakfast or did he pick you up?"

Again, Carl Lee seemed surprised by the question. "That *was* odd. He called and asked me to pick him up a few miles from town, where he'd parked his car. After we ate, he had me drop him back at the car." He seemed really tired and not exactly focused but nothing I could explain.

Tony wondered if the car had been located. He made a note to himself to check on that. "Can you tell me where the car was?"

"From my motel, to the car." Carl Lee carefully drew him a little map. "I don't know the names of any of the roads." He put an X at one intersection. "There was a stoplight here."

CHAPTER NINE

Tony thought the drive over the mountains was a dreadful experience. Not only because he was exhausted and certainly not because Wade was a poor driver, but it was dark, snowy, and the roads were slick. The storm dumping this moisture had started hundreds of miles to the east and was relentless in its march inland.

"I hope Mrs. Cashdollar's there," Tony murmured to Wade. "If we make this trip for nothing . . ." He didn't finish his thought.

Wade steered the patrol car around a clump of slower vehicles. "It won't be for nothing."

Tony was only half listening. His eyes were trained on the road, but his brain was toying with the man's death. "Orvan and Walter heard a banshee in the morning."

"Or maybe someone screaming as he fell," Wade added. "A man like that, a long time paratrooper, jumping without a parachute. It doesn't make any sense."

"No. It doesn't." Tony had known a few avid skydivers. Except for their enjoyment in leaping out of perfectly sound airplanes, they were quite normal. They took care of their equipment, and checked and double-checked every part. Their dead man was not wearing a parachute or a harness. He was holding a fishing pole. Totally unnecessary equipment for skydiving, and there was no fishing spot for miles. Tony didn't like the peculiar circumstances. If he'd been in the plane for the purpose of committing suicide, why take the pole? If he was pushed, why didn't he drop the pole and fight for his life? The only other possibility was he accidentally fell out of the plane. Tony thought that idea was dumber than jumping out of an airplane holding a fishing pole. For the death to be an accident, Franklin would have had to unfasten his seat belt and grab his fishing pole, just as the pilot rolled the airplane. Ludicrous.

Tony's cell phone rang, jolting him out of his bizarre contemplation and the various facts they couldn't match up. The caller was from North Carolina, the local sheriff's office. "Sheriff Abernathy? I'm Sergeant Dupont. My boss tells me I'll be your guide and liaison while you're over here. Anything I can prepare while I'm waiting?"

"Thank you. That's assuming we make it over the mountains," Tony said. "This is quite a storm."

"Yessir, it is at least that. I don't envy the patrols tonight. They may set a new record for accidents." Dupont cleared his throat. "In the meantime, I have determined that Mrs. Franklin Cashdollar is at home this evening."

Tony didn't deny his relief. "Unless she's crazy, she'll still be there when we arrive. I'd guess we're about a half hour away."

"Roger that. Where should we meet?"

"How far away is your office from her home?" Tony had checked the map but without a sense of the space, it hadn't meant much. "If it's relatively close, we'll just meet in your office."

"Yes, it's only a few miles. I'll wait for you there."

The rest of the journey was slow but uneventful.

To keep each other awake, Tony and Wade got involved in relaying news about their extended families. Tony learned that Wade's sister, Karen, a night dispatcher for his department, was taking an online language class. She was learning Italian and Wade claimed it was driving their mother crazy. Karen would practice her new phrases on Mom without translating.

"Maybe I should learn a few Italian words to mess with Karen," Tony said. "Speaking of driving someone crazy, my brother Gus and my sister-in-law, Catherine, did you know she grew up in the Asheville area?" Wade nodded and Tony laughed. "That's not the crazy part. You probably haven't heard but my whole family is going nuts because they are hoarding their little girl."

Wade looked startled. "Not even your mom has seen her?"

"Nope." Tony grinned. "I'm guessing she'll get my brother Tiberius and sister Calpurnia to join her in an assault on their privacy. Maybe I'll get called to come rescue the baby."

"Your mom is not going to behave." Wade peered through the snow. "I wouldn't be surprised if she and your aunt Martha aren't on their way, in this blizzard, for an impromptu visit with Caesar Augustus and Catherine."

Tony didn't refute anything but said, "I see lights ahead."

Wade sighed with relief. "Is Gus going with your mom's love of old Rome in the name game?"

"I sincerely hope not." Tony thought being named Marc Antony had warped him for life.

Tony was relieved to get inside the sheriff's office. Driving into the blowing snow, the headlights had reflected off the flakes and created a solid white panorama. Their last few miles had been snail-like. Inside the sheriff's department building, after being in black and white hell, the lights seemed too bright and the temperature too warm.

It was almost ten thirty at night. If Mrs. Cashdollar was in bed, Tony would be regretful and apologetic, but it would not be the first time he had needed to awaken people in the night to deliver bad news. It made the whole awful process even worse. "I do hope Mrs. Cashdollar is still awake."

Wade and their escort nodded. Their faces reflected his own emotions.

The three men trooped out to the parking lot. Dupont indicated his vehicle. "Y'all want to ride with me? There's not much point in taking two cars, or are you heading right back over the mountain tonight?"

"One car." Tony said, "We'll spend the night somewhere over here. Depending on what Mrs. Cashdollar has to tell us, we might hang around and ask a few questions tomorrow morning. At any rate, I'm not anxious to travel that road again tonight. It's been a long enough day." As understatements went, it was masterful.

Silhouetted against the dark sky, with snow swirling around the decorative streetlights of the expensive neighborhood, Tony thought the Cashdollar house resembled a European castle. It was at least three stories high and had honest to goodness turrets. He couldn't tell in the dark if the home was surrounded by a moat.

Seated in the back seat of Sergeant Dupont's car, Wade made an admiring whistle. "That's a house? Wow, do you suppose Queen Doreen's seen this? It makes the mayor's house look pretty puny."

Tony nodded. He didn't mention that his sister-in-law, Gus's wife, grew up in this same exclusive neighborhood.

Dupont laughed. "We do have a few estates, not houses, around here that seem larger than life. Let's just say the wife and I are not one of their neighbors. And what's really pitiful is my yearly salary is probably less than their gardener's." He turned to the right and headed up a long driveway and eventually parked in a small parking lot. There were no other vehicles in sight.

The three of them climbed out, bracing against the wind, preparing for their condolence call. Tony checked his watch. It was now more than a little past ten thirty, almost eleven. Light shining from several windows gave him hope that Mrs. Cash-dollar was still up.

Immediately after they knocked, Tony could see the shadow of someone coming to the door. He relaxed just a bit; at least they wouldn't have to awaken everyone in the house.

A middle-aged woman, wearing an ill-fitting dark gray dress seemingly designed to add ten pounds and twenty years to her appearance, opened the door to their knock. She did not invite them inside but stood in the narrow space. The lace collar at her throat was probably popular in the 1880s. No way was this the lady of the house.

"Yes?" The woman gripped the edge of the door to prevent it blowing closed in their faces.

"I'm Sergeant Dupont with the local sheriff's department. These men are from over the mountains, from the Park County, Tennessee, sheriff's department." He paused a moment to let her absorb the introduction. "We need to speak with Mrs. Laura Cashdollar."

"It's the butler's night off. He did not tell me to expect you." The housekeeper did not appear impressed by titles, geography, or manners. Her face tightened and her eyes narrowed as if she were trying to decide if she should ask for more identification than uniforms and badges. "Is Madam expecting you?"

Tony thought it was an interesting question but, even so, he doubted the housekeeper was kept apprised of all of the details of her employers' lives. His eyes wandered to the elegant staircase on the far end of the foyer. It curved as it rose, twisting upwards.

He heard Wade answer instead of Dupont. "No. But it is important that we speak with her."

Before the housekeeper managed to decide whether or not to disturb her employer, a cultured, almost musical, voice filtered down to them. "It's late, for heaven's sake. Betsy, just buy ten tickets to whatever they're selling tickets for and come in here."

Tony pitched his voice to carry deep into the house. "We are not selling tickets, Mrs. Cashdollar. I'm Sheriff Abernathy from Park County, Tennessee, and it's very important that we speak with you tonight."

"That is intriguing." The woman's voice sounded like it was moving closer. "Come inside, gentlemen. It's a poor night for a drive, especially one over the mountains."

Tony opened his mouth to agree and fell silent when the lady of the house stepped into the light. She was striking rather than pretty. Elegant. Expensive. Cold. Neither young, nor old, but well-maintained and dressed to stay home in a deep-blue velvet robe trimmed with shiny black fur. Diamond earrings sparkled under the chandelier. It was not exactly Theo's evening ensemble of faded sweatpants and an old T-shirt. Mrs. Cashdollar's smile seemed genuine. Tony found himself wanting to smile in response but fought to maintain a professional demeanor.

Mrs. Cashdollar studied the three men in silence, looking from one to the next. Whether it was the expressions they wore or the fact that a group of law enforcement professionals stood in her foyer after normal visiting hours, she took a step backwards. She had to notice that none of them was smiling in response to her greeting.

"Let's go into the study. It will be much warmer away from the door." Recovering her manners, she turned and led them deeper into the house.

Tony wasn't sure the vast room she called a study was much warmer than the storm outside. At least there was no wind or snow in here. A cheery fire blazed in the enormous fireplace but it felt like the heat was being sucked out and tossed into the sky, along with the smoke. Nevertheless, Mrs. Cashdollar settled onto an armchair near the fireplace and gestured to indicate the choice of chairs available for the men. She pulled a mink throw over her knees and feet. "Would you gentlemen care for coffee?"

Three heads moved from side to side as three voices murmured, "No. Thank you." Two men sat down.

"I have bad news, for you, I'm afraid." Tony remained standing, knowing there was no good way to deliver such news. "Your husband died earlier today in Tennessee."

"Nonsense. He went fishing somewhere near here. He'd tell me if he was leaving town." Laura Cashdollar's eyes sparkled a bit. "Fishing is his passion."

"We do believe that he did intend to fish." Tony slipped his notebook into his hand. "Mrs. Cashdollar, do you know how he traveled to his fishing spot?"

"Call me Laura." Her expression, as she studied his hand gripping the pen, suddenly seemed less confident. "Franklin left here in his Land Rover early in the morning, before breakfast. That's normal. I assume he was driving to wherever he planned to fish." She hesitated looking from man to man. "Was he in a car accident?"

Wade shook his head. "No, ma'am, there wasn't a car involved. Could we check your garage?"

"Certainly." Mrs. Cashdollar waved to the housekeeper hovering in the entry, "Betsy, show one of these gentlemen to the garage."

Wade followed the housekeeper away from the parlor. Moments later he returned, a shake of his head indicated the Land Rover was not in the garage.

"Does he fly?" Tony wrote himself a note to locate the car.

"You mean does he have a pilot's license? Yes. He learned how years ago." Laura Cashdollar pushed a strand of hair away from her face. Her hand suddenly trembled and her expression became less certain. "But he doesn't own a plane."

"Was he going fishing alone?"

"I have no idea." Laura's eyebrows rose. "He doesn't tell me all the details and, well, frankly, I don't ask. One fishing trip sounds like any other to me."

"It's been dark for quite a while," Dupont said. "You didn't expect him home by now? On a snowy night?"

The observation must have hit a nerve. She flinched. "It is unusual for him to be out this late but not unknown. There's a sports bar where the fish stories sometimes are told late into the night. Maybe he's there. I can get you the address." She lifted the lap robe away and stood up. "It doesn't happen often but, he's very good about taking a taxi if he's been over-served."

"No, ma'am," said Tony. "We don't need the address of the bar. Your husband was most definitely in Tennessee."

"We've recovered a body that matches his identification in every way, including fingerprints." Wade's voice was quiet but firm. "It was a clear match."

Mrs. Cashdollar fell silent, staring into the fire, and more or less collapsed back onto the chair. Her head moved slightly from side to side. Tony thought she seemed to be trying to make sense of their words. "There *was* something unusual last night. He received a phone call from his son, Carl Lee. I'm sure I overheard them making plans to meet for breakfast." She looked at Tony, "You must know Carl Lee?"

Tony nodded, waiting.

Her hands twitched on her lap, the firelight catching the facets of the diamonds she wore. "Carl Lee had some meeting and was spending the night over here." She repeated herself. "That's why they were able to meet for breakfast. Did they?"

"Yes. They did breakfast together. Carl Lee confirmed that." Tony glanced around the huge room and guessed the mansion had eight to ten bedrooms, but maybe that was still not enough space to house one stepson. "This is a beautiful home. Carl Lee didn't stay here?"

"No." Laura Cashdollar's voice was firm but she did not elaborate.

Tony thought he'd try a different tack. "What business was your husband in?"

A thin smile crept onto her face. "As I'm sure you already know, he's a retired Army officer. He went to West Point. This house was *not* paid for with Franklin's money. Or my first husband's either."

Tony listened to what she didn't say. There wasn't disdain in the voice, just a simple stating of facts. The information matched what he'd learned from Carl Lee. From what he'd seen of the house, there would be few, if any, people Tony knew who could afford to live like this. Maybe a movie star. Certainly no one in law enforcement unless they married into big money. He was sure a retired cop would have to rob a bank to pay for the furniture, and wouldn't ever be able to steal enough cash for a down payment on the building. "This is your inheritance?"

"Yes. I was an only child, and my family has owned this house for generations. After I die, it goes into a historical preservation trust so it can't be torn down to make way for a mini-mall." Her lip curled a bit over the term "mini-mall."

"And your husband, if you died first, would he have inherited anything?"

"No. Well, yes, a small stipend." A tear slid down her cheek dragging mascara with it. "The bulk of the estate and the house stay intact, together. These historic places require scads of money for maintenance."

"You have no children?" Wade asked.

She looked surprised by the question. "But I do. I have two wonderful sons, Glenn and Jesse, from my first marriage. They were written out of the estate so they wouldn't try to split up the house and grounds. Not that they would, you understand. They're good boys and are just fine with the situation."

Tony wasn't surprised the children would not inherit. Old money knew how to preserve assets. For himself, he was just as glad the building couldn't be torn down. It was architecturally archaic but lovely and impractical. The world did not need another mini-market. "We'd like their names and addresses if you don't mind." The sons might not be as pleased to be disinherited as their mother seemed to believe, or they might have another view of Franklin. Perhaps one less admiring.

"Obviously you've told Carl Lee about his father?" Laura pulled an embroidered bit of cloth from her pocket and dried the tears from her face, smudging the mascara.

Tony found it oddly endearing. "Yes."

"And Joyce?" A flash of anger was in Laura's eyes when she asked the question. "Did you tell her before me?"

"Joyce?" Tony repeated. The word sizzled in the air.

"His second wife." Laura's eyebrows arched higher. "Wife number two does not approve of divorce so she claims Franklin and I are—were now, I suppose—living in sin."

Tony shouldn't have been surprised by the vehemence in her words, but he was. The two women were clearly not friends. His curiosity about Joyce, created when Carl Lee had said the woman moved into the Asheville area after the divorce, intensified. He couldn't help but wonder how far it was to her home from this one.

A tiny whisper in his head told him friendship wasn't required for conspiracy to commit murder. Tony said, "As a matter of fact, we haven't spoken to her yet. Do you know where she lives by chance?"

"Yes." Laura sighed. The long exhalation had a little hitch in it, almost a sob. "I can give you all the addresses and phone numbers you need." She paused. "No one has told how my husband died. What happened? What about the funeral? Is Calvin taking charge of that?"

"I'm sorry, but we have very little information about the circumstances surrounding his death. I can tell you his body was found in the mountains of Park County and has been recovered. An autopsy will have to be done." Tony shook his head. "It's too early to be making any plans."

By the time their condolence call with Franklin's widow ended, it was after midnight and the men were exhausted. A short list of names and addresses gave them something to check the next morning.

Chapter Ten

"I vote for a motel bed and a few hours of sleep." Tony was too tired to think. "Dupont, I imagine you'd like to see your own wife and bed."

Dupont nodded. "I think we've all had enough for one day. There's a clean little motel not far from here. There's no pool or restaurant, but I'm guessing you won't care."

"A bed and a door and a shower." Tony wasn't sure he'd notice if any of those requirements, except the bed, were missing.

A few minutes later Tony sat on the edge of the bed, considering whether or not he should call Theo. Either way, it was going to be the wrong thing to do. If he woke her up, she'd fuss, and if she was waiting for him to call and he didn't, she'd fuss. He picked up his cell phone and called her. Make her happy, let her fuss a bit.

"Are you all right?" Theo was awake and answered on the first ring. "I keep seeing the blizzard on the television. It seems to be all they can talk about. I was afraid you were part of a big accident. Did you run into any trouble?"

"Nope. We're fine. Tired. In a motel." Tony felt too warm and mentally a bit slow. "Love you."

"I love you too. Thanks for calling. Good night." Theo disconnected.

Tony barely managed to press his phone's disconnect button before he was asleep, with the television volume low. He awakened at some point and turned it off, flipped over, and was back asleep in seconds.

Much refreshed after some sleep, Tony felt human again. The big breakfast he'd consumed at a nearby café should hold him for most of the day. Over breakfast, he and Wade had decided to begin their search for answers with the airplane charter company. Tony looked forward to meeting Gentry Frazier, the owner/pilot of the small charter plane company and, more importantly, the man who called Tony to report the accident. After the pilot, they would tackle the stepsons and the ex-wife. In that order.

When Tony and Wade arrived at the charter company hangar, they found two men standing there, next to a small airplane. There were at least three other aircraft in the building. "One of you Gentry Frazier?"

A hand wave of the older of the two men pulled them closer.

"I'm Frazier. This is my mechanic, John Smith." The good-looking, much younger mechanic, was laughing at something the grizzled Frazier was saying, but nodded a greeting. Frazier walked toward them and Smith wiped a smudge off the wing of the pretty little red and white airplane he stood near, then carefully folded the rag and stuck it inside his jumpsuit.

"You here about Cashdollar?"

When Tony nodded, Frazier offered his hand, noticed grease on it, and pulled it back. He wiped it on his pants but didn't extend it again. "Cashdollar called me and said he wanted me to take him over to a fishing spot on the Tennessee side of the mountains. We've done it before, and it worked just fine for both of us."

"Do you advertise, or how did the two of you get together?" Wade looked up from his notebook.

"Yep. I'm in the phone book under 'airplanes, charter.' I

have"—Gentry gestured to the assortment of airplanes in the large hangar—"several choices of aircraft. If I need a copilot, I know a couple of independent pilots who like to pick up some extra money."

Tony said, "How far in advance did Franklin Cashdollar contact you about this trip?"

"Seems like it was the day before. Called out of the blue wanting to take a fishing trip. S'all right by me." Gentry smiled but didn't look happy. "The plan was that we were to fly over the mountains, and he'd rent a car and he'd fish and I'd hang out, and then we'd fly back before dark. Nothing unusual. We've done it before."

"So, what happened this time?" Wade looked up from his notebook.

"Oh, man, I don't know. I never had anyone flip out like that in the air before." Gentry pointed to the biplane. "You see the two seats. He sat in the front one. Everything was fine. He was laughing and enjoying the ride. Snow was falling, but he still wanted to go. I told him it would be miserably cold and he dismissed it. So we took off. Next thing, he's pointing down into a small bald in the midst of the forest and yelling for me to land there."

Tony remembered looking up from that bald—it was not a large space, and certainly not a fit space to land a plane. "And then?"

"And then I said that there was no place to land, and the next thing I know, he was climbing out of his seat, gripping his fishing rod with one hand and waving to me. And he was gone." With a trembling hand, Gentry massaged his chin. His lower lip quivered. "I've seen a lot of weird stuff over the years, but I never saw anything like that."

Wade said, "You didn't report it right away."

"Nossir. I was busy flying the plane." Gentry wiped a fine

line of sweat from his forehead onto the jumpsuit's sleeve. "I love that old plane, but the radio in it sucks. One minute it's working just fine, the next thing there's nothing but dead air."

Tony consulted his notebook, flipping through some of the pages. "What time was this?"

Gentry hesitated. "I might have misspoke what I was saying yesterday. It was actually in the morning, maybe ten o'clock."

"But when you called it in, you claimed it was after two thirty. In fact, it was more like three thirty in the afternoon when you reported it." Tony felt his eyebrows rise. "Why the delay in reporting it?"

"I, uh, well . . ." Gentry fell silent. He slowly moved his head from side to side and swallowed hard. His eyes flickered from Tony to Wade, and back. "I've never had anything like this happen before. It just shocked me so bad, I didn't want to face it. He's never done anything like that before, and the radio going out doesn't reflect too good on my business."

"This was not the first time you took him fishing. Did he always go to the same location?"

"Nope." Gentry scuffed a toe across the cement. "I've flown him a couple of times, different places. He comes scooting across the tarmac carrying that prize fishing pole of his, we fly in, he fishes, strictly catch and release, and we leave again. It's only been a couple of times, and he's been polite but not chatty."

"Did you see how he arrived yesterday?"

"Didn't pay any attention." Gentry looked puzzled. "Didn't he drive?"

"His Land Rover isn't in your parking area." Tony wished some of the dots connected better. "If he drove here, where did his vehicle go?"

"And if someone dropped him off, who was it?" Gentry finished Tony's thought. "I swear, Sheriff, I have no idea how he got out here."

95

"Can we look at the airplane?" Tony hoped standing next to the airplane would help him to understand what happened.

"Sure. Right this way."

Tony and Wade followed Gentry as he led them through the hangar and stopped to stand near an old biplane about the same intense yellow as Theo's little SUV. There was a single propeller in the front, an open cockpit and two wings, one above the other. U.S. Navy was written on the side rear along with a series of numbers.

Gentry's eyes gleamed with joy. "This is my little beauty."

Tony was not an expert, but the plane did look well-cared for. "I'd like to see the passenger seat."

"Oh, sure." Gentry trotted over to a ladder on wheels, a platform at the top. He unlocked the wheels and moved it over to the biplane. "Passenger seat is the one in the front."

Tony climbed up and looked into the two seats, one in front of the other. The single passenger seat was nothing but a bench with a seat belt. Nothing in the tiny space resembled a heater. "With the early snow it had to be freezing up there."

"No kidding." Gentry shrugged. "I don't generally take passengers anywhere in this plane if the ground temperature is not at least sixty degrees because it gets so cold in the sky and the wind chill is amazing. Even when I wear a sheepskin jacket and helmet, fur-lined gloves, and goggles in the summer, it can still sometimes be cold." He shivered and crossing his arms over his chest, he slapped his hands on his upper arms. "I said it was crazy and we should take an enclosed airplane. Told him he'd freeze up there."

"But?" Tony could guess. From what he'd learned so far, Franklin really liked things to be done his way.

"Franklin said he'd be fine wearing his heavy jacket and gloves if I'd loan him a helmet. I always do that anyway. Keeps people's hair from flying around and the attached goggles protect the eyes." Gentry sighed. "I do okay with my business, but it's hard to turn down that kind of money. So I pulled on my long johns and bundled up good, and off we went."

Tony stared at Gentry. "He wasn't wearing gloves when we found him."

Shaking his head, Gentry frowned. "I'm sure I saw them. Brown leather." He studied his own hands as if that would jog his memory.

Wade waited on the floor, unable to see inside. "Are there seat belts?"

Gentry answered before Tony could. "Oh, yeah, and I insist any passenger buckle their seat belt and keep it on. I don't make them strap down into a full harness like those charters who will take their guests on a thrill trip of loops and rolls. Not me."

"You don't enjoy it?" Tony got a bit queasy at the very idea of flying upside down in an open cockpit.

"Oh, yeah, I love it." Standing on the second step, Gentry patted the side of the airplane. "It's awesome fun, but I'm not listening to some screamer and definitely don't want to deal with a weak stomach. This is not an amusement ride, and I'm not cleaning up puke."

Tony continued looking into the passenger seat area and decided that once an adult was buckled in, there wouldn't be much room to shift around and no way to just fall out. The sides of the open cockpit would probably hit Tony in the middle of his upper arm, but he was big. He couldn't suppress a smile. His tiny wife would have to sit on a metropolitan phone book to see out. Leaning over the passenger seat, he twisted around to look up. He was surprised to see the hangar's ceiling instead of the lower surface of the wing. The upper wing had a curve in toward the single engine, leaving the passenger uncovered. If the plane flipped, a falling body wouldn't strike the wing. He looked down again to the airplane's floor, and a glint of silver caught his eye. "There's something under the seat. Wade? You're on."

Gentry shook his head as he climbed back to the ground. He looked angry enough to start a gasoline fire. "No way! Someone better not be dumping their trash into my plane."

Wade climbed the steps, pulled on a pair of latex gloves, and leaning over the side, dug around under the small bench. After a few moments, he retrieved a thermos bottle and held it up for everyone to see.

"Oh, man, I do recognize that." Gentry laughed. An expression of relief erased his confusion. "That man drank more coffee than anyone I've ever seen. He musta had cast-iron kidneys. That belongs to Cashdollar, all right. See here." He pointed to initials FC engraved on the screw top that doubled as a cup. "Every time I've seen him, he's had coffee with him."

"This strap was caught on a piece of metal." Wade carried it down the steps and pulled a bag from his pocket, mumbling to himself. "Lucky I've got plenty of pockets." Once the thermos was in the bag, Wade began filling out a form officially making the thermos evidence. It was easier to do it and not need it than try to fulfill the necessary chain of custody after the fact.

Tony glanced at the thermos. The custom-tooled leather case must have cost a pretty penny. He really needed to quit trying to apply a price tag on everything they saw in this case. "That's a fine piece of leatherwork."

While his deputy worked on his evidence project, Tony gave Gentry a stern look. "Anything else you can think of that we might need to know?"

Gentry appeared to consider the question carefully before he shook his head. "Nope."

After placing the bagged and tagged thermos in a box and locking it in the car, Tony felt relief. For some reason, he was certain there would be evidence in the thermos that would help explain Franklin Cashdollar's attempt to fly. Maybe drugs, maybe alcohol. There were numerous possible chemical tests they could run as part of the autopsy. His office didn't want to pay for anything unnecessary. Searching for exotic poisons could cost a fortune and take months.

If Gentry was telling the truth, and he had no reason to believe otherwise, Cashdollar must have committed suicide. Calvin's questioning of suicide, Tony believed, had been not a question of belief but more a surprised reaction to learning of the man's ordinary mortality.

"One of you guys Sheriff Abernathy?" A female voice called from the front of the building, interrupting his thoughts.

Tony waved.

"Hi, I'm Jackie. I'm an evidence collection tech for the sheriff's office." There was a musical lilt to her voice. "My sheriff thought you might need someone to find and verify, and I quote, 'fingerprints on the wing.' "

Tony studied their new assistant. The middle-aged, chubby woman had neatly contained salt and pepper hair, and a wide grin. She looked like she was eager to examine what he assumed was an unusual location for fingerprinting.

"Yes, our Mr. Cashdollar was not wearing gloves." The absence of gloves disturbed Tony. The pilot had been wearing fur-lined ones. There were none in Cashdollar's pockets or under his seat on the airplane. It was one of those instances of, "what did you expect to see and didn't?"

Jackie opened her case and went to work. Between her expertise and Wade's, whose trained eyes watched her work, Tony was confident that any fingerprint on the wing, in the seating area, and even the pilot's seat, would be picked up, analyzed, and reported in a coherent, clearly worded report.

★ ★ ★ ★ ★

From the airport, he and Wade went to chat with the two Dill men, Laura Cashdollar's sons. The more information they could learn about Franklin's normal behavior, the more likely they could sift through facts leading to his death.

With a little help from their GPS device, they located the Dill brothers' shared office space in a semi-industrial building.

Sergeant Dupont joined them in front of the vintage brick-red building. He smiled, climbing out of his vehicle. "Did you two get any sleep? I slept like a rock."

Tony thought their local guide did look somewhat refreshed in the morning light.

Both Tony and Wade said they had also slept well and thanked him for his recommendation for the motel and café. "We didn't have any trouble locating the airstrip and flight charter company."

"That's good. I'm sorry I couldn't join you earlier. I had to testify in court this morning."

"Business before more business." Tony smiled. "You missed seeing some spiffy airplanes. One of your techs came and checked the airplane for fingerprints. We don't expect anything interesting, but there's only one way to find out."

Dupont nodded. "Never assume anything."

"Let's just talk to both of them together and then we can separate them if there's any reason," Tony suggested and Wade agreed.

Once inside the business office, it was quickly apparent that the Dill brothers had gotten a call from Laura and were expecting visitors. Tony had learned the two Dills were in their early thirties. That was where the resemblance between the brothers ended. One was tall and thin and the other was short and stout. The taller one was blond and blue-eyed and the other was dark chocolate and had such deep brown eyes they were almost black.

According to a quick computer check of their drivers' licenses, they conveniently, at least as far as Tony was concerned, lived in townhomes next door to each other.

The brothers each stood near one of the two large desks, both of which faced the doorway. These were not particle board, assemble it yourself, desks but rather oversized, old-fashioned, valuable antiques. Cherry wood, Tony guessed. There was only a very small desk to separate their office area from the entry and it, too, reeked of old money. A half-full cup of coffee suggested an employee, possibly a receptionist, was away for the moment. The room was larger than it initially appeared because of the exceptionally high ceiling, which was decorated with antique-embossed tin. Modern ceiling fans moved the heated air, and beautiful artworks depicting garden vegetables decorated the silk-covered walls.

"Mom says you won't let her plan a funeral." Tall and blond, this one was Jesse. His patrician features were tight with disapproval but not grief. "Why not?"

Before Tony could respond, the other Dill, Glenn, spoke, addressing his brother. "I imagine they are not through with the investigation." He turned to Tony. "Isn't that so, Sheriff?"

"Exactly." Tony appreciated his understanding. "Your stepfather's body was recovered in a remote area, nowhere near the spot where your mother expected him to be fishing. We need to know why."

Jesse said, "I'm sorry for the attitude, Sheriff. Mom was distraught, and some of her unhappiness wore off on me. How can we help?" He led the way to a small sitting area in the back of the room. More antiques and silk upholstery.

Tony understood how maternal issues worked on sons. Sometimes his own mother's attitudes rubbed off onto him, too. "We need to clarify a few things." Tony settled onto a chair that had looked hard but was, in fact, extremely comfortable.

He opened his notebook. "Your mother explained that neither of you are in line to inherit the house."

The men nodded.

"You don't feel left out?" Tony was curious more than convinced it had anything to do with Cashdollar's death. He just hated dangling bits of information.

Glenn laughed. "Not at all. It's not like either of us are direct descendants of the original family."

Tony's face must have shown his confusion.

"Look at us." Glenn's merriment stopped, his dark eyes turned pensive. "Jesse and me, we're both adopted. Mom and Dad picked us out of cardboard boxes in front of the grocery store, like puppies."

Jesse shook his head. "Not the time for our puppy story, Glenn." He smiled at Tony. "Actually we were available for adoption and our birth mothers found us new homes. Now, except for the bloodlines and the old house, we are Dills. Even our father was only considered a temporary resident in the family house. Family by marriage. I'm surprised our mother ever used either husband's name. It rather spoiled her connection with the past."

Nodding his agreement with his brother's statement, Glenn took over the conversation. "Luckily for everyone, Dad had plenty of his own money. It's a necessary commodity when marriage comes with a family heirloom that is actually a huge money pit." Glenn smiled. "Jesse and I each inherited a fair amount of cash when Dad died. Enough to keep us funded without needing to get real work, and that's discounting the cash we put into our new business."

"What's that?" For no particular reason, Tony guessed the brothers might go into real estate.

"Dills' Pickles." Glenn pulled a business card and a small folded advertising/calendar from his shirt pocket and handed them to Tony. "From the moment we were adopted as kids, Jesse and I talked about our new last name and we always said with a name like Dill, we should have a pickle factory. So now we are in the pickle business. Our company is about to release the first batch. We're taking orders already and, of course, our pickles are strictly first-class—we process cucumbers, okra, peppers, and any vegetable we can get that's certified organic. We're developing gourmet, healthy pickles."

The business sounded like a good one, but guessing he couldn't afford their products, Tony returned to his questions. "What was your relationship with Franklin like? Did you spend much time with him?"

Glenn shrugged. "He was okay, but then we never actually lived with him. At most, we shared a few meals, at holidays, a couple of times a year. Our dad was more fun than Franklin, but he died in an accident years ago."

"We were in college at the time." Jesse stared into Tony's eyes. "Mom was lonely, and Franklin looked good in formal wear—the military posture, you know. It was fine with us when she married Franklin."

"Mostly because we didn't have to live with him," Glenn repeated. "He was totally opposed to anything spur of the moment, even a pickup basketball game had to be on the day's schedule or it didn't happen. Don't you think planning ahead for an impulse game is weird?"

"Well, there is that." Jesse nodded. "Franklin had a lot of rules he lived by. What happened to him?"

Tony thought it was interesting how long it took for them to show any interest in how the deceased came to be in that condition. When he explained the flight to go fishing, the siblings nodded.

"Sounds like Franklin. He did love to fish," said Glenn.

"Did either of you share his interest in the sport?"

Glenn shook his head, and at the same time Jesse said, "I fish a little, but compared to Franklin, no. That man was hard-core. He'd spend twenty hours a day, casting, tying flies, sharpening his knife. A big knife."

"So, his having a charter flight to take him somewhere to fish was not out of character?"

"No." The brothers spoke in unison.

Glenn said, "I thought it was weird he carried a huge knife like he did if he didn't plan to gut something big."

Tony didn't remember there being a large knife on the body, or for that matter, any knife. He glanced at Wade. His deputy was busy drawing a question mark next to the statement in his notebook.

Thanking the men for their assistance and wishing them good luck with Dills' Pickles, Tony, Wade, and Dupont headed for the ex-wife's office.

"What did you think of the knife business?" Tony looked at Wade.

"I think it's very interesting that there wasn't a knife on him when he landed." Wade rubbed the back of his neck. "Or a sheath. A knife that size ought to have a sheath."

"It wasn't in the airplane." Tony hated lines that didn't connect. "Do you suppose he dropped it when he left the plane?"

"Oh, man, if he did, it could be anywhere."

Tony wondered if his initial assessment of Franklin's second wife, Joyce Cashdollar, was accurate, or if it had been colored by the third wife's attitude. Physically, she could have been a sister or cousin to the much wealthier woman. It made Tony wonder if the first wife had been the same body type. He hoped he would remember to ask Carl Lee to show him a photograph of his mother.

"We need to speak with Joyce Cashdollar. Is that you?" Tony

wanted to be certain this was not someone else sitting at Joyce's desk.

"Yes. And you are?" Her eyes narrowed.

"Sheriff Tony Abernathy of Park County, Tennessee, and my deputy, Wade Claybough."

"Let me see your identification." It was not a request.

After he'd introduced himself and Wade, Joyce had checked his badge and identification, asked for references, and even called Carl Lee Cashdollar for a description. After all of that, she still tried to keep Wade from joining Tony when he entered her office, and almost did keep Dupont out. Tony wished he could have a reason to be excluded. Tony couldn't imagine how he'd get into her house if he needed to interview her there. A certain degree of suspicion was good as a personal safeguard— this woman was paranoid.

"May I call you Joyce?" Tony didn't want to just drop the bad news on her like a brick, but it might come to that. First he thought he'd do a bit of subtle inquiry.

She stepped back as if she'd been slapped. "No. Call me Mrs. Cashdollar. I'm a married woman. I won't have you taking liberties."

Having been warned by Laura, the replacement wife, he thought he'd test Joyce's determination. "It's my understanding that you and Franklin divorced some time ago."

"Absolutely not. I do not approve of divorce. He and I took vows in church. We are still married." Joyce bared her teeth like an angry rodent. "He'll burn in hell for his cheating ways."

Tony stood his ground. He thought Joyce's personality reeked of anger, disdain, and jealousy. Why was there such an overblown reaction?

Joyce narrowed her eyes at him. "What do you want here?"

Feeling like there was only one way to get through the personality wall, Tony spoke softly and said, "It's my sad duty, but I have to tell you he has died."

Joyce's expression changed dramatically. The snarl disappeared, and she even produced a faint smile. "Oh, well then, I guess he's already burning." Joyce ran her fingers through her hair, fluffing the curls. "There's nothing to discuss then."

Tony did not agree. "Actually, I have several questions that only you can answer for me." When Joyce's face shifted from anger to satisfaction and now curiosity, she became lovelier and appeared more relaxed than she had when they arrived.

She smiled. "What do you need to know?"

"Were you two often in communication with each other?" Tony said. "Visits?"

"No. Just birthday cards and Christmas fruit." Joyce blinked rapidly, sending a tear down her cheek. "And anniversary gifts. He sent me a gold necklace last time."

Tony didn't think normal people still shared anniversary gifts after a divorce, but what did he know. "Phone calls?"

"Sometimes." Joyce finally sat down on her office chair and rested her hands on the spotless desktop. "I think he was sorry he left me and shacked up with the rich woman."

"Did he ever tell you he was unhappy in his new marriage?" Tony guessed the answer would be no. This woman would be hard to live with. Theo, like himself, had irritating moments, but Joyce did not appear to have any idea of give and take. In their short conversation, Joyce had experienced just about every emotion he could think of. Mood swings made him uneasy. This woman's were hurricane-sized.

"Not in so many words, but we were soul mates and so I knew." Joyce tightened her lips like she'd bitten into something sour. "That rich woman lured him away, but I still get paid."

"Paid?" The word conjured another word. A silent one: Blackmail.

"I guess it's not exactly like a salary, but I'm still on the life insurance we bought together years ago. He's worth a hundred thousand dollars to me now that he's dead. He always said he wanted me to have something, and so insurance was his gift." Joyce continued her rapid speech, her eyes narrowed. "If that brazen woman thinks she can steal my inheritance away from me, too, she's got another think coming."

Tony noticed moisture gathered in the corners of Joyce's mouth, conjuring in his mind, the vision of rabies. This woman was seriously scary. He did some mental math about her income. A hundred thousand to Laura Dill Cashdollar was nothing; to Joyce it would be a tidy nest egg. He did think it was pretty crass to be gloating over the insurance payout during a death notification, but there was no standard of behavior in certain circumstances. Was she totally innocent or not too bright? For that matter, he wondered what kind of person bought life insurance as a parting gift for the end of a marriage. It would only pay out if the insured didn't outlive the heir. Was that the deceased's plan? Was jumping from the plane a way to give Joyce cash or just coincidence?

"Are you aware of any health issues that might have been expected to shorten Franklin's life?"

Calmer for the moment, Joyce sighed heavily and considered his question. "No. As far as I know, he was still in his usual perfect physical condition." Her expression darkened again. "Oh, I see what you're asking. If he was in such good health, I'd probably die first and I'd never get paid anything."

Tony thought the troubled expression on her face meant she had never considered the parting gift might not be as delightful as she had supposed.

Leaving her to her thoughts, Tony and Wade excused themselves.

"Maybe we should talk to Mrs. Cashdollar's staff." Tony had

almost forgotten about them, mostly because he was unaccustomed to the very concept of a butler.

The Cashdollar butler answered the door. "May I help you?"

Tony was somewhat surprised to find the butler was in his mid-thirties, tall, fit, and quite handsome. The butler didn't possess the same attractiveness as Wade, but who could? Tony glimpsed sparkling white teeth, accentuated by a lingering tan. The butler blocked their way, waiting to see their identification.

The three men trotted out their badges and identification. "I believe you were off duty the first time we came." Tony smiled. This was the first honest to goodness butler he'd ever met. He felt his smile grow wider as he thought how suddenly life was like being in an old movie—a castle and a butler. What would be next? A dragon? A ghost on the battlement? He wasn't sure what a battlement looked like.

"Yes, sir, I was." The butler sounded politely detached. "Madam did inform me of the master's tragic end. She is expecting you."

The voice surprised Tony, bringing him back to reality. The accent was decidedly closer to Georgia than Britain.

"If you'll come this way." The butler turned and led them back to the unwelcoming room where they had talked previously. Today though, the fireplace was cold, making the room even less appealing than before. "Wait here." And he vanished through a door partially hidden by a tapestry.

A few minutes passed before Mrs. Cashdollar appeared. Minutes while Tony prowled about the large room, restless and unsettled by the lack of anything he'd call "personal" in this vast room. Maybe because he was so accustomed to seeing living rooms filled with newspapers, televisions, toys, quilt projects, and even a motorcycle in one house he'd visited, that this museum piece seemed unlived in. "There's not even a book."

Wade shook his head, his expression as curious as Tony's own. "They don't live in here."

The lady of the manor, Laura Dill Cashdollar swept through the doorway like a movie star arriving to collect a trophy. She was as immaculately groomed as she had been the first time they'd met. The slacks and sweater she wore looked like they had been made for her, but the obvious strain of the situation had taken a toll on her as evidenced by the red-rimmed eyes. She squeezed her hands together, but a fine tremor continued. Exhaustion and grief. "You have more questions?"

"Yes. Wouldn't you like to sit?" Tony didn't like questioning the grieving, but questions had to be answered.

Mrs. Cashdollar lowered herself onto a wing chair. She didn't invite the three men to sit, but they did, pulling chairs around to form a semicircle at her feet.

"Is there a possibility that your husband might have jumped from the airplane on an impulse?" Tony hadn't wasted much time with preliminaries. "We keep running into inconsistencies and roadblocks."

"No way. Impulse was *not* part of his personality."

"People can change." Tony had lost count of the number of times he was told someone wouldn't do such and such—and yet they had. Cheated, lied, run off with another person.

Laura Dill Cashdollar's expression changed to something like anger. She clearly didn't like be contradicted. "I know, but *he* didn't change. Several times I even tried to loosen him up a bit. Like one time I suggested we just take our plates into the den and eat in front of the fireplace because I was cold in the dining room. He checked his watch and shook his head and said something about it being too late to switch." A sigh followed her words. "One beautiful summer day, I suggested we throw a few things in the car and drive over to the Outer Banks. He looked at me like I was proposing we leap from the roof." She opened her hands, revealing the handkerchief wadded up inside, and wiped her streaming eyes.

Tony thought "leap" was an interesting word, given the situation, but everything Laura said tallied with Carl Lee's observations about his father. Franklin seemed to have been a solid, dependable, organized man. He was not without a lighter side, but definitely not one to leap from a cliff, or an airplane, without checking the altitude, wind velocity, and angle of the sun.

Dupont gave Mrs. Cashdollar a moment to gather herself together again. "Is there any reason you could suggest to explain his jumping?"

"What are you suggesting?" She managed to sit up even straighter. "I'm telling you for the last time, he would never do something like kill himself. I know that as well as I know myself."

"Even if he was ill? Very ill?" Tony spoke softly.

"Was he?" Turning to face him, Mrs. Cashdollar looked relieved by the suggestion. "I had no idea."

"Not as far as we've learned." Tony felt like a cad. "I was just asking."

"That was cruel."

"I'm sorry. It wasn't meant to be cruel. We're just searching for answers." Tony didn't think they would learn anything from this woman. He wanted to chat with the butler. Staff, or so he was told, often know more about their employers than family members. "Thank you Mrs. Cashdollar."

She stood.

"Would you ask your butler to join us?" Tony studied her face. If her expression meant anything, he might have asked if the wallpaper would talk to them.

"Of course." She swept out of the room without looking back.

The butler, on the other hand, sidled in like he was preparing to confess to stealing the family silver. "You asked to speak with me?"

"Absolutely." Tony smiled.

Wade suggested the man be seated.

The butler appeared scandalized by the idea of sitting where the lady of the manor had been seated. He shook his head, took a step back, and stood at attention. Only the military or butler school could produce that posture.

"I presume you have a name." Tony waved his notebook.

"Yes, sir, it's Anderson." His posture did not relax. "The family calls me Anderson."

"How long have you worked for the family?" Tony thought he might as well dive right in.

"Eight years now." A faint smile appeared on the butler's face, but nothing else moved.

"Do you enjoy it?"

The butler's eyebrows did rise on that question, as if he'd never thought about it. "Of course."

Tony wasn't sure why, but he believed the man was lying. Maybe it was his interpretation of a butler's duties—work twenty hours a day and remain invisible. "Go to butler school?"

"No sir, reform school." Anderson relaxed an inch. "Mrs. Dill, that is, Mrs. Cashdollar now, maintains many charitable organizations. Rehabilitation put me in her path."

"You couldn't have been very old," said Wade.

"As they say, it's not the years but the miles." Anderson straightened back into position. "My choices were to either change my way of life or spend the rest of it behind bars." He smiled but his eyes were intensely serious. "I did not want prison."

"Fair enough." Tony smiled. "Did the Cashdollars get along well?"

"Sir?" Anderson appeared scandalized by the question.

"I'm not looking for gossip." Tony tapped his notebook. "It's none of my business if they threw crystal at each other every night after dinner, but I believe anyone who lives in the same building will be aware if there was friction. Were they merely polite to one another? Affectionate? Raging arguments?"

"If those are my choices, I'd say somewhere between polite and affectionate." Anderson almost smiled. "The household is very civilized."

"That's fine." Tony didn't feel like there was more to learn. "Would you ask the housekeeper to join us?"

Anderson nodded and left the room without another word.

The middle-aged woman who had opened the door to them the previous evening joined them. Today's dress was identical and her demeanor was only slightly friendlier. "I'm Betsy."

Tony waved to the chair. Betsy perched on the edge. Her features were nondescript and her dull blond hair was streaked with gray. "Do you live in?"

"Yes, like Anderson, I have an apartment over the garage."

"And how long have you worked for the Cashdollars?"

"I've attended to Mrs. C. for ten years now."

"Do you enjoy your work?" Tony would have stood on his head if he thought she would change expressions.

"Enjoy?" The question seemed to have no meaning to the woman and the word came back to him like an undissolved piece of hard candy.

"Did you like Mr. Cashdollar?"

"He liked things done just so." Betsy finally displayed some emotion. Irritation.

"Specifically?"

Blank blue eyes stared back at him.

"What had to be 'just so'?"

"Oh, well everything. The pillows on the bed. The towels on the rack. The fold on them had to be away from the shower. And ferns. If Mrs. C. received fresh flowers, he always pulled out any ferns and threw them away."

"Did he say why?"

Betsy shook her head. "And I didn't ask."

"Did he yell or threaten you in any way?"

"Oh, no sir. He'd just stare like he couldn't believe you was so stupid." Betsy's eyes narrowed. "Made me feel like dirt."

CHAPTER ELEVEN

After Betsy was excused, Tony and Wade went to the kitchen in search of the cook. When Tony visualized "cook" his brain said, "Blossom or Pinkie," probably because of their affiliation with Ruby's Café. Mrs. Jenkins, the Cashdollar cook, did not fit the mold. She looked barely old enough to buy wine.

Dressed in tight black Capri pants and a spotless white "chef's jacket," the girl had copper skin and hair and brilliant green eyes. Maybe Mrs. Jenkins wasn't quite beautiful, but she was strikingly attractive.

"How long have you worked for the Cashdollars?" The phrase was getting easier.

Mrs. Jenkins narrowed her eyes, thinking, and Tony noticed a line where her artificial lashes were glued to her eyelids.

"Almost a year now."

"Do you like working here?" Wade's turn to ask the question.

"It's all right." She moved a stack of plates closer to the stove. "It's a short-time gig for me."

"Why is that?" Tony guessed it would be dull work.

"When my husband is done working on his master's degree, we will probably move some place bigger and I would like to open my own restaurant."

"Did you interact much with Mr. Cashdollar?"

"Lots of coffee!" Mrs. Jenkins smiled. "He never seemed to care what the menu was as long as I made lots of coffee."

"Yesterday morning," Tony said. "Did you fill his thermos?"

"Of course."

Leaving the Cashdollar mansion, Tony looked at Wade. He could practically hear the paperwork stacking up on his desk from the other side of the mountains. "Let's go home. We can come back to North Carolina later. Maybe something in that thermos will solve the entire case."

Tony watched as Deputy Sheila Teffeteller fidgeted on the chair across from his desk. Not at all her style. She had asked to talk to him almost as soon as he'd gotten back to Silersville. Now back from North Carolina, he was trying to catch up. Piles of fresh mail and reports covered his already messy desk.

He was tired but not exhausted, and although he'd probably be heading back over the mountains at some point, he hoped not to be doing it in a snowstorm. "What's bothering you, Sheila?"

"I think you might not know this, but you should." She paused. "Carl Lee and I are cousins. First cousins. His mom and my dad are siblings."

"No way." Tony had cousins, but they all lived in other states. He and his siblings had moved to Silersville with his mom and dad when he was eight years old. After his father's death, they had stayed, but even so he was variously considered "a foreigner" or, at best, "a newcomer." Of his forty years, deducting his time in the service, college, and Chicago, only maybe fifteen of his years had been spent in Park County. "Why didn't I know that?"

Sheila smiled. "If you scratch the old families, we're all connected at some level. If there hasn't been a marriage, there's been a feud, or some combination of one causing the other."

Tony knew Sheila was younger than Carl Lee, but only by maybe three to five years. "Do you remember Carl Lee's mother, his birth mother?"

"When she married Franklin Cashdollar and moved away, I wasn't born yet. They came through the area several times though, when I was a little girl. I remember Calvin's mom seemed very nice," Sheila added. "But although I met Uncle Franklin a few times, he wasn't my favorite uncle."

Tony believed that instincts are immeasurable and yet sometimes the best guide. "Any particular reason you didn't like him?" Tony lifted his right hand as if being sworn to silence, but he would take all the insight into the deceased he could get. "I won't tell anyone."

"He's probably the reason I'm your sniper." Sheila laughed, but there wasn't much humor in it. "Uncle Franklin claimed females were incapable of being quiet and couldn't be trusted with a gun."

"I'd say your Uncle Franklin is . . . was an idiot." Tony guessed her uncle had made other hurtful and stupid comments about one of the poorest branches of the family tree. He himself had often watched, with awe, Sheila training and at work with her rifle. Her patience was legendary and even knowing where she waited, hidden, he often couldn't spot her. Starting when she was still very young, the Teffeteller children ate a lot of fried rabbit instead of going hungry, thanks to Sheila. Poor man's chicken. "I'll bet Carl Lee already knows, but he won't hear it from me."

Sheila did smile then. "I like Carl Lee. His dad used to send him to stay with his backwoods cousins every summer. We liked it just fine, he was fun, but I always wondered how he felt about being shipped to us from exotic places."

A lurid image of a gangly boy emerging from a crate covered with foreign postage stamps flashed through his brain. "Shipped?"

"Oh, yeah, my mom and dad would get a message that Carl Lee was arriving at the airport on such and such a date and time and would someone pick him up." Sheila studied her feet. "Carl Lee would stay with us and then with his Uncle Calvin and the Queen for part of the time. It had to be quite a contrast in lifestyles."

Tony couldn't visualize Queen Doreen interacting with a gangly boy. "I imagine he had more fun with your family."

"It was good for him to see both families. When I'm not thinking about slapping Doreen just to wipe that snotty expression from her face, she does some nice things; she's just not warm and cuddly." Sheila shrugged slightly. "My view of her is a bit tainted by my childhood. Doreen was always polite, but she was so very clean, and when we were young, soap was not our favorite product. Oddly enough, she didn't want us hugging her."

As a compliment, Tony thought it was fine. If Sheila had liked the woman enough to want to hug the Queen, she'd seen past the icy surface.

"What's the status on our stabbing victim?" Tony talked to Doc Nash, ashamed he'd almost forgotten about the woman Theo had rescued at the grocery store.

"I had to let her leave the clinic." The doctor sounded angry. "She never would say what happened. What about you? Can you charge anyone with assault with a deadly weapon or whatever?"

Tony flipped through the open file on his desk. "The fingerprints on the knife are definitely not all hers."

"There's a big surprise." Doc Nash fumed. "Any idea who they do belong to?"

"Nope. Whoever it is has no criminal history and has not been fingerprinted and put into the system." He glanced at the framed Cashdollar fingerprints and blew out a relieved sigh. He watched the doctor rise from his chair and cleared his throat to stop the doctor from going off on a rant. "You know, it's not as though I even have access to fingerprints unless they're in a criminal database."

"What do you mean?" The doctor sat.

"I mean, even if you have been fingerprinted as part of your job identification, that does not necessarily mean I have access to the information. I don't get to just dig around in everyone's personal information because I am looking for a match." Tony heaved a sigh, not sure what he thought of the system. "Lots of people have never been fingerprinted at all."

"Well, I guess we'll have to do a little more research." Doc Nash removed his glasses and polished the lenses before returning them to his face. "Let me see what I can find."

Tony gripped the edge of his desk. "Doctor, you may not make a house call to check on a patient and start picking up items for fingerprint comparison."

"What if they are my items and I let someone examine them?"

Tony didn't know. He wanted to know who had done the stabbing as much as the doctor did, but if the woman didn't want to talk about what happened, he couldn't force her. "Please don't."

Theo reached into the pantry and retrieved a box of crackers, thinking they'd be nice with some cheese and the leftover stew. She shook the box. Silence. She reached inside and found it was completely empty. It didn't even have the cellophane liner in it. It didn't take much detective work to know that neither the dog nor the baby girls could have done it. That left three males of varying sizes as cracker-thieving suspects. Carrying the box, she walked to the non-kitchen portion of their kitchen/family room and stood in front of the television, blocking the football game. Three heads moved to the right as the guys tried to see around her.

She waved the empty box. "Who ate the last cracker and put the empty box back in the pantry?"

"Not me." Tony was the fastest to reply. He held a baby girl in each arm and nodded at them. "Or them."

"Not me," said Chris.

"Not me." Jamie's words lacked the ring of truth. It only took a glance at his mother's face before he conceded, "Okay, maybe it *was* me but there weren't many in the box to start with."

Theo shook her head and stared. "It's not that you ate the crackers. A box sitting in the pantry makes me think there is food in it."

Jamie laughed. "So, if I left only one cracker in the box, would it be better?"

Tony joined the fray. "Before you head off to law school, James, why don't you run over to Food City and get another box of crackers for all of us to share."

Theo handed Jamie some cash. "Chris, you go with him."

For just a moment, Chris looked like he might want to protest, but he quickly headed out with his brother. "We could have a snowball fight in the park." His words carried through the house as the boys stomped toward the front door.

"Thank you." Theo plopped down on the love seat. "Food around here vanishes at an alarming rate."

"My mom says she still has nightmares about the quantities of food the four of us used to go through." Tony winked. "Don't get her started if you don't want your own nightmares about food flying from the cupboards."

Theo studied her oversized husband. Gus, Tony's oldest brother, was as big as Tony or bigger, and Berry wasn't small. "At least we only have two boys."

"Don't kid yourself. Skinny little Calpurnia could eat her weight in food. Us boys won several bets by putting her into various eating contests. She always won."

"We're doomed." Theo looked at the baby girls, and the nightmare description of Callie's eating capacity only brought more concern. She hoped next year's garden would produce a bumper crop.

"Before you start food rationing, and before the boys return, I have a question."

Tony looked serious, so Theo guessed it had something to do with work. "Okay."

"What do you know about the Teffeteller clan and their relationship to Carl Lee Cashdollar?"

The question surprised her. "I forgot they are related. I was older than them so we didn't hang out together, but I can remember my grandmother expressing some concern about whether they'd all have enough to eat. Sort of like us today. Mammaw said she couldn't believe Carl Lee's dad would drop him off for the summer with people who couldn't afford to feed their own children."

Tony remembered Theo's grandmother as being extremely old, frail, and yet not a woman who would keep her opinions to herself if change in something or someone was needed. "What did she do about it?"

The memory made Theo laugh. "She cooked vast quantities of perishable foods—you know—breads, muffins, and things that could quickly spoil like potato salads and tuna dishes, and then she made my grandfather deliver them to the Teffetellers and say we had too much and the food would just go bad and maybe they could help us out by eating the extra."

"And he did, of course." The old man was a gentleman with a kind heart and married to a woman who was ruthlessly charitable.

"Yes, but still he was embarrassed, so he used to buy bullets for Sheila's old twenty-two. I remember one time, not long before he died, he said that girl had more ambition than either of her folks, and she'd be able to feed the whole family on her own with a little practice."

"I'll bet he never envisioned Sheila as a police sniper." Tony shifted his sleeping girls, hoping they wouldn't have to spend their childhoods trying to supply food to anyone.

Theo shook her head, making her curls bounce. "The idea of her having such a job would never have occurred to him. I can practically hear him flipping over in his grave."

"Is that the thumping, spinning sound I hear?" Tony cocked his head.

"No." Theo leapt to her feet and dashed for the washing machine. "Just a load of towels shifted. If I don't catch it, it will send water everywhere."

"Someone has reported a stabbing outside the Okay." Rex frowned. "Anonymous but stupid. He called nine-one-one from his personal cell phone."

"Who was our genius and who was stabbed?" Tony was surprised. Usually the clientele at the Okay were better behaved than those at The Spa.

"I've sent Sheila to check it out." Rex looked up. "I've got everyone else on alert. It sounds like a trap or a diversion."

Tony didn't doubt it. He really didn't like it. "I'll go to the Okay. Let Sheila know I'm on my way."

It didn't take him long to reach the bar. Its full name was the Okay Bar and Bait Shop. They hadn't sold bait since God was a boy, but the sign remained. Now the Okay was more of an unrestricted clubhouse than a tavern. Sure, the patrons could buy a drink, but it was often coffee or soda pop. The short, feisty proprietress, Mom Proffitt, ran the business, offered advice only when asked, and kept everyone's keys, no matter what they were drinking. Tony loved her.

When he reached the Okay, he could see Sheila leaning against her car, chatting with Mom. Mom looked confused and Sheila looked wary. If she was in a trap, she and Mom could be targets. Sheila was waving the older woman back inside, and Tony could see her lips moving. Through the radio he could hear that Sheila was talking to Rex. The gist was there had been a brief fight ending with a threat to Mom.

Flavio Weems stepped out of the Okay. As one of their dispatch team, Flavio's work had improved tremendously with practice. He shepherded the bar owner back inside. Being off duty and being at the Okay put him in the right place at the right time.

"Flavio," Tony called out. "Come back here after you get Mom settled."

Obligingly, Flavio returned after seeing the bar owner safely inside and loped toward them; his slightly awkward gait was caused by the unevenness of his legs. He wore a corrective shoe, but it didn't allow him to run normally. "Sheriff? What's happening?"

"Rex received a call about a stabbing at this location. Did you see or hear anything?" After the woman with a knife in her back, he was hoping not to have a copycat or an outbreak of anything similar.

"I've been here most of the evening." Flavio's forehead creased as he thought. "There was a bit of a verbal altercation between a couple of guys, and Mom made them leave. There was not even any pushing or shoving, much less a stabbing. The disagreement didn't look serious or like it was about to get worse, or I'd have called in and reported it myself. I'll bet it was a practical joke."

Tony nodded. "Well, let's have a little chat with our prank caller."

He didn't even have to go inside. Sheila tipped her head to

indicate that the man she grasped by the upper arm, mostly to keep him on his feet, was the person who reported the stabbing. Tony couldn't wait to see the drunken prankster's face when he learned how much trouble he was in for making the call.

Maybelle Ruth finally came forward to talk about her own stabbing. She said that with the recent false report at the Okay, one of those bits of information that quickly made the gossip circles, she wanted his office to understand what had happened to her.

"Why don't you just start at the beginning?" Tony rolled his pen between his palms, waiting for her to speak. His anticipation increased when she didn't start immediately.

"It was an accident." Maybelle held several tissues in her balled fist. "The kitchen in my son's house is small and has the door into the yard opposite a swinging door into the living room." She shifted, then flinched as the movement pulled her injury.

"Okay, I can imagine that." Tony made a little sketch in his notebook of a possible floor plan. "Like this?"

Maybelle studied the drawing. "The stove is opposite from the sink."

Tony changed his sketch. She nodded. "Go on."

"My son and I were chatting when his wife came in. I stepped back to make room and backed into the blade of the knife he was holding and then went outside and left them alone together."

Tony believed part of this story was true, but not the whole thing. "No one tried to stop you or get the knife back?" Why, if she backed into the blade, did the son not pull it free, if for no other reason than he was using it? Wouldn't he need to continue slicing whatever? "Nonsense. Are you telling me you didn't feel it?"

Maybelle nodded her head.

Tony glared at her. The slowest mind in the world, even a caterpillar's, would realize the knife had been pulled out of his hand. "Ridiculous."

The two of them stared at each other for several minutes. Tony clasped his hands together, lacing his fingers. He rested them on the surface of his desk. And waited.

Maybelle's fingers fluttered like she was telling an exciting story with sign language. But she wasn't. "It was my fault."

"Convince me."

"It was so crowded in there. They don't have room for me." Tears, real tears this time, filled her eyes. "A young couple needs privacy. It was so confusing and busy in the kitchen. They were hurrying to get to work. I was trying to get outside with their dogs. The least I can do is walk their dogs." She exhaled sharply and dabbed at her eyes. "There's more room in the closet than in the kitchen, and my daughter-in-law was holding the knife and was going to put it away and I got bumped by one of the dogs and sort of fell back. At first I really didn't feel anything and by then I was outside."

"Your daughter-in-law didn't tell anyone what happened."

"I told her not to. She tried to stop me but I promised I was fine. I had no idea the knife was stuck in there and it didn't hurt, really. It was not her fault." Maybelle shredded the remains of the tissue and tossed it in the trash. "I want her to like me."

That statement, Tony believed. "Okay. I'll accept your story. Just stay out of the kitchen in the mornings."

CHAPTER TWELVE

On such a cold day, to find Blossom in his office with a warm apple pie in an insulated carrier was a delightful surprise. His groupie, Blossom Flowers, had cut way back on the deliveries of pies, cookies, and muffins to him. On the taste bud and stomach level, he missed them. On every other level, he was delighted. It meant her life was going well. This pie was a bad omen. He could sense something had changed. Wasn't she supposed to be too busy with her upcoming wedding to bake for others?

"Blossom?" Tony eased into his desk chair, taking care not to topple the stacks of files on his desk and the pie balanced on the top. "What is the occasion?"

The plus-plus-sized woman dug into the tote bag at her feet. "I want you to keep this for me." She handed him a small box, a ring box containing a man's wedding band. "I'm afraid I'll lose it before the wedding. There's so much going on and the house is a mess with everything and . . ." Blossom's words ended in a sob. She covered her face with a pile of tissues and tears overflowed her bulbous eyes. Her sparse, flame orange hair was a mess.

If Tony had learned anything living with Theo, it was to keep his mouth shut when a woman was crying or offer quiet murmurs of consolation and not offer advice, unless she asked for it. One time he'd mumbled something about the situation not being very serious or worth being upset about and he almost got scalped. Probably the only thing saving him had been his lack of hair. He allowed himself to say to Blossom, "I'm sure it will calm down eventually." He vowed he'd rip out his own tongue before he'd inquire directly about the problem.

Blossom gave him the "how stupid are you?" look and blew her nose. "The ring's just an excuse. I need your help."

Tony was curious in spite of himself. "How can I help you?"

"You can ask questions about people. You know, check into their past."

"Not just because I'm nosy." Tony leaned back in his chair. "It's an invasion of privacy if I just dig around in their lives. People have a right to their secrets unless one is a crime."

Blossom's expression turned to dismay. "I don't care. I need to know."

Her anxious, yet woeful, expression fascinated him. He believed Blossom was not the kind of person who spent his or her life poking into other people's lives for entertainment. As if listening to someone else's conversation, he heard his own voice ask, "What do you need to know?"

"Did Kenny have more than one ex-wife?" The syllables poured out of her like they were forming one long word and ended on a sob.

Whatever Tony might have been imagining, it wasn't this. "Do you have reason to believe he does?" In Tony's head he saw Kenny either with his two little girls, or Blossom, or all three, or alone with a hammer or bricks and mortar. Never with another woman, not even in the past with his ex-wife. "It doesn't sound like Kenny."

"I got this." Blossom's chubby hands shook as she reached into the voluminous tote bag near her feet and retrieved a business-sized envelope and handed it to him. Just in case this was a serious situation, Tony slipped on a thin plastic glove. The envelope itself was generic, plain white, with no postage, just the name "Blossom."

Her name had been typed or printed with a computer, making him think someone in the area had taken great pains to cover their tracks. Tony slid the contents onto a clean sheet of paper. A single sheet of typing paper was folded into thirds. Using a paper clip and a letter opener, Tony spread it open.

"Marrying a man who is not available is dangerous. You won't live through your own wedding." Tony read it twice before looking into Blossom's face. Tears slid over both cheeks and dripped onto her blouse. He pulled a couple of tissues from the box on the floor near his desk and handed them to her. "Did you ask Kenny?"

She nodded. Her lower lip quivered and she sank her upper teeth into it. "Kenny says it's bunk and I should throw it away."

Tony was torn between agreeing with Kenny and wondering what kind of enemy Blossom had. The note didn't feel like a prank. "Can I keep this for a while?"

"Yes." Her whole body quivered on a sob. "Who would do this?"

Who indeed? The idea of a sweet, generous woman like Blossom incurring so much hatred seemed implausible. Unfortunately, implausible was not the same thing as impossible. "I don't know, Blossom, but my department will do everything possible to find out."

"Should I cancel the wedding?" Blossom stared at her engagement ring. "What if they hurt one of Kenny's girls? He'd never forgive me or himself."

"Don't cancel it yet." Tony searched for the right way to placate Blossom. "Let me look into this situation. Go ahead with the wedding as planned, but let me know immediately if the least little thing feels wrong."

Blossom's head moved from side to side. "Like what?"

Planning a wedding was about the last thing Tony knew anything about. It was out there with how to build a rocket ship. What would seem out of place? "Honestly, I don't know. Maybe if the person you've been working with about dresses or music or whatever is suddenly unavailable. Maybe if one of your sisters gets a threat. Tell your family. Half of the county population is related to you on either the Flowers's side or your mother's, maybe one of them has heard of a problem."

Blossom heaved herself to her feet. "Will you talk to Kenny?"

"Yes." Tony understood Kenny's attitude, but if there was a jealous girlfriend, even someone who imagined they had a relationship, Kenny would be more likely to know about it than Blossom would.

Tony decided to place the note and envelope in an evidence bag. The moment he decided to take a shortcut or disregard something someone said or did, it was bound to come back and bite him. He took his time, filling out the form, making all the proper notes.

He was about to go chat with Kenny when his desk telephone rang.

"Did you recover the fly rod?" The question had no preamble, no greeting or identification. If it weren't for caller ID, Tony would have been at a total loss. He wondered what she had told Ruth Ann to bypass normal protocol and have the call forwarded to him. Mrs. Cashdollar's cultured voice was barely above a whisper.

Tony wondered where she was calling from. "Yes." He peeked through the open door and saw Ruth Ann, at her desk, a stunned expression on her face. Clearly Mrs. Cashdollar was an expert at getting her way.

"Oh, thank goodness." Mrs. Cashdollar spoke more loudly. "I was afraid it was lost forever."

"Is there something special about it, other than the fact it belonged to your late husband?" Tony was not a fisherman, so to him it had looked like any other piece of angling equipment.

"It is very valuable and of course, Franklin loved it dearly. I thought I might put it in his coffin with him."

"When you say 'valuable' . . . ?" It didn't matter to Tony, but he did like to have all of the information in his notes. "What is it worth?"

"As I recall, I paid about eight thousand for the rod and reel. It was an anniversary present."

Eighty dollars would have seemed high to Tony, eight hundred amazing, eight thousand made him ask her to repeat the number. He must have gasped because she began to explain.

"Well, the rod is special bamboo and handmade, very rare." She went on, "The reel is exquisite workmanship, much like a Swiss watch."

Tony's slow brain finally connected the dots. In Theo's world, it would be the difference between a utility quilt and a work of art—still a quilt. Or, in his world, the difference between a "Saturday night special" and a precision sniper's weapon—both firearms. There were clearly various qualities of fishing poles for the enthusiasts.

"We have it locked up until the circumstances around his death are cleared up and the body is released."

"And when will that be?" The widow's voice indicated her lack of patience. She didn't wait for an answer but murmured "you dolt" and hung up.

"Sheriff? I've got an update on your skydiver."

Tony thought the pathologist in Knoxville must have bellowed into the speaker phone in his office. The voice coming through his own telephone's receiver almost deafened Tony, making him wonder why the man needed a telephone at all. Tony was grateful his receiver hadn't been pressed against his ear but only halfway between the phone's cradle and his head.

"Yes, sir?" Tony moved the device even farther away from his ear before the man nicknamed Dr. Death rendered him deaf. "What have you learned so far?"

"Well, to start with, falling to the ground from that distance broke lots of bones, chipped some, and man, oh man, those vertebrae are one big mess. Actually, to be technically accurate, it wasn't the fall that broke him up but the landing." Dr. Death wheezed into the phone, laughing at his own joke. "No one's putting that spine together without lots of time and good tweezers."

Tony could imagine the truth of the doctor's statement. The front of the corpse had fared better. "Start with the time of death."

"Weeeel, with the weather and all, I'd say sometime between nine thirty and ten thirty in the morning."

"Was he dead before or after the drop?" Tony stared at the growing pile of files around his desk. Something had to be done about the mess.

"Oh, well . . ." Dr. Death sounded a little disappointed when he realized Tony wasn't in the mood to chitchat. "Back to the gory bits. Mr. Cashdollar might have been alive when he landed but had quite a cocktail of substances in his system. It will be a few days before we know what all of them were. I doubt he knew he was in an airplane, much less that he came out of said airplane. If he was alive when he hit the ground, I sincerely doubt he felt the landing."

"And, if he *was* alive, can you give me any idea how long he continued to live after his landing?" Tony found the whole scenario way beyond suspicious. But how obvious was throwing a man from a plane? Who, other than the pilot could have been involved? "I've been told various times when he fell, everything from early morning to four in the afternoon." The time differences were playing havoc in his case. What was the truth, and why was it so hard to learn?

"No way." Dr. Death actually laughed, a grim reaper braying like a donkey. "The facts don't lie. Considering he was dead for a while when you collected him, and the doctor took the initial liver temperature, even if he maybe lived a bit before expiring, your guy had to hit the ground no later than the middle of the morning, as I said. Maybe as early as nine thirty, maybe ten, at the latest ten thirty, for him to be dead at the right time. No way was it after noon." Dr. Death sounded like he was giving a classroom speech. "Science, Sheriff, can only be juggled a little bit."

"And the drugs you found in his system, would any of them make him think he was a bird?" Tony had jumped from a plane, one time. He had been wearing a parachute but hadn't exactly felt like a bird, more like a package falling from a runaway truck.

"Maybe." Dr. Death was not going to offer any guesses. "Like I said, I'll know more when the entire chemical analysis is done. We are going to run the full panel and will know any number of facts, but it's not fast and it's not cheap."

Tony thought he ought to go back over the mountains and have a little chitchat with the North Carolina group; he wasn't sure he could call them suspects. Yet. The body of Franklin Cashdollar might have been dropped off in his fair county, but every sign and bit of information screamed that Park County was merely used for the body dump.

It made him angry.

He told Ruth Ann and Theo where he was going, grabbed Wade, and left the state.

"Have you spoken with Joyce's fiancé?" Sergeant Dupont, their North Carolina liaison, stacked a file under his desk.

Tony was thinking it didn't look much tidier than his own office but one word caught his full attention. "A fiancé?" News that the second Mrs. Cashdollar had a fiancé came as a shock to Tony. When he'd interviewed Joyce, she had been rabid about the sanctity of the marriage vows she'd taken with Franklin, declaring there was no such thing as a valid divorce. Although she had perked up at hearing of his demise. Fast work. "That's a most interesting bit of information."

Wade sat forward on his chair. "Any idea who she's engaged to?"

"Mark Usher. He's a stockbroker downtown." Dupont looked surprised at their interest. "Why?"

"And you know him?" Tony jotted down a note.

"Yes. The man is not a bad basketball player. We have a city recreation league. I'm on the department team, but we've played against his team for years. Not a lot of turnover, you know. New guys come in, but the old guard is still on the bench."

"And she was introduced as his fiancée?"

"Yep, just a few weeks ago. The wife and I ran into them at a restaurant. Joyce seemed pretty lovey-dovey with the guy. And she was wearing a large diamond ring." Dupont made a circle with his thumb and index finger to indicate a very large rock. "Big."

In his mind, Tony could practically see the little sign over Joyce's head that read "Investigate Here." He was sure he would have noticed such a ring if she'd been wearing it at her office. Evidently she wasn't prepared to make a general announcement. He couldn't help but wonder if the fiancé knew his bride-to-be's attitude about divorce. How badly did he want to marry this woman? Or how badly did she want to marry him? Was divorce worse than murder?

It didn't take long for Tony and Wade to track down the stockbroker. Tony handed the receptionist one of his cards and asked if Mr. Usher would be able to chat with him for a few moments about a professional matter.

Obligingly, and with an expression of total curiosity, the middle-aged woman headed away from her desk. A few minutes later, she returned and led them down the hall.

Mark Usher sat at a reasonably clean desk, his fingers flying across the computer keyboard. The receptionist had announced them and vanished again.

"Just one moment please." Usher finished his keyboard work and then stood to shake hands. "What can I do for you, Sheriff?"

Tony and Wade settled into the comfortable upholstered chairs facing the desk. "We're just trying to get all the t's crossed in an investigation."

Usher nodded, looking a bit confused but alert. "And how can I help a Tennessee investigation? You do understand, I'll need a warrant to discuss any of my clients' portfolios."

"It's not about your business. It's more personal. You see, we're trying to clear up a few loose ends in a case." Tony paused. "Do you know a Joyce Cashdollar?"

"Sure." A wide grin split his otherwise unremarkable face. "We're engaged."

Feigning surprise, Tony leaned over the desk, offering his hand. "Well, congratulations! When's the wedding?"

Still smiling, Usher shook the proffered hand. "Well, that has not been announced yet because Joyce hasn't picked the day. Yet." The grin was replaced with a more somber expression. "She says she needs to work out a couple of small details before we set the date."

Tony couldn't help but wonder if having a living spouse, albeit a divorced one, was a small detail to Joyce and Usher. "Such as?"

Usher rested his hands on the desktop. "Frankly, I'm not sure I understand it all. One time, she said she needed to clear up her relationship with her ex-husband. It sounded like she wanted to have him agree to an annulment." The expression on his face echoed his evident confusion.

"She's married?" Tony could play the dumb hick sheriff. "Pretty brazen having a husband and a fiancé, don't you think?"

"No. No. No. She's divorced." Usher rolled his desk chair backwards and surged to his feet. "I won't stand for one more person coming in here and accusing me of having a relationship with a married woman. It's just not true."

"One more?" Tony leaned back in his chair. He sensed he had pushed the right button and was very careful not to smile. "Who else has been here?"

"Her father." Usher exhaled sharply. "The man is pushing eighty, but he's as tough as nails and has an opinion about everything. He doesn't believe divorce exists and doesn't care whose feelings he tramples." Usher turned away and exhaled sharply. For a moment he was silent as he clearly forced himself to regain his self-control. "Joyce has tried to defy him, but so far she always surrenders. The man has got one of those hellfire and brimstone voices." Usher turned back and met Tony's gaze. His whole body slumped in a gesture of defeat. "I can't fault her. I'm not strong enough to defy him either."

"Have you got his name and address?" Tony thought he'd be remiss if he didn't follow a lead like this one; it all but had a neon sign flashing overhead.

"Yes." Usher opened his desk drawer and pulled out a handmade business card, handing it to Tony, "I do need it back."

"Not a problem." Tony transferred the information into his notebook—name, address, and telephone number. "Mr. Wilson doesn't live with his daughter?" Tony was only surprised because he sounded like the kind of man who wouldn't allow a female relative to live alone.

"No. I do know they discussed it, and I think deep down

she's afraid to defy him, but her apartment is small and since there isn't enough room, he lets her be. Plus, the old tyrant lives with her older sister, Mary Elizabeth"

"Sounds like one big happy group."

Not catching Tony's sarcasm, Usher shook his head. "No. Not really."

CHAPTER THIRTEEN

"Well, who thinks it will be fun to talk to Joyce Cashdollar's father?" Tony stood on the sidewalk near Wade's vehicle.

Neither Wade nor Dupont raised a hand. Tony wasn't looking forward to it either.

Dupont said, "He sounds like a tyrant."

Wade nodded. "A man who likes to control women is not necessarily prepared to take on a man, especially a well-trained soldier like Franklin."

"So true." Tony thought the father sounded like a bully. "But what if he thought Franklin's death would be doing his daughter a favor? Make her a widow so he could approve of her marrying again."

"That's pretty twisted. Divorce is worse than murder?" Wade shook his head. "It doesn't make any sense."

"Well, whether it makes sense or not, let's go meet the man." Tony had stopped expecting things to make sense when, as a child, and only after being dared by his two older brothers, he'd climbed onto the roof and tried coming down the chimney like Santa Claus. He'd gotten stuck in the chimney and earned the wrath of his parents for the damage he'd done. "I'm not as easy to fool as I used to be."

The address of Joyce Cashdollar's sister turned out to be a simple home in a small subdivision. As far as Tony could tell the homeowners had been given a choice of three styles. A small single-level, a boxy two-story, or half of a duplex. Mr. Wilson

136

and his older daughter shared a single-level house.

The three men gathered on the stoop and Wade rang the doorbell. Sounds of loud voices and thumping made Tony wonder if it was something on the television or if the inhabitants were moving furniture.

A moment later, a woman who had to be Joyce's sister, opened the door. Her eyes widened in surprise at the sight of three uniformed men standing on the stoop. Tony smiled. "Are you Mary Elizabeth, Joyce Cashdollar's sister?"

"Yes." Mary Elizabeth shared her sister Joyce's hairstyle but wore no makeup and was simply dressed in baggy jeans and an ancient black sweatshirt. It was covered with big spots that looked like bleach had splashed on it.

Tony introduced himself and his companions. "May we come in and chat with you and your father?"

The woman's eyes flickered to her left, toward someone out of their view. A moment later she opened the door wider. "Please come in." Her voice was soft but melodic, and her smile was pleasant.

The open kitchen and living space were warm and inviting. Tony felt surprise when the old man rose from his recliner and reached out and politely shook hands with each of the men.

"Officers?" He waved to the sofa and nearby chairs. "Won't you sit?"

He settled back in to his recliner. "Mary Elizabeth! Get these gentlemen some refreshments."

Tony shook his head. "Thank you, but no."

Mary Elizabeth laughed. "I'll get your tea, Dad. Maybe the others will have a cookie."

Whatever Tony had been expecting after his conversation with Usher, it wasn't this. He hadn't had time to think much about it, but had not envisioned a warm welcome and fresh cookies. Mary Elizabeth looked tired but not obviously down-trodden.

Appearances were very often deceiving. He didn't relax his guard.

Chewing a warm cookie, Tony wondered if they had been warned to expect visitors. It would have taken Usher less than thirty seconds to call Joyce and about that long for her to call her father or sister. In the twenty minutes the men needed for the drive over, Joyce and Mr. Wilson could have rearranged the furniture and popped some frozen cookie dough into the oven to carefully stage this happy family display.

"I suppose you've heard about the accident involving Franklin Cashdollar." Tony didn't see any reason to beat about the bush. "I understand your daughter and Franklin were married for a few years."

"They still are. Married once is married forever." Mr. Wilson straightened in his chair. His chin jutted out like a belligerent two-year-old's, and then he relaxed and leaned back again. "Well, I guess if he's passed on, they aren't married now."

Tony wasn't going to debate the issue. There was a part of him that wondered if the old man had found a way to make his daughter a widow, but he couldn't imagine how. "Can you tell me the last time you saw Franklin?"

The old man squinted like he was trying to improve his focus on Tony's face. "It's been a bit."

Without any reason he could name, Tony knew the old man was lying through his dentures. "I had hoped you might have seen him in the past few days."

"That so?" Mr. Wilson leaned back in his chair, a man of leisure. "Now, why *is* that?"

"I'd like to get as much information about his state of mind and any problems he might have mentioned."

"You think he kilt himself?"

Tony wasn't about to answer the question. He was there to

obtain information, not to give it away. "Why, do you?"

"Didn't seem like he'd be likely to. Maybe he was feeling some well-deserved guilt about cheating on my daughter." Mr. Wilson grabbed two more cookies from the plate. "Now he's burning in hell most likely." He seemed cheered by the idea.

"Anything else you know of that might have been bothering him?" Tony doubted the man had any information, but it wouldn't hurt to ask. "You know, like problems with his health or maybe he had some other concerns. Maybe even if there was something he wouldn't talk about."

"He wouldn't talk about his time in the Army." Mr. Wilson stuffed a whole cookie into his mouth. "I tried to get him to open up, but he was tighter than a tick about it."

"That's not unusual." Tony knew veterans who couldn't stop talking about war and others who never talked about it. "Anything else?"

"Nope." Another cookie vanished, emptying the plate. "Mary Elizabeth. Show these men to the door."

"Say there, Sheriff Abernathy, I believe we've located Franklin Cashdollar's missing cell phone, but not the car." The call came from the local sheriff's office to Sergeant Dupont's phone, and Dupont had put the call on speaker so they could all hear.

Tony sat up straight, his hand already reaching for his pen. "Where?"

"Right where we should have looked when it wasn't found out at the airstrip. The phone was in a regular fishing spot, down by the river, like it fell from the car." The caller sounded embarrassed.

Tony was too excited to care. He looked at Dupont. "His wife kept saying the man was going fishing locally and took the Land Rover. Makes me really curious how long the flight had been planned."

"Makes me really curious who drove him to the airstrip."

Wade reached for his map of the area. "Could he have walked from car to airplane?"

"Yessir," said Dupont. "He could have walked, but I doubt he'd have had time between his son's account of dropping him off at the car and the pilot's account of takeoff."

Tony made a noncommittal sound. "We have only guesses on both sides—the son and/or the pilot could have been off on their timetables."

"True. But, I don't understand why he wouldn't have just driven over there and left his vehicle at the airstrip." Dupont heaved a deep breath. "I sure wouldn't go through all that, would you?"

"Absolutely not. You win." Tony laughed. "The simplest solution is often the best."

"There wasn't a contest."

Through the radio, Tony heard the sound of papers being shuffled. "Is there anything else we should know?"

"Oh, yeah, and the cell phone was found. It was still plugged into the charger. I find it rather refreshing to find someone who is not a slave to his phone, but to toss it out?" Their informant coughed. "We pulled the calls. The last one the previous night was from his son, Carl Lee. The only one after that came in the morning from the pilot who left a message confirming an eight thirty flight time."

"So, when he went out for breakfast, he knew he was going flying?" Tony was just talking. "Why not tell his son? Why have him bring him back to the car? That would leave him without a way to and from the airstrip without walking."

"That is curious. I'm also curious why his son was there that morning of all mornings." Sergeant Dupont hesitated. "Coincidence is really hard to prove or disprove. What did his wife say his plans were?"

Wade laughed. "Which wife?"

"Exactly." Tony said, "There's too many of them. Mrs. Laura Cashdollar, the widow, says he's been on several of these fly and fish outings. She never knows where he's going and says he always tries to be back in time for dinner but sometimes he's not. She couldn't have been more vague about his schedule, and it seemed to me like she wasn't welcoming to Carl Lee."

Wade said, "I find it interesting because everyone else says the man was the king of organization and appointments, but no one knows anything about his plans."

"Amazingly close to my lifestyle." Dupont chuckled. "Well, at least the try to be home for dinner part."

"How's that working for you?" Tony tried to be home for dinner with his family too, but it seemed like there were too often times when that didn't work. Maybe he should vote for his opponent in the next election, no matter who it was.

"Not too good. I did go out to the airport and talked to Gentry Frazier again. He swears he didn't report the jump right away because he was so shaken by the man's behavior."

Tony thought he could read their liaison deputy's mind. "I'm guessing the pilot has nerves of steel. Having some yahoo jumping out of the plane would not rattle him that badly."

"On that we agree," said Dupont. "But he's a businessman, and losing the goose with golden eggs could be more traumatic than losing a poor person."

Tony rubbed the back of his neck, feeling the tension. "Over on the Tennessee side of the mountain, the M.E. is not through with all the tests, and the family over here is getting a bit testy. I get the feeling there's something specific the pathologist is waiting for, but he's a really good poker player."

"That's always extra hard on the family," Dupont murmured. "Are you saying they plan on burying him over there in Tennessee instead of bringing him back to North Carolina for the funeral?"

"I hope it's held in your area." Tony couldn't help but think it would be harder on Carl Lee and Calvin to bury the man in Park County. On the other hand, he'd heard a few nightmare stories about problems taking a body across state lines. "But, as far as the body goes—finders keepers. If our pathologist wants to keep him for a year, he can."

"I'm hoping Tennessee keeps him forever." Dupont's voice held a thread of humor.

"Why?" Tony said.

"Security for high-profile burials is one more thing we don't have enough officers to handle," Dupont explained. "It's not that the gentleman was so important, but that wife of his often draws a crowd. Money has a big voice."

Tony knew that statement to be true. He'd dealt with some high-profile people and they'd created all kinds of headaches for his department. "Have we checked all the traffic cameras in the area of the airport and parking lot?"

"One of them picked up the Cashdollars, father and son, presumably going to breakfast and returning. We have Carl Lee headed out of town and we picked up his vehicle again, off and on, all the way into Cherokee."

Tony wasn't surprised. "But what about that Land Rover?"

"Nope. It hasn't turned up in any camera, which is hardly surprising. Thousands of vehicles pass through the intersection. It will take lots of man-hours to find it."

"I'd guess it wasn't stolen and parked where it was found down by the river."

"No. And about cameras nearest the airstrip, none of them have that particular car stopping there the morning of the flight. Of course it's not exactly in the city." Dupont frowned. "We got lots of cars and trucks driving past, only a few pulling into the field. One's a fuel truck. There isn't much out there since it's a private airstrip. There's a large hangar, a runway, lots of trees around it, and a small parking area."

"No food service or radar?"

"Nope, a windsock is about as high tech as it appears to be."

"Who paid for the plane?" Tony couldn't believe the company didn't have a record of the payment.

"And how'd he get there?" Dupont laughed. "I'm on it, but nobody seems either informed or interested."

"Is the hangar large enough for there to be parking inside? Lots of people with money might expect not to have to walk from their car to the chartered plane."

Dupont said, "Let me make a call."

Tony waited, musing about the business with the Land Rover. There were many traffic cameras scattered about the area; could someone know enough about their locations to avoid them all? And if so, why?

Dupont interrupted Tony's thoughts. "The answer is both yes and no. They do have parking space inside the building and some passengers have parked there, but never Franklin Cash-dollar."

Tony checked his watch. "We'd better get back over the mountains to do some work, Wade. We could play hide-and-seek over here all day and never accomplish anything but waste Dupont's time."

Wade looked surprised when he checked his own watch. He rose to his feet. "Thanks for the help."

They made it home in record time. The highway over the mountain was clear and although busy, not clogged. Another storm system was working its way through but the highway department was keeping up with the snow.

Tony stopped by the office and concentrated on his paperwork. He was determined to spend an evening with his family.

Thinking too hard about work was creating a logjam in his brain.

After dinner, he was treated to a frenzy of Halloween costume improvements. Chris had decided to add more hardware to his cardboard television, and Jamie was switching from football to ninja. Happy chaos reigned.

CHAPTER FOURTEEN

Tony bent close to his wife's ear and whispered, "How would you like to play detective?"

Theo turned to face him. "Are you saying you *want* me to stick my nose into your business? You're always telling me to stay out of it."

"Just a little bit." Tony tried for a stern expression. It must not have worked because Theo burst out laughing, causing the children's heads to turn their way.

"Okay, okay," she whispered. "What information do you need from gossip central?"

"I need to know if someone might have expected to be the next Mrs. Kenny Baines before Blossom won his heart." Tony felt guilty he'd been so focused on the Cashdollar situation he had forgotten about Blossom's concern. "She just called. Another threatening note arrived today."

Theo's green/gold hazel eyes went wide and the lenses of her glasses intensified her shocked expression. "Seriously?"

"Yes, I'm afraid so. I don't know enough to tell you more." Tony hated getting her involved in his business but the information flowing through her quilt shop always had a different slant from the things reported to his office. "Jealousy is not illegal. But threatening to harm someone often leads to the action."

"That's terrible." Theo shook her head. "Who would do such a thing?"

"I'm hoping you'll be able to help me answer that question. I meant to ask you earlier, but with all these trips to North Carolina and the chaos in the rest of the county, I forgot," Tony said. "There's no excuse."

Theo busied herself doing a little light housekeeping in the quilt shop's all-purpose classroom/workroom. The early morning appliqué group was done.

All Theo needed to do to make the room clean was to pick up some loose threads and tiny bits of fabric. The afternoon quilt-club meeting was about to begin. Today there was going to be a special visitor, Mrs. Miyoko Nakamura, a woman whose quilting had won several of the biggest shows in the world. Theo was excited to see the Japanese woman's work up close.

Minutes later, the back room at Theo's shop, the quilting community's unofficial gathering place, was packed with people, almost like a tour bus had disgorged a group. As usual, there was a group of quilters seated around the charity quilt being hand-quilted by a series of volunteers. At the far end of the room, the long-arm quilting machine—an oversized sewing machine on rails that was guided by hand while the quilt remained stationary, and that was rented by the hour—was humming as someone worked on a project.

Theo lost track of the number of times she'd brewed another pot of coffee. The combination of the continuing snowy weather, her regular people, and the Wednesday afternoon quilting club meant no spare room. Word of their distinguished guest had traveled well beyond the county line. Theo only recognized maybe half of the quilters crammed together on folding chairs, waiting for their guest, Miyoko Nakamura.

While they were gathering, Theo's attempt to learn anything about Kenny's love life, before Blossom, was a bust. No one could come up with a single bit of gossip. The overwhelming consensus was that Kenny was well rid of wife number one and had not seemed to even glance at anyone but Blossom in the years since.

The quilting group had show-and-tell, the star of which was a show-stopping, exquisite, priceless quilt made by Mrs. Nakamura, who was new to the area. Theo knew she did beautiful work herself, but nothing like this woman's. Theo couldn't come up with enough words to describe the flawlessness of any of the pieces being shown. Miyoko's large quilt had won several large international shows and deservedly so. It had even been the cover quilt on a couple of international quilting magazines. The photographs had not done it justice.

In contrast to Miyoko's prize-winning, labor-intensive work of art, the quilters were being shown, as their regular club program, a series of small simple projects to make for the upcoming holiday season. Theo's mother-in-law, Jane, was patiently explaining the steps to create festive placemats and a matching table runner.

Gretchen, Theo's only full-time employee, was virtually chained to the cutting table while Theo happily manned the cash register. Theo's business could use a good day. Tourists still trickled through the area but less so now that the brilliant fall colors were all but gone from the mountains. Winter was coming. Or, with the continuing snowfall, had already arrived.

Glancing around the crowded room, Theo recognized about half of the women in the room and neither of the two men. She smiled, relieved to have a good business day.

"My quilt?" The shrill words cut through the general chatter and happy chaos, stopping all conversation. "Where my quilt?"

Theo reached the speaker's side in seconds. Miyoko was a fairly new arrival in their midst. Theo had never been to Japan, but she guessed the two cultures were not interchangeable. She was positive they both shared one trait, something very important: neither condoned stealing works of art. Theo had examined and admired the quilt in question. It was priceless. A glance around the crowded room spotted lots of people but fewer than moments earlier. No sign of the quilt. She pressed a button on her cell phone, one she used only in dire emergencies.

Flavio answered the 911 call. He listened to Theo's explanation and transferred her call to Tony's office line.

He husband answered almost immediately. "Theo?"

"There's been a theft, Tony. A very valuable quilt was stolen." She felt tears rise in her eyes. "In my shop. Please come and bring the cavalry. This is serious."

"I'm on my way."

"My husband is the sheriff." Theo helped Miyoko to a chair and sat in the one next to it.

"He find quilt?" The woman pleaded with her.

"I certainly hope so." Theo wasn't sure how she could handle the guilt and grief of such a loss, from her shop.

Tony and Wade strode into the workroom, only a few minutes later.

Tony said, "I don't want anyone leaving until you've talked to us." He indicated his deputy. "Even if you don't think you have anything to add, you might know some little detail that will be very useful. If you will please return to where you were before the theft was discovered."

Theo watched the ladies grow calmer. The presence of someone who took the theft seriously and who had the confidence of the experienced investigator settled the group. They made their way back to the chairs and tables. The group working on the charity quilt threaded their needles and began stitching.

"Is this about where you think everyone was?" Tony looked at Theo.

"Yes." Theo glanced around. There was more space in the room than before. "We're not all here now. Several people have already left."

"And where was the quilt last seen?"

Theo led him over to a pristine table on the far side of the room. "It was right here on this table, only we had a clean bed sheet spread out under it to keep it spotless. The quilt was unfolded so we could all study it, and there were white gloves to protect it from our hands." Theo's own hands shook as she gestured.

"It was my fault. I shouldn't have put it here." Theo had to wipe the tears from her face. She hadn't really thought about the table being so near the back door and having no chairs on the far side. The theft was so simple. "Anyone could have just folded it up and walked out the back door with it."

Tony didn't dispute Theo's comment, but addressed the group. "Who's not here now that you saw earlier?" He quickly held up a hand for silence. "Just think about it, maybe write yourself a note. I don't want anyone jumping to conclusions or putting a name in someone else's head."

Wade held up his own camera. "Did anyone take pictures of the quilt?"

"Sure, during show-and-tell, a couple of people grabbed their cell phones and snapped a shot. There were no formal pictures." Theo clutched her cell phone. "I have a picture too."

"I want to see those pictures." Tony spoke softly. "There's a chance, not much, that a person's face was captured where it shouldn't have been."

Theo studied the room and the activity, and something struck her as wrong, different. "The men."

"What men?" Tony said.

"There were two of them, neither familiar. While we were at our busiest, right after show-and-tell, one of the men started coughing and then he passed out." Theo frowned. "Several people rushed to help him but he came to almost immediately and said he was fine and that some fresh air would help so Gretchen and I helped him out the front door."

"Was he alone?" Tony studied the route. It would be hard for more than two people to walk side by side.

"I don't know. It was busy and he could have been with one woman or another, but he was definitely not a local." Theo felt rage replace her guilt. "It was a ruse, wasn't it? His partner took the quilt while we were distracted."

Tony couldn't deny it. "He or she probably just folded the quilt up and slipped out the back door with it. Do you remember hearing the bell on the door ding?"

Theo had had him install a bell so they would know when someone entered the building from the alley. "No, but it could have. We wouldn't have heard it with so many people talking."

Tony moved to talk to the quilt's owner, the middle-aged Japanese woman, and Theo came and stood next to her, holding Miyoko's arm, offering support. The two women were about the same height. As tiny as Theo was, it was a rarity to see her next to a similar-sized adult. Tony pushed aside any impulse to comment about their size.

"Mrs. Nakamura is new in town. My husband, Sheriff Abernathy," Theo said in way of introduction. She blinked, pushing tears over the lower lid.

"Welcome to Silersville, Mrs. Nakamura." Tony doubted the woman was happy to be here at all. He'd talked to enough people suffering loss and tragedy that he'd learned patience. Some. "Tell me what you remember."

"Quilt taken." Miyoko gripped the edges of her lightweight silk jacket.

"Miyoko's quilt is a masterpiece." Theo held her cell phone

out for him to see the picture.

The photo showed him a quilt in muted grays and browns, but even on the small screen he could tell it was exceptional. Theo and her friends had trained his eye.

"Was Miss Bessie there when the quilt went missing?" Tony hoped he could solve a case, any case, on this day. Miss Bessie was a local woman who had a habit of picking up things that did not belong to her and replacing them with other items, also purloined.

A slight smile lit Theo's face, relaxing some of the tension in her jaw. "She was, but the stolen quilt is much too big for her to put in her bag, and besides that, I know she had just traded a pair of pliers for a large spool of variegated thread."

"Did you see her do it?"

"Yes." Theo gazed sightlessly into the distance. "She vanished about the same time as the quilt. I forgot about the thread until now. There's no way she took the quilt. It was too big, and she never makes two trades in the same area."

"How valuable is the quilt?" Tony knew at least, as a certified appraiser, Theo would certainly be able to help him with that. "I know money can't replace a work of art or a labor of love, but it will make a difference down the road. *When* we find it."

Theo smiled slightly at his emphasis on "when" but the smile quickly faded. "You want to know misdemeanor or felony?"

Tony nodded.

"Definitely felony. Grand theft quilt." Theo's eyes filled with tears. "It's worth at least ten thousand dollars."

"The FBI has an art theft department." Tony wondered if he should contact his former partner. Max had gone from Chicago PD to the FBI when he'd finished graduate school. He was definitely not in the art theft group, but would know who to contact.

"Yes," Theo pleaded. "Please call Max."

THE COFFIN QUILT
SECOND BODY OF CLUES

Block One:

Sew together a 2 5/8″ square of fabric (A) to one side of 2 5/8″ square of fabric (D). Make 16 sets. Press to darker fabric.

Divide the (A) plus (D) patches into 2 stacks of 8. Rotate one stack to line up opposite colorations. Sew together to make four patch blocks. Press seam to one side. Make 8. Set aside.

Cut the 16 squares 4″ of (C) once on the diagonal. Sew the resulting two triangles onto opposing sides of the (A)+(D) four patches, lining up the long side against the square, with the triangle's corner lined up opposite center seam. Press to triangle. Trim off "ears." Repeat on remaining corners. Square should now measure 6 1/2″. Make 8. Set aside.

Sew 2″ wide strips by LOF of fabrics (A) and (B). Press to darker fabric. Make 3. Cut into 6 1/2″ by 3 1/2″ rectangles., Make 32. On both ends of 16 of the 6 1/2″ strips, sew a 3 1/2″ square of (D). Press toward strips.

Sew remaining (A)+(B) strips—those without squares of (D)—onto opposing sides of the 6 1/2″ pieced center squares, placing (A) along center. Press to (A).

Add the strips with corners (D) to opposing sides, again, placing fabric (A) next to block centers. Press to new strips.

Make 8.

Label Block One and set aside.

CHAPTER FIFTEEN

Tony and Wade asked lots of questions and learned very little about the two people suspected of stealing the quilt. They had not been the focus of anyone's attention. Hopefully Max would be able to suggest their next move.

A call while they were finishing up had come from Mom Proffitt. She begged Tony to bring the homeless veteran, Boston, to her establishment, The Okay Bar and Bait Shop, when Tony had the time and if he, Boston, wanted to.

It hadn't been hard to entice Boston to go to the Okay for a free meal, and the task was made even easier since Mouse had been invited as well.

Now Tony watched as Mom Proffitt took one look at Boston and reached out to give him a giant hug. "Welcome. Now get yourself into that room over there. Food will be ready soon. And take that mangy hound with you."

The moment the man followed her instructions, Mom turned her face away, pulled a tissue from her pocket, and wiped her streaming eyes. When a man, not Boston, bellowed obscenities from the back room she smiled.

"Who is in there?" Wade craned his neck.

"My middle son, Lucas, is home from the Army. Stubborn and broken and miserable."

Tony wasn't sure he should be concerned about Boston, but he wasn't smiling as he looked into Mom's face. "Aren't you disturbed by all the yelling?"

Mom shook her head and laughed but the pain didn't leave her eyes. "At least they're talking. Those two have much in common. Too much, if I'm any judge at all."

"But your son is missing an arm." Wade stated the obvious.

"Yes, and I've talked to Boston enough to understand that man is missing more than an arm. Something even more terrible: his soul." Mom headed toward the kitchen. "Let's leave them alone for a while."

Tony and Wade sat at the bar eating a burger and drinking coffee while eavesdropping on the conversation in the next room. Tony wasn't sure if they were doing the best thing or the worst for the pair of veterans.

"Is that little tyrant your mom?" Boston's voice carried through a lull in the noise. "You poor devil, having no family's got to be better than dealing with that little fireball."

Lucas's voice was even louder. "At least she doesn't have fleas like your furry friend."

"If you don't like him, quit scratching his ears. You're about to rub them bald."

Mom disappeared into the room again with two platters of burgers and double fries and trotted back out without them. "They can throw food at each other for a while."

Tony felt responsible for bringing Boston into this. The man had no warning what was about to happen. "How long do you plan to keep Boston prisoner here?"

"Not much longer. Give him enough time to eat anyway. Having a free meal won't hurt him, then you can take him back to wherever he stays. But if he doesn't come here on his own, will you bring Boston back at the same time tomorrow?" Mom looked into Tony's eyes. "I don't know if I'm doing the right thing or the wrong thing, but I know in my heart I have to do something. If all those two can find in common is hating me and they join forces and work together on a plan to kill me, so be it." Mom's smile didn't reach her eyes. "At least it would be better than watching my son being holed up like this."

"I'm not abducting Boston again," Tony warned. "If he doesn't want to come here, it's over."

The words were barely past his lips when the bar's front door opened too quickly and slammed against the wall. Mrs. Dixon, the veterinarian's wife, strode in and dropped her keys in front of Mom, ignoring Wade and himself. "Where are they?"

Mom nodded toward her office door.

Mrs. Dixon strode past Mom, opened the door, and went inside, closing the door behind her. "I expect you two slugs, and that Teffeteller boy you've been arguing with, to be at my place tomorrow at eight in the morning. Sharp. Or else." The door opened again and she slammed it closed behind her. It was still vibrating as she reached for her keys and gave Mom a sweet smile. "Sheriff. Wade." And she was gone as quickly as she arrived.

Mom Proffitt's jaw sagged, leaving her mouth open. She blinked.

Tony might have followed Mrs. Dixon, but he heard Wade's whisper.

"There was a female drill instructor at Parris Island that sounded just like that. Scariest person I ever encountered. We couldn't wait to crawl into the swamp to get away from her." He looked at the closed door. "You don't suppose?"

"It's possible. I think someone told me they've been here about five years." Tony had to smile. He didn't know how much difference there was between training men and training dogs but guessed Mrs. Dixon was about to shake up three lives, for the better. "I know they came from South Carolina."

Somewhat rested after lunch, Tony pulled to a stop in front of the law enforcement center, rather than pulling into his private parking bay, and glanced around. He was concerned his crazy groupie/writer wannabe might park behind him, trapping the Blazer. A careful study of the people and vehicles around him did not contain a blocky woman with brown hair.

He only needed to check a couple of things in his office, and then he'd be back out on the road. As he walked through the main doorway of the law enforcement center, he could hear the sound of a powerful baritone voice singing one of the old-timey country songs, filtered by windows and doors. It immediately caught his attention. Quentin was sobering up.

Flavio, at the desk, pressed the button to unlock the door into his wing. Tony saw a couple of people sitting in the waiting area, probably there to visit an inmate. One of them held a newspaper, high, covering the face. Tony could see it was a woman, blocky, but with blond hair. An obvious wig. Tony hustled through the doorway and pulled the door closed behind him, holding it until it latched and locked.

"I assume I'm not to let her in to see you." Flavio wasn't smiling.

"You assume correctly. Just let her sit there." Tony paused. "If she gets rowdy, you might suggest she make an appointment instead of just showing up expecting personal attention."

"You'd better go out the back. She doesn't appear to be in a hurry to go anywhere else."

Tony liked to think he was smart enough to follow good advice, so he was careful to slip out the private entrance and drive away from the building instead of going the shorter way. The one that would put his vehicle exactly in her line of sight. He would deal with her later. First he needed to talk to Carl Lee Cashdollar about his father. The young lawyer should be out of the courtroom now.

★ ★ ★ ★ ★

"Nothing is—was—ever simple with my father."

Tony thought Carl Lee looked much older than he had the day before. "How do you mean?"

"Planning a trip to the movies was akin to organizing the Normandy invasion. We could never suddenly decide to do it and then just jump into the car and go. It was more, we're leaving at fourteen oh five and arrive at the theatre at fourteen twelve. Two minutes to get inside, two more to locate appropriate seating." Carl Lee paused to wipe his streaming eyes and blow his nose. "Sorry. I'm actually surprised at how much his death bothers me."

Tony hated asking questions of the grieving. "Take your time."

Carl Lee took a deep breath and exhaled sharply. "If we wanted popcorn, it was purchased after the correct seats were located, and any long line or slowdown would eliminate the possibility of treats."

"Would you consider his parking off-site for a fly in fishing trip to be in character or not?"

"Some of both. That's what's most disturbing." Carl Lee tossed his used tissues into the trash and pulled out two more from the box. "Parking so his car was not likely to get hit, that's totally normal Franklin Cashdollar behavior. I can remember when I was a kid, sometimes we'd walk ten blocks in the rain to avoid church traffic and the problems he foresaw. You know, like the Sunday traffic in Silersville was so awful."

Tony smiled. Most Sundays, two dogs standing in the road constituted a traffic jam.

"But I can't imagine why he'd park there and not plan to drive to the airport. That's probably not normal." Carl Lee stared at his hands. "He specifically had me return him to the Land Rover. I assumed he was driving over from there. Otherwise, why not just have me drop him at the airfield? Really.

157

Wouldn't that make more sense?"

Tony had to agree it would.

Tony decided he was going to have to stop visiting his mother and aunt at their folk museum. He'd no more than arrived when his mom started in and his aunt sang chorus. They were working on plans for their community Halloween party. The two ladies had more complaints than his jail inmates. Bad weather, and no one will come. Good weather, and too many people will come. Pumpkin carving with children—knives or no knives? Candy or popcorn? Afternoon or evening? Free or pay a fee?

"Mom," said Tony, when his mother paused to breathe. "Listen to yourself. Calm down. The kids will all love coming out here because there's fun stuff to do, plenty of candy, and they can see everyone's costumes and be seen without having to watch for traffic." Tony didn't mention the lessening of stress it would put on his department. He did say, "I'm frankly delighted to have some of the goblins safe from themselves. Honestly, I've seen ten-year-olds practically dive under a moving car to get one more piece of candy."

"Now I'm afraid that the parents will just drop them and run. I can't keep track of all those kids." Jane paced back and forth at a dizzying rate. "It's not safe, and my insurance surely won't cover bobbing for apples."

"No. You can't." Tony felt acid drip into his stomach and searched for his antacids; there were none in his shirt pocket. He needed to refill from his jar in the Blazer. "It's your place, your party. You make the rules and make sure everyone understands. No parent or guardian, no kid. It's simple."

He glanced away from his indignant mother to watch his Aunt Martha working with the shared Abernathy slave, young Alvin Tibbles. The teenager and Martha, Alvin's landlady, were busy lashing together cornstalks for decorations. The barn was being decorated with a combination of seasons—a Halloween meets the autumn harvest theme. Except for the witches and spiders and ghosts in the rafters, they could be getting ready for Thanksgiving.

Martha spoke over her shoulder. "Tell my crazy sister to calm down, everything will be fine, and all we'll have to do after the party to be ready for the fall festival will be to ditch the ghosts and goblins."

"I can hear you." Jane headed toward her sister, worry fighting with irritation in her face.

Tony backed away to get out of the verbal crossfire and unexpectedly stepped in something squishy and slippery. It almost tripped him and he felt like he was going to fall backwards. He barely managed to get both of his feet under him again, just in the nick of time.

A very lucky thing, because he would have fallen into a large galvanized tub already filled with water and apples. "What was that?" He studied the ground until he found the culprit. Under a bit of straw, an exceedingly rotten apple lurked. He scooped it up with his hand and instantly regretted it. It smelled vile and felt worse. "That's nasty," he mumbled, but his mother heard him and brought him an old rag.

Hurrying to get the apple goo cleaned off, he turned to study the overall appearance of the decorations. To Tony's eyes, it looked like everything was shaping up nicely. Add some kids in costumes and some sugar, and it would be a party. A couple of ghosts moaning in the rafters wouldn't hurt either.

"While you're here, Marc Antony," his mom continued. "Will you help your brother hang one of those wooden quilt blocks?"

The square in question was eight feet by eight feet of sturdy plywood. It was part of a new plan by his mom and aunt and wife, plus helpers, to hang these things on barns and buildings all over the county. Climbing a tall ladder and hanging one of the monsters required muscle and planning. He was lacking a really good excuse not to help. "Is Gus ready to leave his wife and daughter and play your games?"

"I just called. He's over at Food City picking up some groceries. He said he'll be here by the time you gather everything you need. How long can it take?" Clearly satisfied with her organization, Jane headed out of the barn on another mission.

Tony glowered at her back as she made a self-satisfied exit. He had twisted his shoulder on the last monster they'd hung. He could only hope Gus had developed a less dangerous, or at least less painful, hanging technique.

Sitting at the dinner table, Tony studied his wife's face. Instead of her sweet, kind of perky face, she seemed a bit misshapen, facially, at dinner. He studied it through bleary eyes as he ate. He was relieved when he finally realized it was her glasses, and not her face, that were wonky.

The ice pack resting on his shoulder was helping ease the pain. "What happened to your glasses?"

"Lizzie happened." Theo pointed to the fuzzy haired toddler who was busy dropping bits of her dinner onto the floor and laughing as Daisy cleaned them up. "She ripped them off my face and threw them on the floor. I have to go to the optician's in Knoxville tomorrow morning."

Tony groaned just a bit as he nodded and shifted his ice pack. Their small community lacked certain services. Eyeglass repair was one of them.

Theo's crooked glasses turned toward him. "Why don't you and Gus use the county's bucket truck or whatever it's called instead of climbing a ladder with those heavy boards?"

Awestruck by his wife's genius, Tony blinked. He had no answer.

CHAPTER SIXTEEN

"Tony?" The voice coming through his cell phone was a mere whisper, but he didn't need caller ID to identify it. He'd heard it too many times to fail to recognize it. He'd heard it laugh, cry, whine, and soothe. His wife. "Theo? Why are you whispering? Are you all right?"

"I found the quilt." Her voice raised just a bit. "The one stolen from the shop."

"That's great." Tony knew his wife had stewed and worried and felt totally responsible for its loss. If she had slept a minute since it vanished, he'd be shocked. "Is it damaged?"

"I don't think so. I can't tell from here."

"Here? Where's here?" He thought she was calling from her shop. The cell phone number was misleading; she could be calling from China. His stomach rumbled, irritated by the burst of acid brought on by her words.

"I'm in Knoxville. Remember, I came up to get my glasses fixed?" Rattling and a whine came through the earpiece. "The quilt is hanging in a pawn shop window right across the street from the optician's office. Can you come help me talk to the pawnbroker?"

"Just walk in." Tony couldn't imagine this would be a problem. She was actually overthinking this situation for a change. Theo's normal approach to life was to leap off a cliff and then search for a landing spot. Her reticence only emphasized how much the theft of the quilt had rattled her. "Ask the pawnbroker about the quilt. You know, act like you might be interested in buying it if the owner doesn't come and redeem it."

"Can he sell it?" The volume of Theo's voice rose along with her indignation level.

"Once the redemption time passes." Tony tried to remember exactly how long that was. "If the owner doesn't claim it, it's the pawnshop's to sell."

"Even if it's stolen?"

"Well, no." Tony frowned. "If it is the right quilt, I doubt the pawnbroker knows it's stolen. If I didn't live with you, I'm sure I'd underestimate its value. By a lot."

"Okay, okay. I'll go talk to the man," Theo muttered. "But I'm not hanging up."

Tony heard the bell ring as she entered the store, and a man's voice. "Ma'am?"

Theo said, "Can I look at that quilt?"

"Sure thing."

Tony was treated to a running commentary by his wife. He thought about just placing his phone on his desk and doing something constructive, like paperwork, but then remembered that she was investigating a crime that had happened within his jurisdiction. Patience was a virtue hard to achieve some days, and being too busy was no excuse for negligence.

"Tony? You still there?"

"Yes. What do you think, is it the right quilt?"

"Yes. I'm positive," Theo whispered. "Now what?"

"Is it listed as for sale?"

"No."

"Let me talk to the owner."

After a few minutes and lots of rattling and coughing that made Tony feel like he'd been dropped into some kind of machinery, the voice on Theo's phone belonged to a man.

"You're a sheriff?" Followed by enough coughing to pull loose a lung, and then without allowing Tony to answer he continued, "This little lady claims I've got a stolen blanket."

"Blanket?" Tony could practically hear the sizzle of Theo's thoughts. "I believe she's found a stolen work of art."

"No kidding? It looks a mite faded to me."

"No kidding." Tony wondered what the man knew about art. "What do you remember about the person who brought it in?"

"Uh . . ." Then silence.

Tony thought he'd better make the questions easier. "Okay, was it a man or a woman who pawned it?"

"Oh, I see what you mean. It was a woman."

"When?" Tony looked at the calendar. It had only been stolen the day before. The thief was working fast. He thought he'd make it simple. "Yesterday or this morning?"

"Dunno. I kin look that up I guess. Hold on."

There was a thud like Theo's cell phone had been dropped and then more coughing. Tony wanted to learn more about the stolen quilt and was not quite believing the man couldn't remember the morning. It wasn't even noon yet. At the same time he was seriously hoping Theo wasn't about to import the plague into Park County. Then he heard Theo mumbling about germs as she must have pulled a baby wipe from her purse and started cleaning her cell phone. Finally it sounded clear.

"Theo?"

"Yes."

Tony was relieved not to be talking to the less than brilliant pawnbroker. "Stay there. I'm going to get you some local assistance. What's the address?"

Theo read it off to him. "I'm not taking my eyes off that quilt until your cop friends get here."

"Sounds like a good plan."

★ ★ ★ ★ ★

It took only seconds for his call to be answered by the Knoxville chief of police. Tony and he had met several times and enjoyed a good working relationship. After they went through minor telephone greetings, Tony went right to the reason he called.

"My wife is in your fair city and believes she has found a very valuable stolen item in a pawnshop. A priceless quilt."

"You don't say." There was a clicking sound in the background, like someone typing. "She's sure about the value?"

"Absolutely." Tony had to smile at the understatement. "My wife is an expert."

"What's the address?"

Tony relayed it to the chief.

"Is she still at that location?"

"Oh, yeah. Dynamite wouldn't budge her," Tony said. "She'll be there even if the owner asks her to leave."

"I know how that works. She sounds a bit like my wife." There was a slight chuckle from the chief. Then silence. "Okay, we have a car headed there now, and the detectives won't be far behind."

"Thanks. I can't wait to hear what happens. The quilt was stolen from my wife's shop and she's been devastated by this whole thing."

"Tell her to hang in there."

Theo only had a few minutes' wait before the first wave of Knoxville police descended on the pawn shop. They listened attentively to her description of the theft of the quilt, its general value, and her finding it by accident. "I can't leave it here like this. The pawnbroker doesn't believe its value, and I haven't had a moment of peace since the theft."

The older of the two cops was about Tony's age, around forty. He had the look of a man who thought he had seen it all, until now. He positioned himself to keep the pawnbroker and the quilt in his line of sight. Theo, he obviously wasn't interested in.

The younger of the two cops stared at the quilt and leaned closer to examine it but was careful not to touch it. "That's amazing!" His eyes flickered in Theo's direction. "I've never seen one that beautiful. Look at the detail, the tiny stitches. The itty-bitty embroidered flowers."

Theo felt better. Now there were two people in the room who truly appreciated the quilt's value and workmanship. The chances of the quilt being treated with white gloves and care had multiplied. "You like quilts?"

"Yeah." He moved away from the quilt. "My mom used to make beautiful quilts, not quite like this, but very good." An unguarded expression of sadness filled his face. "She died last year."

"What was her name?" Theo guessed she would know the woman.

"Dorothy. Dorothy Mansfield."

"I knew Dorothy." Theo felt a clog of emotion fill her own throat. The woman had been a very active quilter in the area and knew every quilt shop and possibly every other quilter in East Tennessee. She had been Theo's customer and if not a friend, a friendly acquaintance. "She is missed by many of us."

"Thank you, ma'am."

A second car arrived. Unmarked. The detectives climbed out and entered the pawnshop, coming immediately to her side. "Mrs. Abernathy?"

Theo went through the whole story again, patiently and with as much detail as possible. If she had to do it fifty more times in order to retrieve Miyoko's priceless quilt, she would do it with a smile.

"Not many old blankets come through here." Cheerful and obviously unwilling to believe what he'd been told about the value of the quilt, the shop owner stood behind his counter, with rows of neatly arranged coins, medals, and jewelry inside the locked glass case. "I thought if the owner didn't come back for it, I might give it to my bird dogs."

Theo stared at the idiot and thought she might be having a heart attack. She didn't mind Daisy sleeping on their bed quilt, but as much as she loved the Golden Retriever, she was not allowed to breathe, much less shed, on the show quilts. For that matter, Theo didn't like it when Tony touched them without washing his hands. Boys with peanut butter or mud on them had to stay twenty feet away. In their small house, twenty feet put them into the next room, which was her intention.

Simple rules are easier to enforce than ones left open to interpretation.

Theo considered herself generally easy to deal with, but she never wavered in this rule—don't touch the show quilts. Even she guessed that maybe if there were a person freezing to death near her and if she had no other option handy, like a towel or dry shirt, she might be forced to break her own rule. She wouldn't bet on it. Certainly not a show quilt that did not belong to her.

Theo watched the detectives asking the owner a few questions.

"So, what's the story with this quilt?" The detective sounded casual but his eyes were alert and curious.

The shop owner peered at their badges. "Say, is there something I should know?"

The lead detective shrugged. "Not necessarily." He stared at the shop owner. "The quilt?"

"All I remember is this woman came in, pulled the blanket out of a plastic garbage bag, and said she needed money." The shop owner closed his eyes partway. "She did seem disappointed I didn't offer her more."

"How much did you give her?"

"Twenty-five." The owner checked the back of the tag.

"Dollars?" Theo gasped out loud and almost swallowed her tongue. The quilt had been stolen twice in one day, from the owner and from the thief.

"What else?" The aggravated owner looked like he thought he'd been robbed too. "She has six days left to redeem it."

Theo considered it unlikely the thief would return for the priceless quilt, now known officially as "an old blanket."

"Has your security system got a working camera?" The younger detective glanced up at the ceiling where a camera pointed at the cash register.

"Naw, that's just for looks." The pawnbroker walked to the window and pointed up at an inconspicuous device on a building across the street. The building where Theo's eye doctor had his office. "That traffic cam belongs to the city. You might check with them."

Driving past the newly paved walking path on the edge of town, Tony glanced out the side window of the Blazer, just in time to see Sheila lift her rifle. In a single fluid movement, she rested the butt against her shoulder and her finger tightened on the trigger. She stood sideways to him. He saw a slight lift of her lips into a smile.

Not for the first time, Tony thought of Annie Oakley. Although Sheila was physically taller than Annie Oakley, which Tony knew because he had been doing research on the diminutive sharpshooter for a book he wanted to write. To him, the parallel between the two blond women was obvious. Both had spent their younger years honing their shooting skills and feeding their siblings and parents with game they'd shot. Sheila fired. She held the rifle in position for a moment before lowering it. Waiting.

Curious, Tony left the Blazer and joined Sheila on the path. Hidden by the shrubbery, he hadn't seen the woman with a stroller standing in the shadows behind Sheila until he made the short climb. The woman's eyes were wide with terror, and an infant strapped to her chest was squalling. He turned to see what Sheila had shot. A feral hog, shot in the head, squarely between the eyes, lay motionless just off the pavement. A toddler stood about six feet away. The toddler wore a warm jacket, little blue overalls, and a matching hat with a brim. He was laughing as he entertained himself by walking in circles in and out of a puddle.

"Sheila?" Seeing the mom, the boy, and the dead hog so close together sent a shock through him. He hadn't heard any report about this situation. Of course, there hadn't been time. Not even Sheila could shoot a hog and operate a radio at the same time.

"I've been tracking this not so little piggy, or at least another one this size, for a while." Her face tightened with anger. "In the past few days, I've seen a lot of tracks on this end of town. It's not like these are domestic pigs run wild. They are relatives of the wild boars imported years ago for hunting parties and they'll eat anything. Literally."

"Or anyone." Tony glanced up and down the newly paved walking path that curved into a loop here on the edge of town. Other than a small space with swings and brightly colored horses on bouncy springs, there was nothing but woods and brush. "They're attracted to the picnic areas, and people keep coming up here in spite of the warning signs."

"Yes, and Hairy Rags always claimed they weren't his problem." Sheila wasn't really looking at Tony. She was still on alert, listening.

Tony thought invoking the name of their late and unlamented game warden explained it all. "He was never in favor of protecting people and property from these boars."

Sheila pitched her voice so he could hear and she wouldn't frighten the young mother who was busily reassuring herself that the small boy was, indeed, fine. "This guy probably weighs close to four hundred pounds."

"There ought to be something we can do." Tony couldn't very well have people running through town, shooting pigs. Even a sharpshooter couldn't be certain of getting a clean shot.

"I've heard of plans to poison them. The most fun idea is packing the corpses with something like strychnine, and then let their voracious relatives eat them and have them get the poison in them as well." Sheila smiled. "It won't work here, but the idea has a certain lovely quality."

Tony shook his head. "I hope it doesn't come to that. No one could safely eat the tainted meat, and how would we get rid of poisoned pigs?" The nightmare scenario of the scavenger population having poisoned pork loomed, birds falling from the sky, bodies everywhere.

"Look at her." Sheila nodded to the toddler's mother, now sitting in a mud puddle created by the melting snow, sobbing as she clutched her unharmed child. "Pigs are omnivores."

Tony thought the calm Sheila used when handling a rifle did not continue to her eyes as they flickered over the distraught mother and children. "Let's get this guy out to the dump and let the relatives come for a visit and you can shoot them having a picnic." Tony paused. "At least what's left of him after Claude does his butchering."

"Sounds good to me. In the meanwhile, I think you might want to see about closing off this section of the walkway." Sheila frowned. "I'm going to stay here awhile and see if I can get some of his relatives. But I can't get them all, and sometimes it's really hard to get a good clear shot this close to town."

"I agree." Tony called Claude Marmot, trash hauler and recy-

cler extraordinaire. "Dead nuisance wildlife ready for pickup."
He knew Claude would butcher the piggy and turn him into
sausage that would end up going to feed those in need. At least
the food bank would be happy. Claude, the recycling king,
would not want poisoned pigs in his dump. The father-to-be
would be more likely to lead the villagers on a pig hunt equipped
with torches and pitchforks than to agree with poison.

Fear for others was a powerful motivation. As a father, he
knew it was true.

Tony offered to take the young mother back to town. Still
sobbing, she followed him to the Blazer. By the time he got the
car seats from the storage area in the vehicle's rear hatch,
buckled them onto the seat, and had the children strapped in,
Claude arrived in his car/truck.

While Tony was wondering how they'd get the hog into the
back of the Crown Victoria cut apart and reassembled into a
pickup, groom-to-be Kenny Baines came from a different direction with his heavy-duty pickup. The bricklayer's truck had a
hydraulic lift on the tailgate and he was ready to help Claude
with the piggy.

Before Tony left with his passengers, he heard the crack of
Sheila's rifle again. Two down, countless wild hogs to go.

CHAPTER SEVENTEEN

Tony thought it was amusing that the bystanders waiting for the Halloween parade to begin seemed possessed by the need to shove their neighbors. Maybe their feisty behavior had something to do with the unusual weather pattern. The storm had circled around again, pulling more moisture across North Carolina and into Tennessee, dropping a new layer of snow. A couple of older ladies were using their walkers as weapons, poking people in the backs of their legs before fighting their way to the front. He watched one old guy jab several people with his cane. As long as it looked like friendly combat, he was not getting involved.

Relieved to see his wife standing quietly outside her quilt shop, Tony sidled near her, dodging a vicious blow from one of the feisty parade watchers. "What is going on?"

Theo's big hazel eyes were hidden by a coating of snow on her glasses. She wiped them with a tissue, smearing water over the lenses. "I have no idea. Gretchen just told me the parade was about to start and so I came out onto the sidewalk and I got knocked down almost at once." She pointed to a streak of red mud on her sweater sleeve. "I thought I'd be safer if I stood against the building."

Tony glanced down at his wife. She was much too short to see anything. "Why not watch from upstairs? You'd be able to see everything."

"I'm supposed to wait here and hold the boys' candy as they collect it." Theo held an orange cloth bag in each hand. Hand-drawn jack-o'-lanterns decorated the bags.

Right on cue, Jamie dashed to his mother and dumped a handful of candy into the bag hanging from her right hand. Moments later Chris was adding to the other one.

Tony received only a cursory greeting from either of the boys. He grinned at his wife. "What will you do when the girls are big enough to join in the fray?"

Theo shook her head and rolled her eyes. It was obviously a question without an answer.

"Want me to tell you what you're missing?" Tony looked over the heads of the people in front of them, the ones blocking Theo's view.

"Show-off." Theo lifted her face and stuck her tongue out at him. Two seconds later she said, "Okay, what am I missing? I can hear the band."

"What you can't see is the band members are wearing their usual uniforms, but they all have either clown makeup or monster faces painted on. I'm sure to have nightmares tonight." Tony faked a shiver of dread.

"Well, at least there isn't a pack of zombies." Theo looked resigned to missing the face paint.

"Not so fast, I think the cheerleaders are zombies."

"Okay, okay, I have to see this." Theo squeezed between some observers to get close to the front. The throng was good-natured, and a couple of older viewers moved to make room for her. Sure enough, the high school girls had enough makeup on to transform them from teenagers into the undead. "Ick."

Tony snagged a piece of candy badly overthrown just before it hit his wife in the face. He handed it to a tiny pumpkin with green legs clinging to the hand of a scarecrow.

The moment the parade ended and the boys reclaimed their candy bags, Theo hurried into the communal workroom in her shop.

Tony encountered Maybelle Ruth on the sidewalk in front of Theo's shop. The knife gone from her back, she was fresh and clean, her hair had been combed, and she was dressed in worn, but clean, street clothes. There was color in her cheeks, and although she still looked much older than her fifty-five years, she didn't look seventy anymore. A young man stood next to her.

"I'm Bobby Ruth." He offered his hand. "Her son. I understand I have you to thank for Mom's rescue."

Tony shook his head. "Actually it was my wife." He watched as Maybelle wandered away from the two of them and studied the window display of Theo's shop. There was a spark of interest and longing in her face. Tony had seen that expression on any number of his wife's customers.

"Aren't you Theodore?" Bobby's eyebrows pulled together. "I was told a Theodore found her. And was the sheriff."

"Theodore is my wife," Tony said. "She was named by her grandfather. The old man didn't care that his hero's name on a petite woman would cause numerous cases of confusion."

Bobby seemed distracted. "Mom's been unsettled ever since my dad died. The two of them had next to nothing and we, my wife and I, asked her to leave Kentucky and move in with us. She gets a little social security but not enough to cover all her expenses." He shrugged. "I thought it would be easier than it's turned out to be."

Tony thought the young man's sigh told the whole story. "She's not happy?"

"No." He studied the sidewalk. "She wants to leave but has no place to go, and I don't know what to do. She says she has

173

no friends, and we keep the house too clean for her to have even housework to do."

"Hobbies? Church? Volunteer in the community?"

"She quilts a bit. You know, cuts up our old clothes and sews the pieces together to make blankets."

"Quilting. Yeah, I know a little about that." Tony resisted the impulse to laugh at his understatement. He guessed the distressed young man wouldn't appreciate his sense of humor. "I think it would be good for her to meet my wife. This time without a knife."

"Mom's standing just over there." Bobby paled a bit at the word "knife." "I'll go get her."

Theo was halfway under a table in the workroom when an unfamiliar female voice said, "I was told I had to come talk to you." Startled, Theo raised her head quickly and cracked it on the underside of the table. "Yow." She backed out, hand on her head, and looked up. The voice came from the woman she'd found with a knife in her back at the grocery store. "Pardon me?"

"My son says I have to talk to you."

Theo smiled. "Nobody has to talk to me, but I'm glad to see you up, out, and about." She was about to say something about how she was hoping the woman felt better but didn't have a chance because the woman interrupted her.

"I'll leave then." The woman turned abruptly and took a step toward the front of the store.

"No. Wait. Don't leave. It would be nice if you could stay a bit, maybe have a cup of coffee and meet some of the regulars when they stop by." Theo saw a look of such longing on the woman's face, it made tears well in her own eyes. "Please stay. I'm Theo."

"I'm Maybelle."

Theo dived back under the table and this time emerged with the marking pen she'd dropped. "Do you quilt?"

"Yes." The voice was almost a whisper. "But I don't intend to stay in this town."

"Why not?" Theo could guess. "Once you meet a few kindred spirits, it won't seem so cold."

"I just don't know what to do." Maybelle twisted her fingers together. "My daughter-in-law is very sweet, but nothing I do is the way she'd do it. They've got no kids for me to watch. I don't cook their kind of foods and the house is already spotless." The last words were delivered with a sob. "But I haven't got enough money to live on my own since my husband died."

Just as Theo poured a cup of coffee for the woman, she heard babbling through the baby monitor. "Here, have a seat for a moment. I have to get my little girls and bring them downstairs."

Before Maybelle could protest, Theo dashed up the stairs.

Two minutes later, she returned with the twins.

"What beautiful little girls." Maybelle's eyes sparkled. "May I hold one?"

"Here, start with this one." Theo offered Kara to the unhappy woman. "Kara is a love sponge."

"What a precious little girl." Maybelle cooed and ran a hand over Kara's fuzzy hair.

Kara, always pleased by praise, grinned and unerringly reached up and stuck her finger in the woman's nose. Maybelle laughed and pulled it out.

Theo carefully checked the floor for stray pins and released Lizzie to explore the room, but not before the little girl managed to rip several strands of her mother's hair from her scalp. Theo's hairs dangled from two tiny fingers as Lizzie reached toward a chair. The tiny explorer couldn't walk without hanging onto something, but there were lots of chairs and usually hands available to help her cross the space. Where Kara was a mellow little snuggle bunny, Lizzie had a fierce temper and an independent spirit. It was a volatile combination.

Maybelle was instantly charmed by them both and Theo, being an adoring mother, was equally charmed by the way her children responded to Maybelle. A shadow of an idea came to her. Maybe this could be the beginning of something good for all of them. It was getting harder each day for her to keep tabs on the twins and get any work done. Even a half-day without the tiny tyrants would be wonderful. She couldn't pay much, but Maybelle would have some extra income, a discount on fabrics, a sense of purpose, and, best of all from Theo's point of view, she might not end up pulling her own hair out by the roots.

The parade over, a few of the regular ladies wandered into the shop looking for coffee, quilts, and babies. They greeted Maybelle with gentle enthusiasm and settled in for a visit. Theo thought one of the nicest things about hanging out with other quilters was having a shared interest to discuss. New people were easily assimilated into the group. A simple question often received fifteen different answers and could keep the conversation going for days.

"What's the progress with the barn quilt project?" Theo's favorite of the over-eighty crowd was Caro. "Is this snow going to cause much of a problem?" Caro looked concerned.

"Of course." An acerbic voice came from the doorway. Eileene Bass had arrived. The woman, until recently when her husband passed away, had been almost invisible and never spoke to anyone. Now they couldn't shut her up. "No one can paint or hang anything in this weather. Our project will never be hung in time." She made it sound like a prediction of the world ending.

Caro stood her ground. "If it's already painted on a wooden square, it can be hung in a blizzard."

Hoping to avoid the beginning of another running battle among the seniors, Theo offered cookies. "We've got two of them up already. If you drive out toward Old Nem's chicken and egg farm, you can see one on the old barn out there. And, of course, we managed to get one up on the museum office."

Eileene looked ready to explode. "You're not hanging one on that antique barn are you?" Disapproval dripped from each word.

"No. We are not. These go on private barns with the owner's permission." Theo chased down Lizzie and moved her away from the coffee cup she had been reaching for. Disappointment made Lizzie squall. Kara joined in to support her twin.

Maybelle leaned forward and whispered in Lizzie's ear and the toddler went silent. And then she laughed.

"That cinches it. You're hired." Theo hoped her plan for Maybelle would work out for everyone. "We'll sit down together and come up with a work schedule. That is, if you want to take the job of part-time babysitter for the dynamic duo."

"Really?" Maybelle looked like she'd just been told her lottery ticket was the big winner. "I would love to spend my days with your babies. I would feel useful and not in the way."

Theo laughed. "And I would really, really love a chance to get some of my paperwork done." Theo felt a great weight lift from her, making her almost giddy. Doing paperwork was not her favorite task, but it was flat impossible with the girls helping.

"Um, Sheriff, um . . ." The words came through Tony's radio.

Rex's improbable hesitation completely grabbed Tony's attention. His chief dispatcher hadn't fumbled for words more than twice in Tony's recollection. He automatically tensed, expecting disaster at hand.

"You know the woman, Mrs. Fairfield, the one who keeps her

embalmed husband in the parlor?" Rex sounded more in control of himself.

Tony could still picture his introduction to the happy couple. "I'm still trying to erase tea time with the family from my brain. Why are you bringing it up now?" Tony could feel trouble brewing.

"Well, sir . . ." Rex's dramatic pause lasted only a split second. "Mrs. Fairfield says her husband has been stolen."

Tony pulled his cell phone away from his ear and moved it to the other one. Maybe he needed to have his hearing checked. "Sorry, I'm not hearing well. Say again. Stolen?"

"Yessir, her words exactly." Rex cleared his throat. "No. That's not completely true. She said that her husband's casket, with him in it, has been stolen and she wants him, with the casket, returned. Forthwith."

"Forthwith?" Tony repeated the word. He guessed it was the first time any of his citizens had used that one. Not for the first time, Tony wondered if there was something inside the former Prigmore home that induced crazy behavior in its occupants. Nellie Pearl Prigmore had gone from eccentric to completely demented. Alzheimer's was the eventual diagnosis, but she'd always been odd. Now they had Mrs. Fairfield living there, with her embalmed husband—was it the house that attracted her? Some woo-woo force in the woodwork? Or was it just plain old coincidence?

"Sir, are you still there?" Rex's voice broke into his thoughts. "What should I tell her?"

"Tell her I'm on the way, and send Wade; he'd probably quit the department if I left him behind."

"Roger that, sir." Rex disconnected.

Tony wasn't sorry to get away from the paperwork and other public service issues involving his office. In between emergencies, he was working on a speech for the senior citizens group, explaining a new proposed "buddy system," but his brain was drifting off the subject. He really wanted to explore the new idea he'd had for a book. He'd begun rewrites of his Western, but he didn't like it. It lacked something. Still, he was proud of himself for finishing. Maybe he should turn it into a mystery. He'd decided his years in law enforcement made him want a crime to have a satisfactory arrest. He definitely would not set the novel here. He wanted zero crime in his own county. Hiding from people wasn't going to help.

He headed to Mrs. Fairfield's house. Wade was already there, waiting for him in his official vehicle. His expression was serious as he climbed out, but Tony saw a sparkle of curiosity in his deep blue eyes as Wade approached the Blazer.

"Did Rex tell you why we're here?" Tony reached for his jumbo jar of antacids and put two in his mouth and six in his shirt pocket. He hoped that would be enough to get him through this interview.

"No, sir, but I'm guessing from the number of antacids you're palming that it looks like you're expecting more heartburn than usual." Wade's expression grew more serious. "Trouble?"

Thinking his deputy was both perceptive and correct, Tony nodded. "It has been reported that Mr. Fairfield, casket and all, has gone missing." He kept watch for Wade's reaction. He wasn't disappointed.

"Sir?" Wade's often praised and incredibly handsome face went completely blank. Then the dark blue eyes gleamed with curiosity. "Did you say missing? On Halloween?"

Tony nodded as he reached for the door handle. "I like to write fiction, but I can't begin to make up something like this."

Wade glanced to the home's perfectly normal front door. Three perfectly normal steps led up to the door. He looked back at Tony. "Sir, you have to be making this up. No one steals a coffin and a body. Out of a house?"

Shaking his head, Tony climbed from the Blazer, his notebook already in hand. He wondered if he should take an extra one. "I just know this is going to take a lot of paper."

Wade fell in step next to him and they marched up the sidewalk, climbed the steps, and rang the bell.

Much more subdued than usual, Mrs. Fairfield opened the door and ushered them into what might have been called a parlor in earlier years. A space along one wall was empty except for a long wheeled platform. In another home, the space was large enough to be occupied by a sofa or a large flat-screen television or even a couple of easy chairs and a lamp table.

After insisting she sit with them, and refusing all offers of tea, coffee, and water, Tony cleared his throat. "When did you discover the theft?"

Mrs. Fairfield waved a lace-edged handkerchief in a somewhat theatrical manner before using it to dab very real tears from her cheeks. "I came home from luncheon at the senior center, and was all excited to tell him about something I heard there, and he was gone!" The handkerchief flapped aimlessly and she stood up and began pacing in an agitated manner. "I don't know what to do!"

"Please have a seat, Mrs. Fairfield." Tony was concerned the distraught woman was about to faint. Her color had gone from pink to gray. "You look quite unwell. Should we call for medical assistance?"

"No." Mrs. Fairfield clutched Tony's forearm, using it to help lower herself onto the sofa. "I'll be fine, as soon as you find and return Mr. Fairfield to me. I'm sure I can't sleep in this house unless he's here. In sixty-three years, we've never been apart."

"My congratulations. That is a very impressive number." Wade wrote something in his notebook. He hesitated slightly. "Was he a large man?"

"Oh my, yes, he was a fine figure of a man." Mrs. Fairfield sat up straighter, clearly heartened by their attempt to help. "Not as tall as either of you. He's about five feet ten inches and sadly, a bit overweight."

"You only moved here a short time ago? Maybe a year at the most?" Tony was thinking out loud. He couldn't imagine any motive for the theft. How many people even knew about the casket? "Why Silersville?"

"It was our dream." Mrs. Fairfield smiled dreamily, staring at an old photograph of her husband hanging on the far wall. "We came through this area on our honeymoon and loved it so."

"Did you tell many people about your husband?" Tony asked. "That is, about his continuing to be above ground?" Part of him couldn't believe he was having this conversation.

"Why, don't you read the *Silersville Gazette*?" Mrs. Fairfield looked shocked. "There was a big article in the paper just last week. I thought that delightful Ms. Thornby did a perfectly lovely job of capturing our relationship."

Tony didn't want to explain his own perfectly awful, or at least dreadfully poor, relationship with the *Gazette*'s owner/ editor. He had avoided reading the newspaper the previous week because he wasn't in the mood for another wacko diatribe by the editor. Winifred Thornby and he had not gotten along well since high school. She now took delight in pointing out every flaw and mistake made by him, his department, and his family, and the election year had brought out the worst in her. Even though months had passed since the voting, she was still on an editorial rampage.

"In this article, were there pictures?" Tony could almost bet there were several photographs. News was sometimes hard to come by and feature articles were padded with numerous photographs and quotes.

Mrs. Fairfield clapped her hands in excitement. "Oh yes, and we discussed the problems created by decorating a living space around a coffin. You may not have considered the problems. It's not easy to find the right arrangement. I need to be near my beloved, but I do like to be able to see the television."

Tony glanced up at the large-screen television mounted on the wall. "I'll admit I'm not much of a decorator myself." He very carefully looked over at Wade.

To his credit, Wade's expression remained polite. "I read the newspaper article and found it was very interesting. Is it true that the coffin itself weighs over four hundred pounds?"

"Yes." Mrs. Fairfield looked thrilled that Wade had remembered such a detail. Her enjoyment of the discussion temporarily superseded her grief. "It does have a very special copper lining, which adds a fair amount to the weight."

Their words washed over Tony. He was busy considering the mechanics of lifting and hauling away a full-sized man in a heavy coffin. Six hundred pounds. Several thieves had to work together. "Excuse me a moment." He left Wade and the widow chatting softly and went to the door. He opened it and carefully examined the door frame. Sure enough there were a couple of spots where it looked like careless movers had bumped it, or the thieves had struggled with the weight. "How long would you say you were away today?"

"A couple of hours," Mrs. Fairfield said. "Three at the most."

"Maybe they stole it for the copper," Tony mumbled.

Wade's head popped up and his mouth opened, but then he glanced at the bereaved and closed it again, making Tony guess his deputy wondered why the thieves bothered to take the body with them. It was an interesting question. In fact, Tony was coming up with lots of questions but none he planned to bother Mrs. Fairfield with, at least not at the moment. "Would you feel better if I got someone to come here and stay overnight with you?"

Tears flooded the older woman's eyes. "Oh, could you? I'm

just so upset, and I don't think I can stay here alone. And where would I go?" She sobbed. "Miss Kitty hates being in a carrier." She waved her handkerchief in the direction of a large calico cat perched on a chair near the window.

"No problem." He punched a number on his cell phone. After a brief pause, he said, "I need a female companion to overnight at Mrs. Fairfield's house."

The exhausted woman sagged into the chair. Relief mixed with fear still showed on her face.

Tony leaned forward. "Someone will be here soon to stay with you tonight and will bring dinner. Do you have any food allergies?"

"No-o. That's so very kind of you." Mrs. Fairfield managed a smile. "What can I do?"

Wade answered for Tony. "Do your best to stay calm."

"I'm so glad I didn't vote for your odious opponent." Her face puckered like she'd eaten something sour. "You two are such gentlemen. That other man came to the senior center, just the other day, and wanted to have you recalled. Nonsense. We were almost preparing to lynch him when he finally left."

Carefully keeping his mouth closed, Tony felt relief. Besides being stupid, Matt Barney, his opponent, had probably been patronizing, as if the elderly couldn't think for themselves. Tony's eyes met Wade's.

The deputy caught the message. Wade explained. "But you need to know that your dinner and the overnight companion are *not* connected to the sheriff's office. It falls completely under a volunteer group focused on community concern and assistance."

Mrs. Fairfield looked intrigued. "I don't believe I've heard of that."

Tony wasn't surprised. It was not publicly discussed. The community of churches, charities—organized and otherwise, shelters, and the food bank formed an unpublicized and unofficial safety net for the citizens of Park County. In this case, their caring for Mrs. Fairfield would give them time to hopefully find the missing coffin or at least some time for her to come to terms with being alone or make her own arrangements for a companion.

"It's an emergency fix only. Just for tonight." Tony wanted to make sure Mrs. Fairfield wasn't expecting a long-term companion. "In the meantime, we'll do our best to locate, um, the missing."

As luck would have it, it turned out to be Tony's own mother who was the emergency companion. She arrived, carrying a frozen chicken casserole in one bag and a few of her own personal items in another. Tony whispered to her as he walked past, "See what you can find out."

"On Halloween?" Jane stared at him. "You want me to ask about a coffin?"

"Why aren't you at the museum, scaring little kids?"

"I did. The party is over." Jane rolled her eyes. "Try to keep up, son. Everyone had fun and then went home."

"Oh, no," Mrs. Fairfield moaned. "I don't have candy for the children." Fresh tears ran down her face.

Jane trotted past her son. "I'll be right back. We had some left after the party."

CHAPTER EIGHTEEN

Theo stirred the bright red paint in the can at her feet. Piles of old newspapers and a disreputable old tarp protected the barn floor. An eight-foot square of plywood was propped up against the opening into an old stall, away from the destruction caused by the Halloween party.

With the boys at a second Halloween party and the girls getting acquainted with Maybelle, their new adult assistant, Theo had sneaked out to paint another of the barn quilts. Using a paint roller on a long handle, she had primed the surface with white paint and divided it into a geometric grid with a pencil while it lay on the tarp. Now that it was upright she couldn't reach the top to add the colors. "I need a stepstool."

Tony's oldest sibling, Caesar Augustus, known to all as Gus, grinned at her. He was cleaning the barn after the party and stopped to watch her work. "I don't think a stool's going to be enough extra height. Should I paint the top row for you?"

"I thought you needed to get back to Catherine and the joys of fatherhood. Diapers don't change themselves, you know." Theo teased Gus but knew he was wildly in love with his baby girl.

Jane's voice interrupted their discussion. Tony's mother was wonderful, sweet, kind, a little ditsy, and annoying all at the same time.

"Hi, Mom," Gus smiled and grabbed the brush from Theo.

Jane looked disappointed to find her oldest child visiting the museum without her youngest grandchild. She didn't stay long. "I'm overnight as a companion and I just came back to pick up some candy." As she walked away, she called out, "Next time, bring the baby."

Theo sighed.

"Why do you think Marc Antony is the only one of my siblings who actually lives in the same town with her?" Gus carefully painted within the lines Theo had marked. "She ran Callie off."

"You and Berry don't live far away from her, just in different directions."

"And different counties." Gus made it sound like the county lines couldn't be crossed without a passport, visa, and prior approval by the residents.

"It might be my fault that we do live so close." Theo frowned. "I pretty much insisted we leave Chicago after Tony was shot."

Gus appeared to be considering her words, checking them for accuracy as he continued to paint. "Nope." He turned and grinned at her, looking exactly like a slightly older version of her husband. "Our baby brother is right where he wants to be."

Theo wasn't sure. "After he was shot . . ." The whispered words still had the power to chill her. She swallowed hard and looked up at Gus. "Until then he had run farther away from home than any of the rest of you. First the Navy and then Chicago. For all the good it did him."

"I know that cop. He's been like he is now for his whole life. This is what he was born to do." Gus's face showed no trace of humor. "Plus, he's the one of us kids the most like our dad, inside."

"Cop and pastor?" Theo was puzzled.

"Yes." Gus pointed his paintbrush at her. "And if you tell him this, not only will I deny it, but I'll find retribution. You will pay big time, little lady." He couldn't quite keep the grin off his face. "They are so alike. Well, except for the hair, because Dad looked more like Berry. Both of them went into the saving business. Lives and souls, justice and redemption. Both of them fight for good."

Theo had never seen Gus so serious. A tingle ran up her spine. "I thought it was Harvey Winston's plan for Tony to take over as sheriff."

"Maybe, maybe not." Gus's smiled reappeared. "Maybe Mom said something to the old man, or maybe someone else put Tony's name in the hat."

Theo laughed at the self-satisfied expression on her brother-in-law's face. "You mean like someone who might have to live in the same town with your mom if Tony didn't return to Silersville?"

"Maybe." Gus dipped his brush into the bucket and kept painting. "Maybe not."

Tony wasn't sure if he was pleased to hear that two men, with outstanding arrest warrants, had opened their front doors to his deputies. Each one was expecting trick-or-treaters and found Darren Holt and Mike Ott holding out the necessary paperwork. They'd surrendered peaceably and calmly, and were now in the booking process.

Tony's cell phone rang again. This time, Alvin Tibbles's name appeared on Tony's caller ID. The teenager had already experienced enough grief, loss, and challenges in his short life to rival many adults well into middle age.

"Hey, Alvin." Tony enjoyed talking to Alvin. He'd learned a lot about plants from the botany-crazed young man. And he'd learned a lot about what was going on in his county as well. "Thanks for calling me back."

"Let me guess." Amusement echoed in the young man's ever deepening voice. "You think I might know someone who knows someone who did what?"

Tony was relieved to hear the thread of humor. Alvin possessed a sharp mind. "That's fair. Let's start with the basics, shall we?"

Alvin's response was a hearty laugh. "Okay. No, your kids don't bother me when I'm working in your yard. No, your wife's cooking isn't great, but it's better than I'm used to. Yes, the truck is running much better since the Thomas brothers worked on it. They're still complaining about how your wife's old minivan almost destroyed their reputations as mechanics." He stopped to breathe.

"And my aunt, your landlady?" Tony was delighted by the humor. For a while he'd been concerned about the sixteen-year-old and still kept tabs on him.

"Oh, yeah, I was getting to her." Alvin's voice lowered. "She is certifiable but nice."

"Are you doing anything for fun besides propagating plants?"

"Sat with a girl at the last football game."

"That sounds good." Tony relaxed. "It's been awhile since you showed up at the jail kitchen to eat. I wanted to make sure I didn't need to hunt you down and hand you a box of food." It wasn't an empty suggestion. The boy had needed donations of food only a few months prior.

Alvin was silent for a moment. "I'm eating fine now, but thank you."

Tony cleared his throat. "I do have a favor to ask."

"Anything."

"I don't want you to feel obligated but, if you should hear anything about a stolen coffin and embalmed body being somewhere it shouldn't, please let me know." To his own ears, Tony's comment sounded like something from a grade C-minus horror movie.

"Well, now that you mention it, I have." Alvin's voice lowered as if he didn't want anyone to overhear this particular part of their conversation. "I was going to call when no one was around."

"Really?" Tony sat up straight and grabbed his pen. "Where? Who?"

"I don't have the answer to either of those questions, Sheriff, but there's a Halloween party being planned with supposedly a coffin and a real live corpse." Alvin laughed on the last word. "I guess that would be a real dead corpse."

"What do you know about the organizers or the location?"

"Not much. Supposedly we'll get a text message later tonight giving us the location. I wasn't planning to go. Do you want me to?"

As it had been only a few months since the boy had seen his own mother's coffin and corpse, Tony was not surprised he didn't want to go. He'd be surprised if Alvin attended another funeral for a while, much less a late night in the dark party. "No. You don't need to go, but if you hear more?"

Alvin quickly agreed. "As soon as I know more, you'll know more."

Tony was delighted by this information. There was nothing like good inside skinny to make life a little better for everyone. "Thank you, Alvin. I can promise not to tell anyone where we got the location, not even my staff."

"Well, if I'm the only invited person who's not there, it's not going to be much of a mystery." A trace of humor filtered through Alvin's words. "Not to mention, the whole county knows my connections to you, your family, and your aunt."

"True." Tony didn't think Alvin was complaining, just stating the truth. "And, if you already know about it, it's hardly a closely guarded secret."

"Well, if the ones I'm guessing are involved really are the

party planners, they've got a group IQ of about three." Alvin's amusement resurfaced. "I'll see what I can learn."

Theo had no idea where Tony was. She was grateful the boys were at a friend's Halloween party and didn't need an adult companion as they went door to door. Just answering the doorbell was wearing her out. The toddlers were *not* helping with the candy distribution. She spent as much time grabbing one girl or another to keep them from tumbling down the front steps as she did dispersing treats. Honestly, did all the kids in town need more candy?

And Daisy? The normally well-behaved Golden Retriever was barking hysterically every time the doorbell rang.

At seven thirty, she ran out of candy and turned off the porch light. As she made her way into the family area, she carried both of the girls. A glance at them in better lighting showed dirty smudges and something like glue in their curls. She turned toward the stairs. "You girls need a bath."

Predictably, Lizzie wanted to crawl up the stairs and pitched a fit when Theo insisted on carrying her. She continued to howl until Theo plopped her in the bathtub with a couple of inches of warm water. Suddenly sunny, Lizzie laughed and splashed. The splashing made Kara cry.

Theo thought about crying too but she didn't have the energy.

Eventually, Theo managed to get both of them clean and dry and into their fuzzy duck pajamas. Chris and Jamie returned from the party just in time to kiss their already snoozing sisters goodnight.

Theo fell asleep on the couch while watching them sort their candy and small prizes. The favorites seemed to be the vampire teeth.

★ ★ ★ ★ ★

"Sheriff?" The boy's voice on the telephone was barely above a whisper.

"Alvin?" Thank goodness for caller ID. Tony was instantly concerned, though. It sounded like the boy was gasping for breath. A hideous nightmare bloomed in his mind, one born of watching too many horror movies with his older siblings. "Are you all right? Where are you?"

"I've found your missing coffin." Then silence. Disconnect.

Tony immediately began pushing buttons trying to get Alvin back on the phone. Nothing. He stared at the clock. Twelve minutes to midnight on Halloween. The sound of his own heartbeat hammered in his brain. Was there a way to trace the location of the disconnected call? He called dispatch. "Where is the coffin party?"

Karen Claybough, Wade's sister, was working the night desk. "I just got a call about it. It's up on the mountain near the old cemetery. Do you know the spot?"

"I think so." Tony would not swear he'd be able to find it. "I need someone who grew up in those hills."

"Then wait a second. I'll get you Wade or Darren. They both grew up playing in those woods, hunting rabbits. They'll know the place." The click of her keyboard almost drowned out her next words. "There haven't really been tombstones up there since I was little."

Tony paced and swore and stared at the clock; seconds were ticking away. His phone chirped, call waiting. Tony pushed the button. "Wade?"

"No. It's Alvin."

"Thank heaven." Tony exhaled, surprised to find he'd been holding his breath. "What happened?"

"I'm up here in the old cemetery. I must have gotten under the wrong rock and lost service." Alvin's voice sounded strained.

"We're coming up there." Tony forced himself to speak calmly. "Find yourself a safe place."

Alvin didn't say don't come. "There's a lot going on up here. It's not just the coffin. Someone must have robbed a moonshiner. There's a lot of white lightning and some weed." He panted like he was running. "You'll have to arrest two thirds of the high school."

"What about you?" Tony hated to think the boy had been drinking.

"You might smell some alcohol on my breath." The boy whispered. "I didn't swallow any, or not much, I just rinsed my mouth with it so they wouldn't think I was a spy. Cripes, it's nasty stuff."

"I'm sure you're right." Tony wasn't a big fan of moonshine. "We'll probably just round up everyone and haul you to the jail as a group. Then we can release you and most of the others to their parents."

"Everyone gets off?" Alvin sounded either angry or disappointed.

"Oh, no. Not a chance." Tony was not going that far. "We will arrest the body snatchers and whoever brought the booze, if we can find them. I hate these parties."

Alvin's voice became clear and calm. "In that case, you should know the snatchers are Doc, Shorty, and Slim Carpenter."

Tony might have guessed. The Carpenter boys were often unsupervised and dumb as dirt. "How are the coffin and Mr. Fairfield?"

"Oh, fine." Alvin started laughing, a hearty laugh. "Not even the Carpenters were willing to open an occupied casket. Especially not on Halloween. They claimed they stole it just for decoration, but everyone knows the truth. They had planned to open it, told everyone, and then chickened out."

"Thank goodness for that." Tony checked his watch. "I hope

to be there in half an hour or so."

With the navigational help of Wade and Darren, Tony put the Blazer in four-wheel drive and followed a snow-covered, narrow, winding road, more of a path, up the side of the mountain. Once, decades ago now, a community had existed here, but now the only signs of it were a couple of rotted cabins and a plot of weeds and trees surrounded by a low row of worn stones. The cemetery. The moon cast a pale light through the clouds, reflecting from the well-polished casket of Mr. Fairfield. It glistened like a lake in the surrounding dark, snow-dusted vegetation, although it tilted as if it had been dumped there rather than placed. A couple of citronella candles sat on the slope of the lid but provided little in the way of illumination or atmosphere.

The three Carpenter boys were easy to find: two were passed out and the third one was throwing up on his brothers. Tony guessed the biggest problem he and his deputies were about to experience was deciding who was going to have to transport them. He wished they could use a pickup and just toss them all into the open truck bed like logs. Unfortunately, they needed to transport them safely. Having a teenager bounce out of a pickup could have lasting repercussions. He sighed.

Wade stared at the coffin. "These idiots are not making our lives any easier. Should we get Mayor Cashdollar up here with his hearse, so we can get Mr. Fairfield back where he belongs?"

"I'll make the call. In the meantime, you can try to use a bit of fingerprint powder." Tony shook his head, watching the swirl of snow falling from the trees. "And take lots of photographs. I don't know why I'm always surprised by the things people do for entertainment that can get them arrested."

Wade flipped out his favorite fingerprint brush. "I'll get started."

"Since there are lots of them and not many of us," Tony said, "we'll have to drive them down in shifts." He radioed Karen and explained the situation and the numbers. "Wake up everyone you think we'll need."

"Yes, of course." Karen paused. "You don't need the doctor?"

"Thankfully not. We've managed to avoid shooting anyone so far." Tony was tempted. "And Mr. Fairfield is not any more dead than he was."

"Hang on," Karen said.

He thought he might have heard Karen snicker before she put him on hold. Maybe he should have his ears checked.

A moment later, she said, "I'm back. I'll stay in touch, but it is Halloween night and my phone bank looks like Christmas. I ought to get paid extra for this."

Tony didn't disagree, but he knew she actually enjoyed her job. Her brother, Wade, once said that Karen was born telling everyone around her what to do and when to do it. Dispatch was the perfect job for her.

CHAPTER NINETEEN

Ferrying the partygoers down the mountain turned out to be a bigger job than Tony expected. The road was so narrow it was virtually a one-way, one-lane path. There wasn't any place where it was wide enough to allow vehicles to pass, so they had to send a load of kids down and then return empty to pick up more. Mike had the fun job of ferrying the partygoers down the mountain and coming back to pick up others. With every member of his department on the mountain, except J.B. Lewis, the county's usual night patrol, and Sheila, Tony prayed there would be fewer calls than normal for Halloween.

The mayor and owner of Cashdollar Mortuary, Calvin had to wait in line like the others. The hearse was long and powerful and made it most of the way up the mountain just fine. When the road became impassable, he climbed out, dressed in worn jeans, a sweatshirt celebrating Tennessee football, and heavy leather gloves. He wasted no time, but opened the back door on the hearse, the beams of his headlights centered on the casket. "I'll need help. I can't get any closer."

Calvin, Tony, and the two available deputies lined up on either side of the coffin and lifted. It didn't budge. They all stepped back, eyeing the casket with some concern.

"Holy cow, she wasn't kidding about its weight." Tony didn't look away from the gleaming wood. "Why would anyone have to have such a heavy coffin?"

Even Calvin was shaking his head. "It's not one I would

recommend. There's no reason I can see."

Tony said, "I heard it has a copper lining." His words produced nothing but frowns on every face.

"So we need even more strong backs." Wade studied the remaining partygoers. "There's not much muscle left up here."

"Mike should be back up here in a minute." Darren looked down at the coffin. Swirling across the dark wooden surface, illuminated by flashlights, was a flurry of fine white. "Is that more snow?"

A gust of wind swirled the flakes. Definitely new snow. Tony toyed with the idea of just quitting his job, driving down the mountain, and leaving his official vehicle parked in the sheriff's bay, with the keys in it. It would be ready for his replacement, whoever that might be. The moment passed after he considered that the idea of a special election might leave them only Matt Barney on the ballot. He took a deep breath and it erased his insane impulse. He refused to inflict such a waste of skin on the citizens of Park County. "Okay, let's think. How did three skinny kids steal this and get it up here? Surely we can reverse the procedure?"

Wade was the only one of them besides Tony who had been to Mrs. Fairfield's home and seen the casket on-site. "Mrs. Fairfield had it on wheels. There is no other way for that woman to be able to move it from the wall over to the table for tea."

"That's right!" Tony slapped him on the back. "Wade, you're a genius."

"Does that mean I get to go home, snuggle with my wife, and eat leftover Halloween candy while you juggle Mr. Fairfield?"

"Ha! Let's find some wheels." Tony looked at the undertaker. "Calvin?"

"Certainly. I use wheels all the time. But . . ." Calvin's eyelids drooped with fatigue. "I don't have any with me. Not only that, they're not exactly designed for off-road work, if you catch my meaning." Calvin continued to study the coffin, clearly considering its awkward position and the distance to the hearse.

"But how'd those skinny guys move it once they were up here?" Wade stared at the distance between the coffin and the Carpenter boys' pickup.

Tony said, "I'll bet they just backed the pickup almost to Mrs. Fairfield's front door, and then pushed the coffin into the pickup bed from its display stand. Once they got it up here and parked with the front end of the pickup facing uphill, they probably all three pushed the coffin and it slid out right where it is now." He mentally measured the distance to the hearse. "I'm sure they never planned to return it."

"Oh, I have an idea," Calvin interrupted. "I'll have to go back down to town. I'll need to leave the hearse here because we'll need it later."

"We'll wait. Why don't you ride down with Mike? He'll take you wherever you need him to." Tony was not leaving the casket here unprotected, even if they all had to wait until sunrise. He hoped he wouldn't need a wooden stake but thankfully there had been no rumors of the deceased gentleman having vampire tendencies. "Off you go."

While they waited for the funeral director to return, Wade finished his photographs and Darren held a protective tarp over Wade's head and the coffin. Tony was in charge of the flashlight. He hoped the batteries were as long-lived as the advertisements suggested. Dark, snow, and a coffin didn't appeal to him.

Wade looked up from his work. "Nobody saw those little ferrets shove a coffin into the bed of a pickup?"

Darren groaned. "Are you kidding? With all the thick, overgrown vegetation and tall privacy fences in that neighborhood, I'm not surprised. Those lots are huge and every one of them is overgrown. Six grown men could have a sword fight in the front lawn and none of the neighbors would have been able to see a thing."

Nodding his agreement, Tony moved slightly away from the others but kept the flashlight focused on their work. Cell phone service in this spot was okay, if not great. Theo would worry if he didn't call when he was out this late. "I'm not sure when I'll get home."

Theo's voice was fuzzy, like she'd been asleep. "I know you are not out having fun."

"No fun," Tony agreed with her understatement. "But wait until you hear what we have been doing."

After what seemed like an endless wait, Calvin returned, driving a huge pickup pulling a wheeled trailer. On the trailer was a device that looked like a combination of a pulley and winch system on wheels. As Calvin backed it into position, Tony saw there were also several large chains and a bracing arm.

Calvin climbed down. "I'll need some help."

"Sure thing." The fascinated viewers leapt to lend a hand. "What do you need?"

"This gizmo works sort of like a crane. We need to slip these hooks into those rings near the coffin's bottom." Calvin handed the hook he was holding to Tony. "There's two on each side."

Obligingly, Tony slipped the first hook in and stepped back to attach the next one. Wade worked on the other side.

"Don't twist the chain." Calvin's words were muffled by the sweater he'd pulled up over his mouth. The snow was getting thicker and the air colder.

Following Calvin's directions, Tony and Wade got the support chains clipped on correctly. It was so cold now, Tony could barely feel his fingers after handling the chilled steel.

Calvin said, "The rest of you—we're going to lift this coffin with the winch and move it to the hearse. See the roller platform in the back? Slide that out."

Everyone hustled to do his bidding.

Calvin hit the power button on the winch and the cable tightened and slowly lifted the casket. It seemed steady, almost like it was too heavy to swing. Calvin manipulated it over to the rear of the hearse where the rollout waited for its cargo. Calvin had clearly practiced this maneuver. He moved the casket into position, and pushed the button to relax the tension on the chain. He signaled for his assistants.

Tony and Wade jumped forward and unclipped the hooks.

Calvin gave the coffin a gentle push and sent it rolling smoothly into the hearse.

The entire crew heaved a collective sigh of relief. Maybe they would get off the mountain before dawn.

Calvin cast a professional eye over the coffin. "Don't get too excited. The night's not over. We'll still need a lot of strong people to carry this into the house. At least it doesn't appear to be really damaged, just a couple of small scratches. We can patch the finish easily enough."

"That's quite a gizmo, Calvin." Tony studied the contraption on the trailer. With it, he had actually done little to help.

Calvin nodded his agreement and brushed the snow off his hands. "I've only needed this in a few cases."

Tony knew "case" was mortician-speak for burial. "What's it for, really?"

"If there isn't a service, I can handle a burial single-handed."

Calvin and his hearse led the procession down the mountain. Wade followed in the pickup, hauling the winch.

Tony eventually brought up the rear. He was the last to come off the mountain, but he consoled himself. At least the sun wasn't up. Yet. There was lots of work to be done. He guessed they had about twenty kids to process or lecture and parents to call. Some of the kids were just innocent and stupid, and some were ringleaders. He didn't love this part of his job.

★ ★ ★ ★ ★

A pale, exhausted Mrs. Fairfield answered their knock. Dispatch had called to inform her of their coffin rescue and she insisted she could not wait until later in the morning for her husband's remains to be returned. Sleep, even with such a compassionate friend in the house, had eluded her.

Jane, now officially labeled compassionate, didn't look any better than Mrs. Fairfield. Tony frowned when he saw his mother's bloodshot eyes and pale face. "I'm guessing you didn't get any sleep?"

"She couldn't stop crying, much less go to sleep," Jane whispered, her voice ragged. "We've been playing cards. For hours." Jane stumbled to the sofa, more or less collapsed onto it with the side of her face pressed against the armrest, and stared into space.

Unlike his mother, Mrs. Fairfield suddenly seemed invigorated by their arrival. She offered tea and cookies, bustling around like she'd had a good night's sleep and a lot of caffeine.

Tony carried his camera inside. He wanted to take a few photographs of the home's interior and the now-empty wheeled display table. It was, in fact, sturdy stainless steel, with four locking wheels. "Have you cleaned this?"

"No, no, your deputy was very insistent that I not touch it, much less clean it."

Wade twirled his favorite fingerprint brush. "I'm ready when they are."

As if awaiting a cue, the hearse pulled up outside. Calvin backed the vehicle close to the front steps. It put the coffin up about to the level of the top step. The cart was a couple of feet taller. "We need more muscle."

Tony's deputies had scattered on other calls.

Karen informed Tony that help was already on the way. She had called for more assistance. The two-man ambulance crew arrived. The EMTs immediately started discussing the difference between hauling someone out of a building as opposed to hauling someone in. "How much does he weigh?"

"We're guessing about six to eight hundred with the custom box." Tony counted. With the two newcomers, they had five men. Surely that would be enough.

"No kidding." The biggest of the new arrivals flexed his muscles. "If we roll the table over here, and lift on the count of three, I'll bet we can heave it up here in one smooth move."

"Actually," Calvin interrupted. "Now that we are on fairly level ground, I have a power table that can lift it up another foot. That will make it a bit easier." He cracked a jovial smile. "No matter what the job, it's all about the toys."

"Please stand away from the door, Mrs. Fairfield." Wade moved the woman to the sofa.

With plenty of muscle, the extra foot supplied by the lift, and determination, the men heaved the coffin up and into the house, setting it with care onto the white cloth covering the wheeled table. Seconds after receiving heartfelt thanks from everyone, the EMTs vanished, their radio crackling with a new emergency.

Mrs. Fairfield smoothed the corner of the cover on the top of the table. "I always leave this on, but I can unbutton the skirt and wash it. Plus, I have several different ones. I'm particularly fond of the Christmas skirt. Lots of felt trees and sequins on it." Grinning widely, she wiped her streaming eyes. "Would you like to see it?"

Tony glanced at his watch. It was three in the morning. "Would you mind showing me at a later time? I still have a lot of work to take care of tonight." Contacting the parents of their party kids promised to be lots of fun.

"Of course, of course." Mrs. Fairfield might look brighter than she had when they arrived, but Jane looked ready for her own coffin.

"Come on, Mom, I'll drop you off at your house. You can get your car later."

Jane didn't protest but followed her youngest child down the steps. He didn't bother with formalities, just picked her up like a child and put her on the passenger seat of the Blazer.

Wade stood nearby. He didn't look any better than Tony felt.

"Wade, go home. You'll be on duty in a few hours." Tony blinked when the headlights of a vehicle coming down the road struck him. "I don't think our little felons will run far tonight."

Wade nodded.

"Archie will probably want to do a little legal research to see how many crimes we can charge the little perverts with."

Wade paused as he was climbing into his vehicle. "I was there, and *I* don't believe it. Who would?"

By the time Tony had crawled into his own bed, the morning was not new. He was sound asleep in seconds. It felt like he had slept maybe ten whole minutes when his phone rang. The hideous, insistent ringer had his attention, but he was contemplating throwing the nuisance out the window.

"What?" His voice sounded croaky, even to his own ears. His throat felt raw and sore.

"Sheriff?" Rex was on duty.

Tony mumbled, trying to stay asleep. "No. He's gone far away."

"Sir?" Rex sounded unsure who had answered the phone. "Is that you?"

Tony groaned again and tried to clear what felt like a wadded-up sock from his throat. It hurt. Could the sock have razor blades in it? "Yes. I think it's me." He felt stupid and dizzy and couldn't decide if he was hot or cold.

"Are you coming in to your office?" Rex spoke with more confidence. "Our fearless prosecutor wants to talk to you about the Carpenter boys."

"Tell Archie I'll take a quick shower and be right down." Tony didn't wait for a response, just disconnected and swung his feet off the bed and onto the floor as he sat up. He swayed when the room felt like it started to move. He stumbled into the bathroom and turned on the shower. A glance in the mirror was not reassuring. His eyes looked bleary and bright red where there was supposed to be white. Tony tried swallowing a glass of water, but the throat clog remained. His shower was brief, and he shaved quickly before pulling on a clean uniform. None of the normal routine seemed to be improving his overall condition.

"Theo," he croaked as he went downstairs. Daisy, the Golden Retriever, lifted her head from the sofa and wagged her plumed tail in a half-hearted greeting. She looked as tired as he felt and didn't bother to leave the furniture. Theo and the kids were gone, so he received no sympathy before he left.

The greeting from his staff was unenthusiastic. Mostly it consisted of, "You look awful," or "Whatever bug you have, please don't share it with me."

Ruth Ann pulled out a filter mask and a jumbo canister of disinfecting wipes. She did not express any sympathy for his condition. "I don't have time to be sick." She began wiping every surface she could reach.

Archie Campbell took one look at him and borrowed a wipe from Ruth Ann. He carefully cleaned his hands and the arms of the chair he was seated on. "If I'd known you were carrying the plague, I'd have insisted on a telephone conference."

Tony was not in the best mood, and their attitudes were not improving it. "Well I'm here now, and you're here, so let's do it."

"Okay." Archie pulled out a sheaf of papers. "We can charge your body snatchers with breaking and entering and theft. I don't know if you can place a value on a deceased person, but the coffin is expensive. The copper lining alone must have set the widow back a pretty penny."

Tony raised a hand to stop the torrent of words. His head was threatening to explode, and he could barely follow Archie's quick explanation. It felt like the mucus in his nose was backing up into his ears. "Bobby snabbing?"

Archie was silent, processing the question. "Oh, you mean body snatching? Is there such a law? Shouldn't that man have been buried long ago?" His well-manicured fingers drummed on the chair arm. "I do know it is either illegal, or should be, to keep a human body or stuff one."

"Taxidermy?" Tony shuddered at what he considered a horrifying thought. "It was bad enough thinking he was embalmed. You think she stuffed him?"

Ruth Ann knocked on the door frame. "I think you'd better take this call, Sheriff. It's Mrs. Fairfield. She claims she has a confession to make."

"I can't imagine what." Tony held up a finger to keep Archie in place, and silent. "Mrs. Fairfield?"

After a muffled sob, Mrs. Fairfield began, "Sheriff, I should tell you, I've been lying to you and to everyone else in town."

"How's that, Mrs. Fairfield?" Tony forced himself to loosen but not release his grasp on the receiver. He wasn't sure how much more of this case he could handle. Body snatching, midnight revels in an ancient cemetery, the idiocy that kept him out all night and was now rewarding him with a pounding headache and the feeling he could end up in the mucus hall of fame. His throat threatened to close completely.

"Mr. Fairfield is not in that coffin. I lied to you and everyone." She sniffled. "I paid to have a sculpture made. It looks real enough through the glass, but it's not really Mr. Fairfield. He's buried in Ohio, where I moved from."

Tony was fascinated. In his tenure as sheriff, he had encountered some wackos, but Mrs. Fairfield was edging ahead in the race for the wackiest. "Why?" It sounded like "By."

"Should I disconnect?" she whispered. "We could talk another time."

"No. No. This is fine." Tony wanted to get this case over with. "Why did you get the sculpture and why lie about it?"

"Well, I did want to keep my beloved husband at home with me, but I was told it was illegal." Her voice grew stronger. "The makeup artist at the funeral home said she could make a sculpture that would look just like him, and there isn't a law against owning a sculpture." She released a giant shuddering sob. "I just can't bear to lose him again."

Tony stared at the telephone. Nothing in Sheriff School had addressed such a bizarre situation. "It's fine. I'll be in touch." He disconnected, staring at Archie. "We have a change in our crime."

Archie leaned forward, grasping his expensive pen in his professionally manicured hand. "What now?"

"Well, to start, there was no bobby snabbing." Tony pulled out his handkerchief and blew his nose. "There was a sculpture snabbing."

Archie managed to look both relieved and invigorated. "All righty then, now we are getting somewhere, legally speaking. We can have the sculpture appraised for its value. That will determine part of the charge. Plus, as I understand it, the coffin is lined with copper. They don't give that away. By the time we add up the value of coffin and sculpture, we should easily move into felony range."

"Yes," Tony agreed. "But those little ne'er-do-wells thought they had a real body."

"True. I don't think it matters, though, what they did or didn't think. Thinking's not illegal, you know." Archie released a big sigh. "At least the little ferrets won't have the really cool body snatcher title they were hoping for. They probably thought it would give them some status in prison. Now, it's just plain thievery."

Tony thought Archie was absolutely correct. The Carpenter boys were about to be disappointed. He smiled, feeling better just thinking about their misery.

"All right, let's see what they have to say. Do the little darlings have an attorney?" Archie clicked the button on his pen.

"They do. They are busy having a group discussion right now," Tony said. "Carl Lee Cashdollar is their attorney."

"Of course he is. Heaven forbid the family would pay for a lawyer. Our poor overworked, underappreciated public defender, Carl Lee, gets to have all the fun." Archie's voice was filled with anger. "I can see him now, struggling to get a lucid answer out of a trio of hungover teenage thugs while still dealing with the loss of his father. The man should have some bereavement time off."

Tony couldn't dispute Archie's assessment. The county didn't have a huge budget for anything, much less free legal advice. There were only a couple of attorneys' names on the list, which was one more than they'd had a few months ago. It didn't help. Carl Lee's new co-advocate had recently gone on maternity leave.

A knock on the door frame attracted both men's attention. Ruth Ann, still armed with disinfecting wipes, said, "Carl Lee and his clients are waiting for you in the greenhouse."

Tony and Archie trudged down the hall. The small interrogation room was packed. Carl Lee, plus three Carpenters, and a social worker assigned to them because the youngest Carpenter was only thirteen. The boys were dressed in jail orange and wore handcuffs and shackles. Deputy Darren Holt stood at the door. His hand rested on his taser. "Do you want them all at once?" Tony looked at Archie.

Archie looked at Carl Lee.

Carl Lee shook his head.

"Let's just deal with the youngest first," said Carl Lee. He sighed. Then he sneezed.

"Holt, take the older ones to the jail," Tony instructed. "Hold on. I'll get a jail deputy to help walk them over." Tony spoke softly into his radio but leveled his stare on the two older boys. "We don't want anyone developing delusions of turning this into a three-ring circus."

While waiting as Deputy Holt and the jailer shepherded the older brothers out of the room and headed to their separate holding cells, Tony noticed an expression of relief mixed with resignation on the social worker's face. He couldn't find her name in his mucus-filled head. He apologized and she laughed. A pleasant woman doing a necessary, but not a fun, job.

"I'm JoAnn Nesbitt." She offered her hand.

"I knew that." Tony smiled but kept his hands by his side. "I have some wretched cold virus that stole my brain. Let's just say we shook hands."

"Thank you for the warning." JoAnn settled into the chair next to her young client. She glanced at the teenager and then nodded to Calvin. "Sit down, Mr. Campbell, and let's get on with it."

To Tony, it felt like ten hours passed between the initial introduction and the removal of the youngest Carpenter to a juvenile unit. He glanced at JoAnn Nesbitt. The social worker looked older than she had when she'd arrived, and sat staring at the empty chair after young Carpenter had been led away.

"Ms. Nesbitt, are you staying for the brothers?"

"No!" She rose to her feet. "That is, I believe only this one of the pack is a juvenile. I believe I've had quite enough fun for one day. Gentlemen, you all have my thanks and admiration."

Tony's hearing was a bit fuzzy but he thought he heard her say "good luck," as she slipped through the doorway, moving fast.

THE COFFIN QUILT
THIRD BODY OF CLUES

Block Two:

Using 14 squares 3″ of fabrics (B) and (D), draw a diagonal line on wrong side of the lighter of the two fabrics. Place right sides together. Stitch 1/4″ from both sides of the drawn line. Cut on line and open, pressing to the darker fabric. Clip "ears" and trim blocks to 2 5/8″ square. Make 28 squares.

Stack the squares with fabric (B) in lower right corner. Remove 14 squares, rotate (B) to lower left corner. Place this stack above the other. Sew upper stack squares onto lower stacked squares—being careful not to rotate them. Press to dark. Turn half of the 14 rectangles and align next to remaining stack. A pinwheel of (D) should be seen. Sew together.

Turn to the back, hold the seam near the center with thumbs, and gently twist. It will release a stitch or two, forming tiny pinwheel on back and allow you to press each end of the seam to the darker fabric and lay flat.

Using 14 of the squares 4″ of fabric (B), cut once on diagonal. Sew resulting triangles to the pinwheel block on two opposing sides, press to triangles. Sew remaining triangles on opposite sides. Press to triangles. Trim. Blocks should measure 6 1/2″. Make 7. Set aside.

Cut the seven 7 1/4″ squares of fabric (B) diagonally twice in X, making 28 large triangles with long side on straight of grain. Cut the remaining 3 7/8″ squares of fabric (C) once diagonally. Take care not to stretch the bias edges of triangles—sew the long edge of one (C) to each diagonal cut on fabric (B) and form a rectangle—flying geese block. Press to darker fabric. Trim carefully to 6 1/2″ by 3 1/2″ block Make 28.

Using 14 of the flying geese blocks, place the triangles of (C) next to two opposing sides of the pinwheel square, pointing away from center. Sew. Press away from pinwheel.

Sew 3 1/2″ squares of fabric (B) on each end of remaining 14 flying geese rectangles. Press toward points. Sew onto remaining opposing sides of pinwheel blocks, forming star. Press.

Label Block Two. Make 7.

CHAPTER TWENTY

Tony was not going to have the other two Carpenters in the same room at the same time. "Let's see what Carpenter Number Two has to say." He blinked. His tired and now cold-infected eyes felt like they were on fire in his head. He half-expected to see flames in his reflection on the small window.

Carpenter Number Two, as Tony thought of him, was the smallest of the brothers. Wiry and short, his arms were bones covered with sinew. Tony guessed he could beat up both of his larger brothers at the same time. He had *fight to the finish* and *no surrender* written all over him. Unfortunately for Park County, he had the same two mottoes written all over his jail records. Carpenter Number Two had apparently arrived angry and then got worse. Brothers One and Three had never said anything slightly derogatory about him or had even implied that Number Two had ever been part of any criminal endeavor. Other witnesses had reluctantly spoken against him. Secrecy was crucial to their continued good health.

Tony put Number Two in shackles for the interview. There wasn't a single person in law enforcement in the adjoining states of North Carolina, Kentucky, and Virginia who was stupid enough to let him sit unchained. To date his offenses had not crossed into anything that would get him life imprisonment, but if he wasn't just a little careful, he was going to accumulate enough bad deeds to keep him away from the rest of the world for a long, long time.

Number Two slouched as well as he could with his arms and legs chained to each other. He glared at Archie Campbell and then Tony. "You've got nothing."

"Shut up." Carl Lee prodded his client with the point of his pen before looking at Tony. "He has nothing to say."

As irritated as Tony was, he felt sorry for Carl Lee. He'd hate to have to be even nominally on Number Two's side. "Okay." Tony tapped on the door and spoke to Darren. "Take this one back and bring in the smart brother."

The reaction he got was a lot like dropping a match on gasoline. When Tony was still a boy, his brothers Gus and Tiberius had blown up a wasp nest with a firecracker while he and their sister watched. This was just about as exciting.

"You think he's smarter than me? He can't do anything unless I tell him to." Number Two's shackles rattled and spittle flew from his lips. "He's too dumb to . . . um . . ." He stopped talking the second his brain managed to send a feeble message to his mouth. "I mean. Well, you know."

"Oh, yeah." Tony had to smile. "I do know." He loved having it all recorded on video.

Carpenter Number One, the oldest, didn't have the will or the brain to come up with a plan, criminal or otherwise. Tony doubted the boy could add French fries to a sandwich order, if it wasn't part of a meal package. Number One was the best looking of the three brothers. He was tall, well-muscled, and he even combed his hair. Rumor had listed several teenage girls recently giving birth to his offspring. Number One didn't claim any of them but his denial was not going to convince the paternity tests being run.

Strictly speaking, Number One was not unintelligent. The boy could read and passed the tests moving him up the school ladder; he was just . . . just . . . Tony searched his brain and thesaurus for the word he needed. Obtuse? No, maybe imperceptive.

Tony had gone to school with the Carpenters' father. Like Number One, he had been a good-looking youth with no ambition and no moral fiber at all. The three Carpenter boys currently in his jail were not the only Carpenter offspring. A couple of older ones had left the county before Tony took office. He was sure they were either in jail, or about to be, in some other lucky sheriff's jurisdiction.

No matter what other traits and appearances they possessed, or who the mother was, every single known or suspected Carpenter, son or daughter, had the same, very distinctive lobeless right ear. Somewhere along the way, something had created the odd genetic pattern.

"Who do you suppose gets invited to the Carpenter family reunion?" Wade had asked once. "Just the ones with the name, or do they add in the ones with the undeniable appearance?"

Tony had been in the process of lifting a mug of coffee to his lips. Wade's comment created an unplanned movement, sending a plume of coffee sailing from the mug. After Tony had cleaned the coffee he'd spilled off his desk, he gave some consideration to the question. "It seems unlikely that no one in the families has noticed the resemblance. Still, I imagine the party is open only to the official offspring."

"Well, I'd just as soon not get invited to that party." Wade didn't smile. "They're not in the same socially deviant league as the Farquars, but still, I can't imagine spending that much time with them en masse."

Tony agreed. The Farquar family had managed to produce enough deviant felons to populate not only their jail but the state penitentiary. The leader—if a word like that could be applied to a man like Angus Farquar—made the Carpenters look clean, sweet and law abiding. "We've stalled long enough." Tony blew his nose and gulped some water. "Let's go see what he has to say."

Carpenter Number One sat quietly in his chair. He wasn't fidgeting or playing with his shackles. He stared quietly at the papers spread across the table with no evident curiosity.

"Mr. Cashdollar." Tony moved in and took a seat. "Have you had a chance to talk to your client?"

"Yeah." Number One's voice was flat, without any expression. "I didn't do nothin'."

"Oddly, that's not exactly the information I've received from witnesses." Tony thumbed through a large stack of papers.

"Someone musta paid them to lie." Number One spat on the floor.

Carl Lee leaned close to his client and whispered furiously in the ear with no lobe. "Or else" were the only words said loudly enough to be heard across the table. Judging from the way the young man's spine straightened, whatever Carl Lee said to him seemed to have been received as it was supposed to be. Carl Lee sat back, glanced at Tony, and gave a little nod.

"Would you like to confess?"

Number One looked like he'd rather spit on the floor again, but he said, "Yes, sir."

"You'll get to clean the floor when you're done with your confession." Tony was not going to let the weasel get away with possibly infecting one of their office mice with some Carpenter family disease.

When the bell on the shop door rang, Theo glanced up and recognized Miss Dawson. She was the newer of the two third-grade teachers at the county's elementary school.

Her first year in Silersville, Miss Dawson had Chris as a student. Tony and Theo had met her, of course, during parent-teacher conferences and other school events. Because she liked the boy and he liked her and his grades were good, there had not been many conferences.

Perky. That's how Theo always thought of Miss Dawson. She was long-limbed and lanky and could frequently be seen jogging with her long dark hair pulled into a bouncy ponytail. Her passion, besides teaching, was long-distance running. There was a photograph in her classroom of her crossing the finish line of the New York City Marathon.

If Miss Dawson had a social life, it was led quietly. There had been a few teachers over the years whose names appeared on the newspaper list of DWI's. The school board frowned on that, and rightly so.

Theo was surprised to find the jogger in her shop. She was dressed in her teacher's garb and still managed to look like she was poised to dash out. "Mrs. Abernathy?"

"Yes." Theo smiled and walked closer. "Miss Dawson. How are you?"

"What lovely colors." The teacher turned in a slow circle. "I'm not sure I could pick my favorite."

"Thank you." Theo waited, assuming now that the teacher was looking for a donation of some merchandise as part of a fundraiser for the track team. "Can I help you?"

"I hope so." Her expression became quite intense. "You know Blossom Flowers pretty well—at least that's my understanding—and I need you to help me stop her from making a terrible mistake."

As a conversation opener, Theo thought it was mesmerizing. Miss Dawson had her full attention. "Yes, I've known Blossom for a long time. What's the problem?"

"Well, I don't feel like I know her well enough to announce, at least not to her, that I think she's making a mistake by marrying Kenny Baines. She might take it the wrong way."

Blindsided, Theo wondered how a statement like that could

be taken the right way. "You have some reason not to approve of Kenny?"

Miss Dawson sighed. "I didn't express the problem very well because I'm so upset. I'll start over." She took a deep breath and let it out. "I saw Kenny kissing another woman, just yesterday. I don't know Blossom very well, but I think she deserves better."

The idea of Kenny cheating on Blossom was ludicrous, but not theoretically impossible. Theo didn't have enough facts. "Where did you see this?"

"I happened to be visiting the parents of a student. They live in Kenny's neighborhood." She sighed again. "Please remember, I know Kenny and his girls from school. I'm not a stalker and I have no personal interest in the man."

Theo smiled. "I appreciate your clearing that up."

"Anyway, I was climbing out of my car, checking my papers and jotting a last-minute note, and about that time, Kenny pulled into his driveway. All of a sudden the woman next door to him rushed out of her house, ran over to Kenny, and planted a major kiss on the man. She wore nothing but a sheer peach nightgown."

"And did he fight her?" Theo had to admit it sounded suspicious.

"I don't know. I went into my student's home." Miss Dawson shook her head. "It could have meant nothing, but it bothered me and I'd hate to see anyone get hurt."

Theo called Nina. Her best friend taught French at the high school.

While she did not know Miss Dawson well, she did know the woman had a decent reputation. In all matters. Nina said, "I can't imagine she'd make up a story like this one, just to break up Blossom and Kenny. She doesn't have a boyfriend, at least not as far as I know, but I'd guess Kenny Baines is not someone she's interested in."

"Well, you've lived here as long as I have—actually longer, because you stayed here while we were in Chicago," Theo said. "I've never met Kenny's neighbor woman, have you?"

"Oh, yeah. Kenny I trust. The neighbor, not so much." Nina's voice held a note of anger. "I know exactly who she is. She was one of my ex-husband's playmates."

Tony dipped a spoon into the jar and scraped some of the crystallized honey into his tea. His throat was closing up. He was at home, so he didn't bother to stifle a painful groan. He glanced at Theo. "Don't you need to be at work?"

"About Kenny's next-door neighbor," Theo began. "What's she like?"

He quickly cut off her question. "You don't need to know about that woman."

"Why not?" Theo seemed surprised by Tony's reaction.

He was usually more guarded than this about his opinions, even with her. Tony began humming, pretending he couldn't hear her.

She poked him in the ribs. "Your groupie is getting ready to marry a man *that* woman is reportedly too familiar with, if you get my drift. We can't let Blossom make a terrible mistake if there's something she should know. Tell her."

Tony knew he'd lost the war without ever getting started. What words would Theo find more tantalizing than, "I really can't talk about it." He sighed. "Promise me. You can't tell anyone, especially not Nina. Even though she's been hurt."

Theo promised.

Tony knew his wife was actually very good about keeping promises and secrets. It was when she was left in the dark that she tended to get into trouble.

"We've had a few calls over the years from the neighbor about her." Tony thought he'd just give his wife the overview. Theo sure didn't need any details. "The woman has some powerful delusions or fantasies. I know she is under medical care, but sometimes it isn't enough. At times she has called to report Peeping Toms, obscene phone calls, none of which are real, and she dresses very inappropriately."

"Can't her husband buy her some flannel jammies and dispose of, or at least hide, the sheer things?" Theo was happy none of their neighbors ran loose in lingerie. If they did and she kept the kids in the house, the curtains would have to be closed all the time. The prospect of being continuously locked inside with four active children gave her chills. "And Kenny?"

"She creeps him out." Tony finally smiled. "I think he likes the husband okay, but he's very concerned about having his little girls encounter her when she's off her medications. Even if he wasn't planning to move into Blossom's house after the wedding, I suspect he would be moving soon."

Tony thought he'd better talk with Kenny about the possible problems created by his admirer. As might be expected, the unexpected bad weather had kept Kenny at home. "Not great weather for a bricklayer."

Kenny smiled, seeing Tony on his doorstep, and ushered him in. Tony had left Wade slogging through paperwork. This was not expected to be anything more than a social call.

"Coffee, Sheriff?"

Tony accepted a cup and settled at the kitchen table. Kenny's living room looked like it had been rocked by an explosion of some nature. Papers and books, and even Christmas decorations, littered the room. "Having fun?"

Kenny groaned. "I'm not enjoying sorting through all this. It's my own fault. I kept putting it off, but the wedding's only a few days away now and I'm sure as heck not moving all of this into Blossom's house. We're starting a new life, not just moving trash from the old one."

Tony had to agree that sorting through papers was not his favorite job either. "So everything's on track for the wedding?"

"Yes, of course." Kenny cocked his head to one side as if listening to words Tony had not said. "Is there something I should know?"

Tony swallowed a large mouthful of coffee. "Blossom came to see me this week. And brought a pie."

Kenny laughed. "She just can't quite give you up."

"No. It's not that." Tony hesitated a moment. "She feels she can't ask for anyone's help without somehow paying for it."

"Help? What's wrong?" Kenny did look wounded now. "She couldn't ask me?"

"She's been getting threatening notes." Tony pulled a six-by-ten-inch, sealed, plastic bag from his pocket and placed it on the table in front of Kenny. It had a serial number on it and the word in the largest print read "Evidence" and was followed by "To Be Opened by Authorized Personnel Only." The victim's name was listed as Blossom Petals Flowers. Other highlights on the bag were "Chain of Custody" and "Case Number."

While Kenny stared at the bag, Tony flipped it over. Sealed inside the bag was a typed note. It read: "Kenny is mine. For your safety, leave town." Tony watched as Kenny read it over and over.

Kenny finally looked up. Confusion creased his forehead, pulling his eyebrows into a single line. "Why? Who?"

"I—we—don't know." Tony shook his head. "It is not my job to give advice to the lovelorn but some of the threats go way beyond what I tend to think of as junior high behavior."

"What's that?" Kenny blinked.

Tony thought Kenny was having trouble absorbing all the information. "You remember, things like, if Johnny says he likes

Sally more than me, then he can't come to my birthday party."

"I forgot." Kenny's dark tan paled a bit.

"About something you heard?"

"No. I forgot that my sweet little girls will hit that phase long before I'll be ready." A faint smile lifted the corners of his lips and vanished again. Anger replaced all hint of humor. "But why would someone threaten Blossom? She's so sweet and nice to everyone."

"What about your neighbor?" Tony watched for a reaction. He wasn't denied one.

"Ridiculous." Kenny's fingers pressed so hard against the surface of the table, it made half of each fingernail blanch. "That poor family. I'll admit the woman is hard to raise children around, but she is really very nice and is extremely apologetic when her medications are balanced properly."

"Okay." Tony did believe the story was true. It matched both the husband's explanation and the woman's. "Have you noticed anyone making doe eyes at you or smiling too much or . . . or anything?" Tony wasn't sure how to phrase it. "An ardent admirer?"

Kenny's expression went from dumbfounded to almost amused to livid; all passed quickly except the anger. "She wouldn't dare."

Tony reached for his pen. "Who are you talking about?"

"Aspen." Kenny's face retained a fair amount of anger. "Aspen Flowers. She's one of Blossom's cousins."

"Which one is she?" Tony had met all of them at some time or another, but that branch of the Flowers family tree was less sociable and a whole lot less wholesome than Blossom, her mother and father, and all of her myriad sisters.

"She's the one that works at Kwik Kirk's convenience store out on the highway. You've seen her. She's too thin, and cranky all the time, maybe because she wears her ponytail too tight."

Tony thought Kenny's description was spot-on. He knew exactly which clerk he referred to. Tony thought Sourpuss would suit her for a name. "Why would you think it might be her?"

"Aspen's been popping up everywhere I go, like she's following me. If I go to the hardware store, she's looking at hammers; if I stop for gas, she's at the next pump, smiling at me." He narrowed his eyes. "Sure, it could be a coincidence, but it doesn't feel right. Too much, even in a town this size. And, she's always smiling and needing help with something a two-year-old could handle. She's come over to my house bringing me food. Really? I'm engaged to the world's best cook, and she's bringing me bad cookies—coals to Newcastle comes to mind. In this case, burnt coals." Kenny took a deep breath. "And there are phone calls, day and night."

"Caller ID?" Tony finally managed to interject a question.

Kenny nodded. "But there's no name, just a number. The same number again and again." He handed Tony a small piece of paper with a clearly written telephone number. The impression of the pen had come almost through the paper.

"Did you ever have a relationship with Aspen?" Tony hated to ask but it might explain the whole problem.

"No. I'm just an ordinary guy, not rich, not handsome, and Blossom is the woman I love." Just saying her name made Kenny's smile extend across the entire lower half of his face. "I don't even mind if she bakes *you* an occasional pie. You've been good about helping her, and I know there are some men who might have taken advantage of her sweetness."

"Anyone else show extra interest in you, or her?"

Kenny shook his head.

CHAPTER TWENTY-ONE

The sound of Quentin's baritone voice filtered from the drunk tank into the jail kitchen. Daffodil Flowers Smith, whose kitchen it was, in everything except title, sighed and said to Tony, "I'm sorry to hear that song again."

Tony sighed too. Quentin Mize had been a frequent visitor to his jail until a couple of years earlier. He'd gotten clean and sober and started working for Gus, Tony's oldest brother. Quentin's best friend, Roscoe, had done a lot for Quentin, including finding him the construction job. Quentin's last binge had been months earlier. "Last I heard, he was doing well."

Daffodil poured herself a mug of strong, black coffee and sipped it meditatively. "I heard him start singing early this morning when I came in to start breakfast."

Knowing Quentin didn't usually start singing until he was almost completely sober, Tony sighed, then thought he was starting to sound like a lovelorn teenager.

"Isn't he still working for your brother?" Daffodil said.

"As far as I know." Tony hesitated, choosing his words carefully. "But Gus is taking a break from work. He and Catherine are taking a few days of personal time." Tony expected they would surface soon. If not, he and Theo and Jane were likely to descend on the family uninvited. After years of disappointment and miscarriages, Gus and Catherine had received the gift of adoption. One baby girl.

"That's right." Daffodil laughed. "I did hear that he and the missus got themselves a seven pound and nothing dictator. Dictatress? What's a female dictator called?"

Tony didn't know either but he agreed with the rest of the summation.

While they were talking, the head jailer had joined them. The man had run the jail for at least ten years, and knew all the tricks and most of the inmates.

"No wonder Quentin's feeling lost." The jailer poured himself a cup of coffee and entered the conversation. "He's ready to leave."

Tony dialed Roscoe's cell phone.

Roscoe picked up on the first ring and the moment Tony identified himself, Roscoe cut in, "Have you heard anything about Quentin? He's not answering my calls."

"He's safe. He's locked in the drunk tank, but he's about ready to leave. What do you think, should I take him home?" Tony was glad Quentin had someone who cared.

"Oh, man." Roscoe exhaled sharply. "Well, at least he's safe."

Tony heard more than mild concern in Roscoe's voice. "What's going on?"

"I have to take part of the blame. Since me and my lady love, the missus, moved, he's got no one up there on his mountain." Roscoe cleared his throat. "That's not a good thing for someone like him."

Tony absolutely agreed. "Have you got any suggestions? If he doesn't change or we can't change something in him or in his life, I see nothing but disaster ahead."

"If he could find a lady love like I did, well, everything would be different, wouldn't it?"

Tony's math skills weren't bad, but he couldn't figure what astronomical odds there were against some dream woman waltzing into Quentin's world. "You met Veronica at a meeting for lovers of vegetable weaponry." Tony knew that wasn't technically accurate, but Roscoe didn't object. "What are Quentin's interests, besides drinking?"

"Singing." Roscoe hummed a little tune, off-key. "If we could get him on one of those reality shows, with his voice he'd knock 'em dead."

Certainly his breath could kill someone today. Tony thought those words but he said, "Not a bad idea. I'll see what I can find out about auditions. We're less than a day's drive to Nashville. If there's ever an audition over there, one of us could drive him over."

Roscoe hesitated. "It's hard to imagine that working out well until Quentin gets hisself a bit more stable. Maybe we could start with finding a place for him to practice singing in public."

"A better one than the county drunk tank, I hope."

"Yessir. And not a bar. I was thinkin' maybe a church might want him. Which one has the best choir?"

Tony enjoyed the choir at the Methodist church, but he suspected the better singers in town were not a part of it. They made up with enthusiasm what they lacked in talent. "Maybe the Baptists?"

"That'd be good. No booze. And a little religion wouldn't hurt him none." Roscoe quieted. "There could be a female going there who's pretty desperate."

The vision of Quentin courting a desperate woman was, at least on second thought, not a bad idea at all. Tony wondered if it would be better to look for a woman who had never met Quentin or one who had never given up on the idea of redeeming him. Some women, he believed, loved to think they'd gotten a broken soul and mended it. At least Quentin had a job and land. If he built a house or replaced his decrepit trailer with something more functional, and added some indoor plumbing, the place could be very nice. Quentin owned, as the last living member of his family, a large undeveloped piece of real estate.

Land rich and money poor.

Roscoe said his goodbyes and Tony continued to sit and think. Strictly speaking, his job as sheriff did not include the duty to reform anyone. Reforming Quentin would make his job easier though. Tony hurried over to Theo's shop because he couldn't wait to hear her reaction to his playing matchmaker for Quentin.

He wasn't disappointed.

"How are you planning to engineer this little romance?" Theo was incredulous. "Arrest some poor woman and put her in the next cell? Have a Sunday school field trip to the jail or a jail trip to the church?" Theo waved her hands as she paced back and forth. "Seeing a hungover Quentin in badly fitting orange jail clothes is sure to make any number of hearts go pitty-pat."

One of Tony's favorite pastimes was winding Theo up and watching her reactions. She wasn't disappointing him. Her expressions had covered the gamut from shock to amusement. He whispered, "Maybe we could hold a singles lunch at the jail. An old-fashioned box lunch with decorated cartons." Tony fought hard to sound serious and not burst out laughing. He sneezed instead. "Or maybe it would be more effective to handcuff a woman to the Blazer and drag her up the mountain."

Theo finally surrendered. Her merry laughter filled her office.

"We could hold a raffle." Tony was semi-serious now. "It would serve two purposes: win lunch with your future spouse, lunch and conversation, and add some dollars to the food bank."

"Whatever you do, don't let Quentin not talk." Theo frowned. "Put him behind a curtain. He *can* win over a girl with that voice. It's like chocolate."

"Actually," he turned serious. "I thought maybe you and your quilters could help."

Theo stared at her husband. Surely she hadn't heard him correctly. "You want me to find what?"

"A girlfriend for Quentin." Tony flashed her what she often called his pirate's grin.

She usually thought it was charming, but this was ridiculous. He'd trapped her into many things with that smile, and a sinking feeling grew in the pit of her stomach. She was doomed. "A what?" She hoped if she asked the same question enough times the answer would change.

Tony's smile remained. "I think you know just about every female in the county and many who live fairly near here."

Theo sighed, fearing she'd lost. She certainly wasn't going to argue against her wide and varied acquaintanceship with an astonishingly diverse assortment of women. Between her quilt-shop customers, the women she'd known since childhood, the members of the church, and women she'd met at various other sites, she felt like she did know most of the females in the area. "But Tony, it's not like Quentin has a lot of good selling points."

"You like him." Tony looked very pleased with his statement.

"True." Theo felt the trap close around her ankle. "I like cheese puffs too. That's not the same as finding him a girlfriend. And as for that, why your sudden interest in his love life? I know you have plenty of work to keep you occupied." She narrowed her eyes. "Shouldn't you be on your way to North Carolina? I heard you have work to do there."

"There are several of us who are concerned. He's up on that mountain now without his friends. No electricity and drinking stale water he stores in old milk jugs." Ignoring her comment, Tony hesitated. The smile disappeared and left his face completely serious. "Roscoe and the professor are very concerned about Quentin being alone. Roscoe says they invited him to move onto their property but Quentin refused. He says he is not leaving the family land."

Theo mumbled a token last protest, "Still, Quentin's not going to be an easy sell."

"I didn't say it would be easy." Tony draped a laughing baby over one shoulder and nibbled on the back of her knee. "Talk to the quilters; one of them might have a desperate old maid in the family."

Intrigued by Tony's request, Theo followed him down the stairs from office to workroom carrying the second twin. As he handed the baby back, he whispered, "Now's as good a time as any to start your new project."

When he left, Theo carried the girls into the workroom and handed them over to a couple of older ladies who stretched their arms out the fastest. Maybelle wasn't expected for another fifteen minutes. Nothing ventured, nothing gained, she thought, and said, "Does anyone know of a suitable woman for Quentin to date?"

Silence fell as the meaning of her words sank in. Several women looked like they were chewing on their lips to keep from laughing.

"I might." Two words softly spoken in the far corner of the room attracted the full attention of every woman in the room. "My second cousin's daughter, Amy."

Theo felt like an iron filing being drawn by a magnet. She was powerless to resist. Seconds later, she stood next to the speaker, Eileene Bass. "Tell me."

"Well, Amy's a nice woman, a bit, um . . ." Eileene hesitated. "Bossy."

"Bossy?" Theo repeated like a robot. "I'm bossy too. What else?"

"She was married right out of high school, but it didn't last. I'd bet you've seen her around. She works at the post office."

The final two words hit a nerve. Theo jumped. "The tall

woman with the serious expression?"

"That's her," Eileene said, "Her ex totally destroyed her self-confidence as far as dating. Among other things, he told her she was stupid and bossy and no fun."

Theo wondered what made people say such cruel things. Even if they were true, wasn't there a kinder, more helpful way to encourage small changes. "Is she?"

"No." Eileene laughed, a rarity for the normally sour woman. "When you get to know her and she relaxes a bit, she's sweet and very funny."

"Who's her ex?" Susan, one of Theo's favorites of the younger quilters, had moved closer, listening to the conversation. "He sounds like a real piece of work."

"His name is Ralph and you're right, he is not very nice at all. He spends more time drinking at The Spa than anything else. That's probably why you don't know him." Eileene shook her head slightly. "Ralph peaked in high school, wasn't bad looking, and his prospects weren't bad. A small college was seriously scouting him for their basketball team."

"But?"

"Ralph didn't want them. He thought one of the basketball powerhouse universities was sure to come begging for him." Eileene's lips twisted in disdain. "None of them came close to wanting him, so he never left town, never furthered his education, and kind of puts the 'L' in loser."

The Spa was an ill-fitting nickname for a local bar. Theo knew its original name had been The Spot but now no one bothered pronouncing the last T. Its clientele consisted of generally unpleasant, unsavory, and usually unemployed citizens.

"And your cousin?" Theo said. "When did she realize he wasn't a winner?"

"Oh, it took a little while. She loved him in high school, believed his story, married him, and went to work so he wouldn't have to balance a job along with his studies and practice sessions. When he didn't go to college, he didn't go to work either. It turned out he liked being supported financially by his wife, but she wised up pretty fast. Turns out he *was* practicing *something* while she was working, but it wasn't basketball." The woman looked like she wouldn't bother to call 911 if the man was having a heart attack. "They were divorced within six months of the wedding."

"I don't know what to do." Ruby sat in Tony's office. Her hands folded and refolded a tissue as Ruby's gorgeous brown eyes filled with tears. "Mike thought you might have a suggestion."

Tony had heard Theo comment from time to time about the unfair advantage held by women with brown eyes. A single tear in big brown eyes broke both hearts and rules. Ruby's tears were genuine, a mixture he suspected of fatigue and concern, and he felt their impact, encouraging him to volunteer to help.

"What's the problem?" He handed her a box of tissues and tried to visualize Theo's green/gold hazel eyes. They were beautiful, amazingly so, and intelligent and full of fight and wit and he loved them. But, well, they weren't brown and didn't scream *protect me.*

Before Ruby had a chance to say anything, her husband, Deputy Mike Ott, came into the office carrying their tiny, precious, brown-eyed daughter. The baby was sleeping on her back, draped across her father's arm, one of her tiny arms dangling, limp as a rag doll. Dammit the bloodhound slouched in and collapsed close enough to Ruby for her to be able to pet him without changing position. The dog looked exhausted, and his drooping eyes and skin seemed to be hanging lower than usual.

Mike looked into his wife's face and said, "Did you tell him?"

Ruby shook her head. "I was trying to decide what to tell

him and how to tell him."

"Tell me what?" The mysterious conversation erased all thoughts of eye color from Tony's mind. He hoped this wasn't Mike's notice of intent to leave the department. He mentally shook the idea away. Paranoia was not a good trait.

Balancing the baby, Mike reached for Ruby's hand with his free one. "Just give him the highlights for now."

Ruby sighed and looked directly into Tony's eyes. "You won't be surprised to learn that I run a casual and unregulated shelter for broken families."

Tony did know about it. He also suspected she was involved in transporting fleeing spouses across state lines and into safer areas, sort of a modern underground railroad. "Do I want to know more?"

Ruby ignored his question. "There was a woman who showed up with two children the other day."

Mike interrupted, "We have no idea how she found us. That's the scary part."

Ruby's dark eyes flashed with anger or irritation, and Tony wasn't sure if the nameless woman or Mike's interruption was the cause.

"As I was saying, she just showed up on our shelter doorstep, claiming to have been battered by her husband. Prudence Holt was on duty at the time. When Prudence asked her about any injuries, she said she didn't have any." Ruby sighed. "We'll call this woman Alice."

Tony started to see Ruby's problem. "We all know there are other forms of abuse."

Ruby nodded. "Alice had two children with her, a three-year-old and a six-year-old." Ruby stopped massaging the dog's ear and stared into the distance. "The kids were nice enough, seemed kind of bored, but they did not seem traumatized or bruised either."

"How long ago was this?" Tony thought he could check for a missing woman with children. Maybe the report would shed some light on the problem. He wasn't at all surprised that Deputy Darren Holt's wife, Prudence, was also part of this group. Not only did Prudence hold strong feelings about how women should be treated, she was the undisputed arm wrestling champion in the area. He wouldn't fight Prudence on a dare.

"Alice arrived on Tuesday. On Wednesday I had to confront her about the rules." Ruby checked her pocket calendar. "She said she didn't have to follow my stupid rules or come to the support meetings. She claimed her attitude was because she knew we would be sending her on down the line."

"Pretty rebellious for one of your rescues." Tony could feel Ruby's discomfort.

"No kidding." Ruby finally smiled. "I like it when they start to show a little spunk and a little less, 'I deserve to be beaten 'cause he wouldn't have hit me if I did everything right.'"

"So, you're suspicious about why she sought you out, how she found you, and now maybe where she went?"

"That, and because we're taking care of another, truly pitiful woman whose life since she ran away from her home, at least until now, has been foraging for food and clothes in other people's garbage." Ruby bit her lower lip. "This morning, this other woman came to me with thousands of dollars in cash. Said she found it spilling out of one of Alice's bags. Said there was more money in the bag than in a bank. I made sure she put it all back."

Tony sat back, stunned. A runaway with lots of cash could either be in a world of trouble or be the cause of it. "Does this Alice know what your husband does for a living?"

"No." Ruby seemed to relax a bit. "No one knows who we really are or where we live or what we do in life. I was afraid for the other woman if Alice finds any of her money is missing and turns on her."

"But you are doubly suspicious of this Alice woman because she can afford hotels, transportation, protection, and she's been staying in our little backwater for no apparent reason."

"Unless she stole it from someone truly evil." Ruby shivered. "Rich people are as often guilty as the poor or middle class. Abuse is a crime that crosses all segments of society."

The baby started fussing in Mike's arms, and he handed her to Ruby. His eyes met Tony's. "I've tried to find out something, anything, about this woman without giving her location away to the bad guy or involving your office in any way."

"And?" Tony knew he wasn't going to like the answer.

"And there's nothing." Mike shook his head. "No one claims to be missing a wife and two children. No one seems to be missing a boatload of cash. And the little information we ask the women for when they come to us, all of hers seems fictitious. Lots, if not most, of our victims tell lies about their names and locations, but the painful truth is still evident."

"So she's lying. But why?" Tony leaned forward. "Is she hiding from her abusive husband whose money and children she's running with or . . ."

"Maybe those aren't her kids and she borrowed them, and somewhere their parents are either counting their rental money or she took them and they're hoping if they cooperate, she'll return them." Mike shook his head. "Whichever, I think she is hiding with us for a different reason."

"No matter how you look at it, we need to move her and the other woman." Tony looked at Mike. "We are now officially involved in this. Put out her description and all the warnings about who else might be hunting for her. If that money is stolen, the owner, husband or not, will most likely be looking for it."

"Now then, Ruby, you're smarter than about anyone I know and you have had some experience with bad husbands." He tipped his head toward Mike. "I gather this one is an exception."

Ruby laughed, a real laugh filled with joy. "He is a keeper."

"So, what is your gut telling you?" Tony thought the change in her expression from joy to despair told the whole story. "You wanted to help, and she's involved you and your rescue system in a very public, potentially disastrous situation."

There was no trace of the happy woman from seconds earlier. "We have to move everyone away, as quickly as possible and without using any of our normal routes." Ruby's dark eyes filled with tears. "If I thought it possible, I'd say this woman, Alice, was paid to find us, paid to expose our fragile souls to someone who hasn't stopped hunting."

Tony felt her words like blows to his gut. Ruby was right. He could feel it too: someone had breached her security and was planning to close in and destroy them. Soon. "Pack the women and children up and get them all out of their current locations."

"And take them where?" Ruby wasn't arguing; she was hoping for help.

"How many do you have?"

"We have Alice and her two children plus one other woman who has one child and a small dog." Ruby stared at her trembling fingers as if surprised there weren't more to protect. "So only two families."

For a moment Tony considered locking the whole bunch in the jail for safekeeping. Not a good plan. And then he had an idea. They could send them to the most isolated, most unlikely place to stash women and children until they could be safely moved. "Hold on." He dialed his brother Gus's cell phone. When Gus answered Tony skipped the small talk. "Is Roscoe with you? I need to talk to him."

Seconds later, the distinctive nasal voice spoke. "Sheriff?"

"Roscoe, can you and the professor hide a few people for

me?" He cleared his throat. "I wouldn't ask, but it's a bit of an emergency."

"Sure. I'll call my lady love and tell her you're a-coming."

"Thanks Roscoe, I owe you one." Tony disconnected. "Ruby, you get those women packed up and tell them I'm coming. Then I want you to take your baby girl to your café and stay there, in plain sight."

Ruby didn't hesitate. She was gone before Tony said more than, "And Mike. I'll go get them and let you explain the details to Theo."

Luckily there were only the two women and three children. Tony called his wife's cell phone. "Theo, honey, I need your car, and then I'll need you to drive it somewhere." He must have sounded as urgent as he felt. For a change, his wife didn't ask any questions, but just agreed. "I'll come by and pick it up. In the meantime, please don't report it stolen."

Five minutes later, half of which he used to get the seat moved far enough away from the steering wheel for him to fit inside so he could actually drive the yellow SUV, he was following Ruby's instructions to the safe house. Hidden in plain sight, for sure. The little house was in the middle of town. Prudence Sligar Holt waved him around to the back door. In less than ten minutes they'd loaded all the residents and their few belongings, including a small mongrel dog, into Theo's SUV. "Stay down." And Tony headed back to the quilt shop.

By the time he returned, Mike had filled in Theo, telling her of Tony's master plan.

Tony parked behind the shop and at an angle so no one could see inside the driver's door when it was open. He didn't think anyone was watching but didn't want to risk someone spotting his passengers.

In seconds he had gotten out and Theo climbed behind the wheel and moved the seat forward so she could reach the pedals again. She lowered the window. "Don't forget to pick up the boys after school," she said. "The girls are fine staying here with Maybelle."

Tony almost laughed at her micro-managing in this situation. He whispered in her ear, "Love you." She kissed him.

CHAPTER TWENTY-TWO

As she had been instructed to do, Theo drove around town. She'd been given a list of seemingly normal things to do, errands, just in case she was being followed. She headed sedately for the edge of town. On the way, she stopped for gas. Went to the ATM. Ran into Food City and picked up a few items. All the while her heart was pounding. She must have checked her watch over fifty times in twenty minutes.

Trying to seem as relaxed as possible, she climbed back into her unmistakably bright yellow SUV and whispered to her passengers, "I'm sorry I had to leave the windows rolled up. I'll get you some fresh air now."

"Bless you for doing this." A frightened female voice in the far back whispered, "I'm Alice."

It was enough to give Theo the courage she needed. "I'm sorry y'all have to be so crammed in."

"We're fine." The voice came from a woman folded onto the floor instead of sitting on the front seat. "This is just fine. You can call me Darla."

Theo smiled. If Darla, crouching and badly cramped, was able to smile and lie about her comfort, and her name, Theo could drive. She held to her normal speed and headed out to the small farm on the border of the county and federal land. She thought that Roscoe, the professor, and Baby the bear might as well have moved to the moon. As she came around the final bend in the road and could see the house, she slowed down. In the pasture, surrounded by a split-rail fence, she could see the crane-like features of one of the intriguing couple's trebuchets. This new version of an old siege weapon sat in a former cornfield.

As they had gotten farther from town and seen no other vehicles, her passengers had gradually risen from the floor to buckle themselves into the seats. All of them were sure no one would see them out here.

"What is that thing?" A child's voice.

Theo was relieved to hear, finally, a normal-sounding question from a curious child. Theo explained the medieval weapons as she drove past. "It's really fun to watch it kind of back up and fling things—like it's throwing a ball overhand."

"What do they fling?" The child hesitated on the last word.

"Oh, fun stuff now. Back in medieval times it would have been rocks, but now my friends send pumpkins and overgrown zucchini flying through the air." Theo was delighted by the smile she glimpsed in the rearview mirror. "When they hit the ground, they splatter vegetable bits over everything nearby."

"There's no quilt." Darla spoke, her eyes glued to the house and yard. She looked ready to jump from the car and run.

"No." Theo reached over and patted the woman's leg. "These are trusted friends, but they are not part of the regular transportation."

"Why are we here?"

"Someone has broken our trust." Theo felt a knot form in her throat. "We'll see you safely away, but we have to handle the transportation differently."

"Is that necessary?" The woman in the far back frowned. "We've come this far. Shouldn't we stick to the original plan? I want you to turn and take us back."

Theo felt a tingle at the base of her neck. No one ever complained or offered resistance. These people were desperate.

Not even the shelter or facilities where they came from originally had been able to protect them. She glanced over at the woman who had been on the floor next to her. Wide-eyed, Darla looked back at Theo, but her breathing was suddenly very shallow.

Slowing to make the turn into the drive, Theo flashed her headlights instead of using the turn signal. Relieved, she watched Roscoe trot toward her, his arms waving to make her stop. Her errands had taken long enough to allow him to get here before she did and he'd had plenty of time to talk to Tony.

"What happened?" Alice, the woman in the far back, sounded angry more than frightened.

"I don't know." Theo stopped her car and lowered her window and stuck her head out. "Let's see what he says."

Roscoe whispered an almost soundless question in Theo's ear. "Which one?"

Theo's answer was almost inaudible, but Roscoe heard every word. He trotted around to the far side of the SUV. "Ma'am, you and your young'un and the pup are to come with me." Roscoe reached for the front passenger door handle. "I'll take you to your next stop."

Looking back at Theo for reassurance, who forced a smile and nodded, the woman known as Darla picked up her well-worn purse and climbed out. Her daughter and the mongrel joined her and then Roscoe shut the door, came back around to the driver's door, and whispered to Theo, "You're to take these other ones back to the house where they'll get different transportation. Your husband says it's too dangerous to have all the eggs in one basket or something like that."

Theo did manage a laugh. "Okay, that sounds like him."

Roscoe patted the SUV like it was a dog. "Only now you've got the bad egg." The sound of his hand striking the car covered his words, not the look of worry on his face. He clearly didn't like the situation. "Come back for this group."

Theo waved goodbye to Darla's entourage. "Safe travels." She backed down the narrow drive until she reached the road, then headed back to town. Watching the remaining passengers as she pretended to check the road behind them was easy. Knowing the doors in the back could only be opened from the outside, a setting Tony had enabled on the car to keep one of the children from doing something potentially tragic, insured they would not try to jump out.

"Sheriff?" Rex glanced up from his bank of electronics and looked at Tony, who was standing near the front desk, pretending to check the jail visitation paperwork. "What is your wife doing?"

"I imagine she's either working or just running a few errands." Tony trusted Rex with his life and that of his family and every member of his department. Still, he refused to voice his concern about her involvement in the domestic rescue group. "Why?"

"Just hearing some chatter. It sounds like your deputies are trying to keep an eye on her and stay away from her at the same time." Rex shook his head accepting the explanation. "She's so little and seems so sweet."

Tony heard the silent, "but." He grinned. He could guess what Rex might have encountered. Instead of answering, he nodded his agreement. No doubt about it. Theo could be a bit feisty.

Rex went on with his thought. "But when she gets mad—I saw it once—it was like someone had dropped dynamite down a well."

"That's my girl. Take no prisoners." Tony glanced at his watch for the hundredth time since Theo had driven off with people he pretended to know nothing about.

The front door of the law enforcement center swung open

and a man Tony had never seen before strode inside, followed by an obviously angry Sheila. He was swearing the whole way. He was built like a rutabaga. Huge shoulders, heavily muscled arms, and a thick neck tapered to a powerful chest and much narrower waist and continued down to short legs and small feet, maybe size eight. They looked half the size of Tony's own. Being dressed in a purple shirt and cream-colored slacks only added to the root vegetable appearance.

Tony might have smiled and greeted the stranger but the vitriol spewing from the man's mouth as he walked away from Deputy Sheila Teffeteller sent a wave of adrenalin through him. This man was bad. Because of the possibly dangerous situation Theo was in, Tony's internal gauge was already on high alert, and this man was pushing the needle higher.

"You heard me. I'm not talking to some know-nothing, dumb-broad deputy. I'm going straight to the top." He ignored Rex but stared at Tony's badge. "You the sheriff of this wasteland or just another Barney?"

"I am the sheriff of this beautiful county. You're welcome to go somewhere else." Tony stood as tall as he could, which was a good foot, maybe more, taller than the rutabaga. "Front door's right behind you. Sooner's better than later."

The rutabaga bared his teeth. They were white and straight but totally fake.

Tony wasn't sure if his expression was supposed to be a smile or a growl. From his own viewpoint, it was simply unpleasant. He waited.

"We've got business." The huge arm muscles under the purple sleeve flexed as the man dug into the small attaché case he carried in one hand and pulled out some papers and a couple of photographs.

"What kind of business?" Tony was curious.

"You'll see." The rutabaga shuffled through the papers and

handed one to Tony. "I'm here for Evelyn and the child she stole, a minor child." He held up the photographs. "These ring any bells?"

Tony studied the pictures but didn't touch them or take the papers. He knew the woman in them as Darla. He didn't have to lie. "I've never heard either of those names."

"Oh, come now, Sheriff, we both know what's going on here."

Tony was serious. He had no knowledge of the woman or the child other than their appearance. "Why don't you come with me to my office? Maybe we can get to the bottom of this."

"Sounds good." The rutabaga strutted through the doorway.

"You'll have to leave your gun here." Tony unlocked a steel cabinet just inside the normally locked door. "House rules. Mine."

For a moment, it looked like the man was going to refuse, but he didn't. He pulled up his pant leg and exposed an ankle holster. He gently placed the semi-automatic in the cabinet. "I'll want that back."

Tony said nothing, just locked the box and turned and led the way to his office.

The rutabaga trotted after Tony. Tony imagined the two of them looked like a bulldog chasing a coonhound.

"Ruth Ann, I'd like for you to come in and take notes." Tony strode past her desk. Something in his expression, or that of his companion, turned her from her normal, intelligent, I-can-do-it-better-than-you self, into a weak, sniveling air brain. It was what Tony was hoping for.

Tony settled into the chair behind his desk and his guest sat facing him. Ruth Ann perched on the other visitor's chair and toyed with her earring. Tony found himself wishing she had chewing gum in her mouth. It would complete the vapid expression.

"So, now, sir." Tony rested his hands on his desk. "Why are you here?"

"I told you. I'm here to collect these two." He waved his paper.

"Yes, that's what you said. I gather you're a private detective, but I don't know you, and I don't know either of them." Tony forced his hands to stay still. "Where are you from?"

"Kansas City." The rutabaga looked a bit surprised he'd answered.

"And these two are presumably missing persons?" Tony leaned forward, his curiosity unfeigned. Tony really wanted to know how this man had come to be here.

"Yes."

"Why would you expect me, out here in the Tennessee sticks, to know anything about these city people? They are obviously not from around here. And, what are we? Maybe seven or eight hundred miles from Kansas City?" Tony was seriously curious about the answer. How had a detective, private or otherwise, picked tiny Park County, Tennessee, to search for a missing mother and child? The only answer, of course, was a breach of the system.

"I'm not at liberty to give you that information." The rutabaga studied his fingernails. "Have you seen them?"

Tony answered honestly. "I don't have who you're looking for. And if these photographs are accurate, I don't have their location either." Which, since Theo had not called to report her location and neither had Roscoe, was true. For all he knew, the entire carload of people could all be sprawled on the couch in his own house, watching his television.

"Well, I can tell you this." The expression on their visitor's face turned confiding, like he was doing something special, just for Tony and Ruth Ann, just because they'd been so nice to him. "She has some kind of shirttail relative in your county."

"No kidding!" Tony leaned back in his chair as if he was settling in for a long conversation but his surprise was real. "Who's that?"

The rutabaga glanced at his papers. "A Pinkie Millsaps."

"No kidding!" Tony repeated, as he found himself seriously short in vocabulary. He forced some enthusiasm into his voice, but his brain was busy connecting the dots. Pinkie was a strong advocate for women and men being equal. After the way her sister had been treated, she despised domestic violence. He could imagine Pinkie telling a stranger how to find her if help was needed—a shirttail relative would get the red carpet treatment. How many others knew her name and her connection with the rescuers? "I know Pinkie; she works a local café."

Ruth Ann piped up. "I know Pinkie too."

The rutabaga glanced over at Ruth Ann. "Shut up."

Tony considered climbing under his desk to avoid being hit by the ceiling falling when his assistant exploded. Thankfully, Ruth Ann continued to play her role of an air brain with talent and enthusiasm. The rutabaga had no idea what he was messing with, but Tony guessed Pinkie would be treated to a full description of both the rutabaga and Ruth Ann's assessment of him. The volunteers would be on high alert, and still nothing official would come from his office. The thought made him smile. "Say, if you're going over to the café, would you like some company? The food is good."

"I suppose." The rutabaga didn't look very pleased.

"The pies are a specialty. I recommend the apple." Smiling, and continuing his self-imposed role as the lovable but less than bright sheriff, Tony led the way, stopping to retrieve the rutabaga's firearm. He'd bet Ruth Ann was already talking to Pinkie before they got out of the building.

"Pinkie's almost always down at Ruby's Café at this time of the morning." Tony kept his dumb-hick expression in place.

"She's the breakfast and lunch cook."

Clearly struggling to maintain his role as the polite visitor, the rutabaga man feigned a salute. "It's nice you want to come along."

"Sure, why not?" Tony did *not* want to go anywhere with this man. He also didn't want him harassing Pinkie. The middle-aged grandmother was one of his favorite citizens, and if he had to guess, she was quite likely to be involved in the disappearance of a runaway wife. Not only was Pinkie all about respect and equality, but her sister Sally had suffered at the hands of her own husband, Possum, for years. Now Possum was dead and no one was sorry. Both ways he looked at an encounter between Pinkie and the rutabaga meant someone was going to need protection. Reinforcements sounded like a good plan.

He led the way in the Blazer and called for Wade to meet him at the café. The rutabaga followed in his late model sedan. Tony would bet the back doors of the car could only be opened from the outside. In that, it would resemble Theo's SUV, but hers was to protect children; the rutabaga's would be a prison.

Ruby's Café hadn't changed its name, location, or basic menu for half a century. Each successive owner had become Ruby, including one man. The current Ruby had her name legally changed and then married one of his deputies. It was a popular place to eat for locals and tourists alike. The interior was always clean and freshly painted white with an old-fashioned counter with cherry-red vinyl-covered stools, red booths lining two sides, and a few tables with chairs in the center.

Blossom Flowers, preparing for her wedding, spotted him and Wade, and bustled through a swinging door, presumably to greet them. The arrival of the rutabaga-shaped man caused her to turn in midstep and return to the kitchen.

A glance at Wade's face confirmed his own impression. The pastry cook and the private detective had already met.

When the slab of Tony's favorite apple pie was delivered to him, a small note accompanied it, dropped onto his lap as the pie hit the paper placemat. It would have been amusing cloak and dagger stuff in the movies, but in real life, it sent a serious warning. "He's a bad man and a liar."

Tony hoped to keep the conversation on the quality of pie. "This is some of the best pastry in the state."

"Where's this Pinkie?" The rutabaga waved his fork in the air while talking through an oversized bite of fresh pumpkin pie.

Watching the open-mouthed mastication made Tony lose his appetite. Almost. He still finished his favorite pie but was careful to keep his eyes on his plate.

As if waiting for the men to finish eating first, Pinkie came to the table. In her fifties, Pinkie was a free spirit. She rode a motorcycle and had tattoos. She had recently taken to dyeing her graying hair pink. Surprising no one, it wasn't pinkish gray; it was wild magenta. "Sheriff?"

Tony introduced her to the rutabaga. "He says he's got a few questions for you."

Pinkie tilted her head to one side as if listening to a second conversation. "Not your questions, Sheriff?"

Tony shook his head slightly. "Wade and I will wait for you outside." His words were meant for the rutabaga, but he was staring into Pinkie's eyes. He hoped she understood what he was saying. She was welcome to tell any lie she liked. He would not be there as a witness.

She winked. Message received.

Tony and Wade waited in the sunshine. There was no conversation, just the moment of peace. The snow on the café roof was melting. A couple of droplets joined forces and fell into the small puddle below the overhang. The sky was becoming a brilliant clear blue, not the most common color here in the Smoky Mountains. Maybe it would turn into a perfect autumn day.

Only a few minutes later, the rutabaga joined them.

"Did you learn what you needed?" Tony tried for slightly obtuse. Maybe he'd use the phrase "slightly obtuse" in the book he was writing. He thought it sounded colorful and yet descriptive.

The rutabaga snarled. "Nothing but a bunch of dumb hicks in this town. I'll bet you boys are married to your sisters."

Tony didn't respond.

Tony had always promised himself that he wouldn't ask anything of Theo or Ruby or any other suspected part of the sisterhood moving abused women and children through the county. What he didn't know, he couldn't report. But now problems were circling close to his home and to the residents of the county where he was sworn to protect and serve. Somewhere along the line, the wrong person had been given information, and that was bringing big trouble into the county.

When Theo returned to town with Darla, her daughter, and the dog, Tony and Mike Ott met her in the parking lot of the grocery store and moved them into Mike's personal car. As they drove away, Theo's beautiful hazel eyes, magnified by the lenses of her glasses, swam with tears.

Tony stood by his Blazer, watching. "Theo, honey." The words sounded okay in his head. "I have to ask you some questions about the sisterhood or whatever you call it."

Theo frowned. "Please don't."

"I'm not going to ask you for names or even how long this has been going on or exactly how it works." Tony fell silent, wondering, but not asking how it began. "This is not part of the county's official shelter and protection system."

"No." Theo's eyes did not meet his. She stared into the distance. "These poor souls are only passing through. They are delivered to us from another shelter. Hiding. Waiting to go on."

"Theo, honey," he began again. "Someone very, very dangerous is looking for one of your transitory people, probably that
woman who just left with Mike."

Her eyes did meet his then. "How'd he find us?"

"I'm guessing he sent an agent pretending to be a victim to
search for her. Them."

"Oh, no. So, the woman with the two children *does* work for
him?" Theo sagged against her car, looking both aged and child-
like. "We've always been so careful."

"How long is always?" Tony seemed to remember something
happening not long after they had moved to Silersville. He had
still been a boy but he'd heard whispers in the kitchen. Doors
opening and closing. His mother calling, "I'll be back in just a
bit."

"I don't know. Forever." Theo wiped a stream of tears from
her face with the heels of her hands. "My mammaw was
involved, and eventually I was enlisted."

"Go on." He moved to her side and wrapped an arm around
her waist, holding her closer to him. "I gather it's like an
underground railroad."

"Exactly." Theo shivered. "They come here terrified and yet
forced to trust in the kindness of strangers. They stay until
someone picks them up." Theo's hands turned palms up. "No
one talks about it, and I have no idea how the message is sent,
or to whom. My job is to take them food and clothes and check
the quilt hanging near the house."

"Tell me about the quilts." It was so common for there to be
quilts hanging on or near the houses in the area, they could be
an obvious symbol to someone, once you knew the way it
worked.

"Different patterns mean different things," Theo said. "Like
'room here' or 'full' or 'not safe.' "

"The underground railroad."

"Precisely." Theo's head bobbed. "But different. These messages are for the couriers, not the victims. We feed them until someone else comes and takes them on."

"So how do you know where to take the food?" Tony was not about to address having a pitiful cook like herself in charge of feeding the runaways, or at least supplying some of the food. Maybe that was to make sure no outsider guessed her role.

"The quilt is changed." Theo smiled as if reading his thoughts. "All I have to do is drive past and look at the quilt. If it's the old one, I just keep going. If it's changed, I check in. The runaways aren't just dumped off, you know."

He whispered in her ear, "No, remember? I don't know."

Theo's head moved up and down, acknowledging his problem. Her curls brushed against his chin and he found himself enjoying the smell of Theo's shampoo. Finally she said, "It's a little harder these days because fewer new homes have clotheslines. Those new homes have to have a banner, you know, like a flag."

"What about the neighbors?" Tony wondered how deep this group went. If Theo's grandmother had been part of it, it certainly wasn't a new invention.

"There are a couple of houses, not next door to each other, but near other members of the club, so to speak. Places where the changing quilts would be easy to see."

Anger started growing deep within him. Some really bad guy was threatening the safe passage of future desperate families, and now possibly his own people. He couldn't even imagine the possible danger to his wife and mother. "Do you ever have men coming through?"

"Oh, yes, but they are the minority." Theo managed a slight smile. "We do not discriminate. Not on any basis."

"Did Harvey Winston know about your system?" Tony didn't

want to ask the former sheriff, because he couldn't do it without giving out more information than desired.

"I'm not sure." Theo fiddled with her curls and kept her eyes averted.

Tony thought his wife looked about five, a sulky five. He knew she didn't want to talk about details. To be honest, he didn't want to know. He preferred to think she wasn't involved. Actually, he preferred to hope there would be a day when the legal system worked perfectly and no one needed to run. People running, he understood, needed help. People hiding, waiting, watching—fearful. The very idea made his heartburn erupt in flames. He was not a naïve boy. These angry partners were a danger not only to the escaping victim, but also to everyone else who tried to help. Not for the first time, he considered the best punishment for abusers would be to turn the table on them.

Tony opened his mouth, thinking he might convince her to quit the group. Her endeavor was worthwhile, but the potential for danger definitely existed. Tiny little Theo's lips curved into a sweet smile. She looked about as old as she had the first time he saw her, standing behind the screen door on the house they now shared. She had been forbidden to go outside. According to her grandmother, the world wasn't safe. Tony pressed his lips together. Theo wasn't seven any more.

Theo laughed at his expression. "So now you know."

"Know what?" Feigning ignorance, Tony poked at one of her curls, avoiding looking into her eyes.

"How I feel when you get a call and leave." Theo rested her palm against his cheek. "No one is being stupid, but . . . would you have us abandon them?"

"No." Tony considered the uncertainty of safety. In a world where a sinkhole could swallow a house or a tornado could flatten a town, there were no guarantees or safeguards. He sighed. "Just . . ."

Theo finished for him. "Just be careful?"

He nodded, and gave her shoulders a squeeze. "And if I ever yell 'duck,' please don't look up for a bird in the sky."

"You be careful, too," Theo said. "Everything is fine."

CHAPTER TWENTY-THREE

The Knoxville police sergeant, Paul Martin, in charge of working the stolen quilt case, called Tony early in the morning. Saturday in law enforcement was like any other work day. "I think we've found your quilt thieves. The camera system shows a couple leaving the pawn shop with empty hands."

"Awesome." Tony couldn't resist saying the word. His head was filled with mucus, but it wouldn't stop him from working. "If we can clear up the theft of that quilt, my wife will be your biggest fan."

Martin laughed. "Does she bake cookies?"

"None you'd want to eat." Tony didn't see any point in telling a lie. "But I do know someone who bakes like a dream. I'll bring you a couple of dozen of the best chocolate chip cookies you've ever eaten the next time I'm in the city. Not today, but soon. I'll get the warrants signed and drive on up."

He needed to be sure to get back in time to attend Blossom's wedding.

"Deal," said Sergeant Martin. "Grab a pencil, and I'll give you names and an address. Let me know when you're around here, and I'll meet you. The pawnbroker has promised to testify. He said this makes his business look bad."

Armed with the warrant, Tony and Wade drove to Knoxville and parked around the corner from the house. The couple's address had not been hard to find. It was just an ordinary home, just off Kingston Pike. Sergeant Martin pulled up behind them, and the three men headed for the front door. Wade peeled off and went to watch the back door, just in case someone decided to slip away.

Tony and Martin's knock brought a messy but clean woman to the door. "Mrs. Harry French?"

"Yes." The woman glanced over her shoulder in the direction of the blaring television.

"We have a warrant." Tony saw surrender on her face the moment he said the words. "Is your husband here?"

"Yes."

"May we come in and talk with him?" Sergeant Martin politely requested.

"Yes." Swallowing hard, Mrs. French stepped back, allowing them inside. She tipped her head in the direction of the sound. "He's napping in there."

"Please put your hands behind your back," said Tony.

A sob was her only protest.

Tony leaned down and handcuffed Mrs. French's hands behind her. "You're under arrest for grand theft."

They continued into the living room. Sure enough, sleeping soundly in his chair was the man Theo had described.

"Mr. Harry French." Tony spoke loudly right next to the man's ear. "You are under arrest for conspiracy to commit a felony."

The man sat bolt upright, causing the recliner to close up with a loud thud. "What the . . . ?" He fell silent as he looked at the two men in uniform. His eyes never moved above their badges. "What's going on here?"

"Will you stand up please?" Sergeant Martin gave the man a moment to comply. Seconds later, he too was neatly cuffed. "Just for fun I'll read both of you your rights, although we don't have to, because we're not planning to ask you any questions."

"I know why you're here. It's all my fault." Mrs. French

started crying. "We were passing through Silersville and stopped in the quilt shop. I thought we might find a gift for Harry's aunt. She quilts. Then everyone was looking at that quilt. I never felt so helpless. I needed that quilt so bad. And I told Harry I thought I might die without it. I just moved closer and closer until I could almost touch it."

"My dear," Harry managed to interrupt.

"No, it was all my fault." Unable to get a tissue, Mrs. French wiped her dripping nose on her shoulder. "Harry pretended to pass out and I picked the quilt up and slipped out the back door."

Tony could see that happening. "Why pawn it?"

"After we got it home, it didn't look right in the house. Harry said it was too dull and he'd rather it was blue." She looked up into Tony's eyes. "We needed money. I really thought we'd get more for it."

"As you should have. Its value is in the thousands; therefore, you committed grand theft." Tony thought maybe she didn't understand the seriousness of the crime. "It's a felony."

"Thousands?" Harry couldn't have looked more surprised if the quilt was said to possess the ability to fly. "It's an old blanket!"

"Don't let my wife hear you say that." Tony felt no sympathy for the couple. Just because they didn't know the appraised value of the quilt did not mean they could just walk away with it.

Sergeant Martin helped Wade and Tony get the couple into Wade's car, then grinned. "They don't look too comfortable back there."

"They'll be fine. It's less than an hour drive." Tony shook hands with Martin. "As soon as we know if they'll confess or insist on a trial, we'll need the quilt returned."

"It's my understanding that the quilt is receiving preferential treatment in our evidence lockup." Martin grinned. "By all accounts, your wife's note explaining how to handle it, store it, and protect it was *very* detailed."

Tony laughed. "I'm sure it was."

Tony watched Sheila running across the park. Her blond ponytail wasn't bouncing like it might if she were jogging; instead, she was sprinting and it streamed behind her like a golden banner in the late afternoon light. Only a few remnants of the most recent snow remained. Running along beside her, Not Bob looked like he was keeping up with her pretty well. Not Bob actually had a perfectly decent name, Will Jackson, but the nickname he'd gotten when Sheila rescued him from an attacker, was the one that stuck. The man's greater muscle mass gave the impression of slower movement, but his longer legs covered more ground with each step than hers.

Tony was glad to see her improved social life. He wanted all of his deputies happy with their lives. Stability was hard won sometimes, especially with the demands of law enforcement. It was not exactly a nine to five desk job.

"Do you think he can catch her?" Theo's soft voice startled him. She had made no sound walking barefoot to stand next to him. "She's pretty quick."

"Yes, I think he can. And I think he might even be able to run as fast as she does."

"He's nice." With a laugh acknowledging his play on words, Theo squeezed closer to him, trying to get a better view. "Does he get along with Mama Teffeteller?"

"I haven't asked. Sheila is entitled to a private life." Tony thought living in such a small county was akin to a tightrope walk. He often knew more about his neighbors than he wanted to. "She hasn't said anything to me about Not Bob or her mama."

"It's almost time for Blossom's wedding." Theo smiled. "I can't wait to see her dress and her cake."

Blossom and her extraordinary gown filled the front of the church. Constructed of ivory-draped satin, the dress had ruffles and bows and silk roses all over it. Theo saw a couple of love birds, thankfully artificial ones, attached to the train. Jewels. Sequins. Embroidery. If it could be sewn or glued onto fabric, it had been. Theo guessed the dress weighed almost as much as she did. Blossom wore it well. A wreath of colorful flowers anchored a sheer tulle veil, covering most of her thin, bright orange hair.

Kenny's two little girls had escorted Blossom down the aisle looking like two small lavender tugboats guiding a sparkling white ocean liner into port. Surprising Theo, and probably most of the congregation, none of Blossom's myriad sisters were attendants. Theo guessed it was easier to choose none than to choose one or two of the baker's dozen and possibly create a long-term argument within the family.

Aspen Flowers surged to her feet when Kenny reached for Blossom's hand. Her mouth opened, and two of Blossom's sisters jerked the woman down onto the pew and stuffed a handkerchief into her still open mouth. Those who witnessed the brief episode smiled and nodded their approval.

Ruby was the only adult female attendant, stunningly gorgeous, as usual, in a simple purple gown. There was sure to be a bit of good-natured complaining from her friends about the lack of lasting baby weight. Theo thought it was really not fair. Theo's babies were already ten months old, and she still had another ten pounds of baby weight to lose.

Surprising everyone, Kenny had asked DuWayne Cozzens to be his best man and DuWayne had accepted. Their rivalry for Blossom's hand had been public and avidly scrutinized. From the outside, the two men seemed evenly matched. The county residents had been keeping score. Every present one of the men gave to Blossom, each date, dance, and glance, was discussed endlessly over coffee at Ruby's Café, in hair salons, at the grocery store, and daily at the quilt shop. Privacy was impossible. Until she made her decision, Blossom's choice of grooms could have gone either way.

Knowing the number of times Blossom had delivered a pie to Tony, especially during her very public courtship, Theo leaned closer to Tony. Her husband was probably as close to a confidant as Blossom had. "Did you guess she'd choose Kenny?"

Tony shook his head. "Did you?"

"No." Theo smiled at the happy couple moving back down the aisle, rings exchanged and vows made. The newly married couple held hands and moved slowly toward the front of the church, stopping from time to time to greet a person special to one or the other. Both looked radiantly happy. Behind them the lavender girls skipped and pretended to toss more flower petals to the congregation. When they strolled past Aspen, Blossom reached down and pulled the handkerchief from her cousin's mouth. Defeated, Aspen slumped on the pew.

The reception was simple. Everyone gathered in the church's fellowship hall. The normally utilitarian room had been transformed by Blossom's sisters into a bridal bower. They might not have been the attendants, but they had worked together on the decorations as a group gift. Tablecloths, floral centerpieces, and lace and lavender tulle swags were draped around the room and attached to the walls with tiny purple birds and sequined wedding bells.

Punch bowls and platters of food covered the serving tables. A chocolate fountain, set up on one side of the room, was surrounded by various cake bits, cookies, and fruits and marshmallows, and was the favorite treat of the horde of children. Some decided against catching the melted chocolate on treats and simply stuck their fingers into the dripping stream of chocolate. Theo laughed, watching her boys enjoying the treats. There was enough chocolate drippage and spillage to conduct a national test for stain removers.

Blossom Flowers Baines had baked her own wedding cake. As highly decorated as the bride and almost as large, the huge confection could serve everyone in the county and still have leftovers. Glancing at the crowd, Theo guessed there were not many residents of Silersville who were not in attendance. Even so, there was plenty of cake. It wasn't just immense, it was decadently delicious.

Next to it sat the only slightly smaller groom's cake, a red velvet creation shaped and decorated to resemble Kenny's new, fire engine red, four-door pickup. Tony whispered, "It looks life-sized."

Theo watched Tony eat at least three slices of cake, starting with the bride's white cake, moving to the groom's red velvet, and back again to the white. Whatever Blossom put in the icing and between the delectable layers was sinful, addicting, and Theo had to force herself not to lick the plate. At least not in front of witnesses.

Nina and her date, Doctor Looks-so-good, congratulated the happy couple and came to stand near Theo.

"What does she put in those cakes?" Nina scraped her spoon across a barren plate.

"I don't know." Theo ran a finger across the almost spotless surface of her plate and licked it. "It's probably illegal so let's not ask."

"Are they going away on their honeymoon?"

Theo nodded. "They are keeping the destination a secret, but Kenny's folks are going to be staying with the girls."

"I'm not sure I've ever met his family." Nina glanced around.

"Is that them standing with the Flowers women?"

The couple in question was indeed Kenny's family. They were smiling broadly. The couple, surrounded by the whole contingent of Blossom's sisters with their families, filled one end of the large room.

Theo and Nina were so busy eating and chatting, they weren't paying close attention to everything around them. A flurry of activity and laughter made them turn, just in time to see Blossom's bouquet flying through the air. Nina caught it reflexively to prevent it from hitting her in the face.

The resulting cheer and applause made Nina's face turn scarlet. Theo laughed. The color really didn't match the red in her friend's hair. Doctor Looks-so-good managed a grin. Theo was getting desperate to pump her best friend for information. Did Blossom know something? If so, how dare Nina not share with Theo!

"They say there's someone for everyone." Theo stared at a couple standing near the cakes.

"Who's *they*?" Tony was distracted, watching something on the other side of the room. He thought he saw his new groupie disappear behind a lavender swag. Either the woman went everywhere he did or his imagination was running amok.

"I don't know." Theo had on her highest heeled shoes and still could barely see over the children. "But there's Quentin standing with a girl. And he's talking to her."

"No kidding. So it did work." Tony turned so fast he almost knocked his wife over. He grabbed her upper arms to stabilize her as she teetered on her fancy shoes. He looked down, smiling into her eyes. "Are you all right?"

"Well, at least I have your attention now." Theo was clearly curious about what he was finding so fascinating. "What worked? What's going on?"

"I'm not sure. There's some kind of fracas over near the cakes."

"Oh, no, you'd better hurry over there." She waved her open hands, palms facing him, shaking in mock despair. "What if they get cakenapped or eaten by dinosaurs?"

He leaned over and kissed her neck, just below her ear. "Mock me, my pretty, and I won't introduce you to Quentin's date." He was gratified to hear her sharp intake of breath. Before he could say more, his cell phone vibrated in his pocket. "Hold on." He pressed the phone tightly against his ear. "What was it? When? Is everyone all right?"

Theo looked disappointed. "Do you have to leave?"

"No." He tried to look worried, but doubted he was doing a good job of it. Good news made his acting pitiful. "Katti had her baby and named it Pumpkin. Everyone is fine."

"And?" Theo laughed. "What's the baby's real name?"

Tony couldn't tease her anymore. "Danielle. Marmot the varmint has a baby girl."

Roscoe and his wife, Veronica, strolled by just in time to hear the news. "Well, if Claude Marmot and I can find a wife, surely there's hope for Quentin." His wide smile displayed sparkling white, straight teeth.

Theo gasped. "Your teeth!" Roscoe was famous for having some of the worst teeth in the county. Had, now, past tense. "They're beautiful!"

"Yes, ma'am, they are mine." Roscoe grinned. "Bought and paid for. Nina's man gave me a discount. Says I'm good advertising."

The change in his appearance was stunning. "You're a handsome man now."

Veronica winked at Theo. "I always told him so."

The Coffin Quilt
Final Body of Clues

Lay out blocks three across and five down. Starting with Block 1.

Layout sequence is 1/2/1, 2/1/2, 1/2/1, 2/1/2, and last row 1/2/1. Rotate the block 1's to have the center four patch blocks all pointing the same direction. Sew top together.

Measure through center and both edges of length. Hopefully the measurements will be the same. Cut 2 1/2" wide strips of fabric (B) to the average those measurements. Cut 2.

Repeat measuring process with the width and cutting 2 1/2" strips. Sew 2 1/2" square of fabric (D) on each end of the shorter strips. Make 2.

Sew long strips of (A) on the long sides of quilt. Press to border. Add the short strips with corner squares to top and bottom. Press to border.

Repeat process with 4 1/2" wide strips of (A) and 4 1/2" squares of (D).

Quilt as desired and bind with 2 1/2" strips of (A).

Chapter Twenty-Four

"An outbreak of ghosts?" Tony stared at Matt Barney, his recent opponent in the sheriff's election. "You make it sound like the measles."

Barney didn't smile. "I don't believe you're taking this seriously. Maybe I can start a petition to have you removed from office."

Tony pretended he hadn't heard the idiotic statement. In spite of a couple of editorials in the *Silersville Gazette,* he'd won the sheriff's job by a landslide in August. "Even if we are having a paranormal invasion, just what do you suggest needs to be done about it? They aren't stealing cars or silverware."

"How can you be so sure? I heard that Old Nem's hens quit laying."

Without any facts to the contrary, Tony assumed that if indeed there were no eggs, it was more likely it was because the hens were ancient like their owner. "No one has complained to me about it, and the county egg production is actually not one of the myriad jobs of *my* office."

"Your office?" Barney lunged to his feet. "This office belongs to the people, the citizens of this county."

"Okay, then, get out of the citizens' office." Tony surged to his feet. Matt Barney was not a small man, but Tony was taller, and younger, and had an array of weapons at his disposal.

"I'll go," said Barney. He narrowed his eyes. "But I'm going from here straight to the newspaper. I think the citizens have a right to know what you think of them."

Tony hated arguing, especially with someone incapable of reason. "If they wanted you in this office, they would have voted for you. Now, get out. I have work to do."

He settled down to study the reports faxed to him.

It had taken much longer than hoped for but, at last, the smudged fingerprints on the thermos found in the airplane were identified by a North Carolina latent print specialist. They belonged to none other than Carl Lee Cashdollar, and were partially entangled with those of the café waitress.

Tony couldn't imagine a motive for Carl Lee to be involved in his father's death. Why kill a man whom you rarely saw and against whom you *said* you had no animosity? Tony's lack of imagination did not make his friend innocent or guilty.

He and Wade dropped into the lawyer's office without making an appointment. Carl Lee looked busy but not concerned about their visit. "What's up?"

"Your fingerprints turned up on a thermos filled with coffee in the airplane. The one your father jumped from." Tony didn't ask a question or mention that the tests for extra substances in the coffee were not finished yet. He simply watched and waited.

Carl Lee stared unwaveringly, meeting Tony's eyes. Silence. A single shake of his head was his response.

Tony said, "Did I ever tell you about an incident I was involved in as a rookie cop in Chicago?"

Surprise lit the attorney's eyes. Another shake of his head.

"My partner and I got a call to a high-rise apartment building. We were only around the corner and easily the first to arrive on the scene. A man's body lay face-down on the sidewalk. It was not pretty and it was obvious, even to a rookie, that he had fallen farther than a single story. We glance up. I'm not sure why, but it's what we all do. It's a good thing we did, because we had to jump back to avoid having a suitcase bash us as it fell. It was followed by three white dress shirts in their store wrappings and a gift box containing a bottle of very expensive women's perfume." Tony paused. He hadn't planned to tell this story, but he might as well finish.

Carl Lee shifted on his chair. He was listening carefully to the story. "And?"

Wade sat silent.

"The detectives arrived. We pointed out the window the items had fallen from, or actually been dropped from, up on the eighth floor. We had counted. And a couple of the detectives headed up to chat with the woman in the apartment."

Carl Lee was leaning forward now.

"So, Max and I are guarding the body and taking names of the curious when this beautiful woman steps forward and she says, 'That perfume is mine. I want it.' " Tony suddenly felt like he was back on the sidewalk, half nauseated by the heat of the day and the smell of blood. "I asked her how she knew it was hers, and she says to me, 'That's my husband, and we live on the fourth floor of this building. Every time he goes out of town on business, he always takes three new white shirts and brings me a bottle of perfume when he comes home.' " Tony shrugged, wondering again why he was telling this story. "So that's how she knew it was her perfume."

Carl Lee and Wade both stared at him. Their identical expressions of confusion and befuddlement said it all. He was exhausted and still paddling upstream.

"Okay, I didn't tell the story right. The man never left the building. Let's forget I ever mentioned it." Tony opened his notebook and looked into his friend's face. "Your fingerprints are on the thermos, so I know you had to touch it. I'm going to sit here until you tell me when and why."

Carl Lee flinched but nodded. He began recounting his steps, speaking softly but out loud. "I had to go to Asheville on business, but I wasn't sure I'd need to spend the night. I took an overnight bag just in case I did." He sighed. "So I called my father after I was already in my hotel. We made plans to have breakfast together. He told me where to pick him up. The next morning, I showered, checked my email, and then I drove over and found him waiting in his car. It was parked right where he said he'd be. He climbed out of his car and into mine, and I drove both of us to the café. He said there was no sense in having two vehicles parked in the same lot." Carl Lee paused, thinking, then smiled, clearly relieved. "Now I remember. Dad had his thermos with him because he said he'd opened it while he was waiting for me to arrive and accidently spilled a lot of the coffee and wanted to top it off while we were at the café. We ate our breakfast, and just before we paid the check and headed back to his car, he passed his thermos to the waitress and headed to the restroom. She topped it off with the coffee in the pot she carried, and I took it and screwed the lid back in and set it next to his plate." Carl Lee tried to smile but failed. "My father was a coffee fiend. He drank it by the gallon."

The story made perfect sense and Tony believed it. That didn't mean he wouldn't check with the waitress on his upcoming return visit to North Carolina. "What was the name of the café?"

"My working idea is that something in the coffee made Franklin think he could fly. It would be easy enough for someone who knew about his coffee addiction to add a little something to the thermos." Tony looked up from the growing file. "What do you think, Wade?"

"Sure, it's possible. Franklin seemed to have some definite patterns." Wade looked up. "Let's say someone who knew about his coffee addiction added something to the thermos. They may or may not have known about the fishing trip. Maybe they expected a traffic accident to cover up the poisoning."

Tony leaned back in his chair and swallowed a big gulp of his own coffee. "Franklin drank the drug-laced coffee, and even though it was diluted by the café coffee, maybe there was enough of the substance to make Franklin think he could fly, without a plane."

Wade nodded. "So he unbuckled the airplane seat's harness and climbed out of the plane, maybe thinking he was on the ground at his fishing destination. And splat. The end."

"We need to find out where the thermos was before the coffee spill." Tony felt sure the report would show there was something extra in the contents.

"I see a trip over the mountains in my future." Wade stared into his empty cup. "Let's do it."

"Yep. Grab your pen and toothbrush; we're going back to North Carolina. There are too many gaps and detours. Someone knows about his transportation and also why this happened. I do not believe this was a suicide. Period."

Tony called North Carolina and set up a meeting with their liaison. Sergeant Dupont sounded happy to accompany them around the county and promised the weather would be better for this trip to North Carolina.

It was. They made the trip easily. Wade drove while Tony alternated between writing notes to himself and getting updates on his smart phone. "Uh-oh, this report shoots another theory." Tony didn't give Wade a chance to reply. "The laboratory reports show there was nothing in the thermos but coffee and water. Even the water had only the normal minerals for this area."

"Man, I was so sure the coffee had to be laced with goofy juice of some kind." Wade's head moved from side to side.

"Something that made him think he had wings of his own."

"Me, too." Tony released a long slow sigh. "I thought there would be diluted drugs or gasoline or something that would make him lose touch with reality."

"It's crazy, the whole business. Or rather, he did something crazy." Wade kept his eyes on the turns in the road. "Unless he wasn't crazy but was frightened or upset enough to just jump."

"Suicide?" Tony had to admit there wasn't any reason to rule it out entirely. Families were so often bewildered when they were given the news. "The autopsy didn't show anything like advanced cancer or other medical conditions that might inspire him to shorten his own life."

"Maybe someone over here will be able to add some insight."

"Won't hurt to ask." For no particular reason, and certainly without evidence, Tony did not believe the suicide theory. He was convinced the man had deliberately, and with malice aforethought, been murdered. He couldn't see how or why or by whom.

"Was Franklin prone to impulsive decisions?" Tony thought they'd start with the second wife, this time. Tony felt like they were getting nowhere. Maybe during their return visit, Joyce would be ready to share secrets with them. "Not a chance!" Joyce Cashdollar snorted as she laughed. "That's just too funny!" The more she laughed, the funnier she seemed to find Tony's question.

"It's been awhile since your divorce." Tony hadn't realized he was such a comedian. "Could he have changed? You know, loosened up a bit after retiring from the Army?"

Joyce calmed and gave his question serious consideration. "Not likely. I'll admit we haven't spent any time together, you know, really, in years. He could have, you know, if he'd had a stroke or something. Otherwise, no."

Tony shifted in his chair, sensing she had something else to say.

"His attitude kept him from being a brilliant leader and working his way up. Once he made colonel, it became clear that was as far up as he was going. He would never be a general, much less the general of generals." Joyce twisted the large diamond engagement ring on her finger. "Once, in an interview with his superiors, they told him they needed a leader who, as the saying goes, could think outside the box. Franklin wanted the box, a lock, and a key, but lacked the magic touch."

"What about personally? Did he ever talk about his relationships with his son or first wife, or, now, the third wife?" Tony didn't feel like they were getting any closer to understanding the man or what motivated him.

"When we were dating, he talked some. Franklin didn't go into the details of their lives or relationships. I think he loved his son and first wife very much, but he kept his feelings and memories of them carefully contained." Joyce shook her head. "I never heard of him losing control of anything."

Tony couldn't help but wonder about the eventual cost of living such a tightly organized life in a world filled with random events. He asked Joyce about the flexibility issue. "How had he dealt with plans made based on factors out of his control, like an inaccurate weather forecast?"

"Shockingly poorly," Joyce said. "It was very difficult for him to change plans on the fly. He was a very intelligent man, but he would sit and think and rethink until he came up with an acceptable new plan. One time we were traveling from San Francisco back to Tennessee to collect Carl Lee, and the flight was cancelled; some equipment issue." Her lips squeezed tight. "It was not good. Franklin stared at the screen, the one flashing 'cancelled,' then looked at me, and I could tell he had no idea what to do next. I took our tickets to the rebooking station and got us new flights. He never said a word."

"That's a beautiful ring," Wade interrupted. "You didn't mention your engagement the last time we visited."

Joyce's lips tightened. "It didn't seem appropriate at the time." Her eyes widened as she realized what he was implying. "How did you know?"

"You failed to tell your fiancé the engagement was secret."

"Oh." A slight shake of the head was the end of her statement.

Sergeant Dupont was running toward them, waving a paper and laughing. He climbed into the back seat of Wade's patrol car. "Look at this." He held out a photograph of Gentry Frazier driving through an intersection near the airstrip. The time and date on it was during the time he should have been flying Franklin Cashdollar over the mountains. "He wasn't flying the plane."

"Let's go back to chat with the supposed pilot." Tony checked his notebook. "Who would know better than he what happened?"

"Gentry Frazier didn't immediately report the accident," said Dupont. "Now we know it was because he wasn't involved. Didn't see it happen."

"Who do you suppose *was* flying the airplane?" Wade asked.

Dupont shook his head. "Gentry might not have known about it until Mrs. C. needed proof her husband was dead. She wanted a body because there's a funeral to plan and an estate needing proof of death."

"Murder for hire?" Wade suggested.

"I don't think so. Maybe it could have been some revenge business between the pilot and Cashdollar. No wonder Gentry was in a snit."

"He didn't want to rat out a friend and didn't want to take the fall." Tony considered the ramifications. "It looks bad either way—covering up a crime or just ignoring it."

"What if he really doesn't know what happened?" Dupont sighed. "Let's say you loan a friend your car, he drives it out of state, picks up a sack full of stolen pharmaceuticals, comes home, and gives you back your car."

Tony picked up the thread. "So one afternoon, you come out of your office, ready to get home to the family, and the local drug dog is staring at your car. The vehicle is surrounded by crime scene tape and a group of happy cops."

"The dog's handler is smiling like he just won the lottery," said Wade.

"You know you haven't done anything wrong, but you can guess someone did, and left you with the evidence of a crime." Tony had heard of real cases of just that type of bad behavior. "What do you do? If you accuse your friend and he denies it, you figure you're screwed. So you call him and he offers to try to help cover it up."

"Only instead of helping, he makes it worse." Dupont's voice was a rumble of sound. "I don't know about you, but I'd be mad or scared or some bad combination of the two. So, I'm out on bail, and I confront my friend, insisting he go with me to the cops. He refuses and calls me every name in the book, so I whack him with a golf club and he still won't confess. Now I'm guilty of assault."

Tony couldn't disagree. "Or maybe it doesn't go that far. Maybe there's not enough evidence to convict you, but if you can't get your friend to confess and you haven't been convicted, at least not yet, but everyone is looking at you like you're scum, no one will trust you, and then your business heads for the toilet."

It was Wade's turn to add to the story. "About the time you've severed all ties and offended your friends, you learn that the drugs were not stolen by your buddy but actually by your wife's ne'er-do-well cousin, and he was storing them in your car. You turn him in. Soon you've got no friends, your wife is leaving, and even the dog won't talk to you."

"We've been in this business too long." Tony laughed. "But, there is always the chance that someone will man up and say, 'I've been so bad. Please, lock me up.' "

"Dreamer." Wade and Dupont ended the story together.

"We find it very interesting that you claim to have flown Franklin over the mountains, but we found a traffic camera with your car and your face driving through an intersection when you claim to have been in the airplane, somewhere over the mountains." Tony stared into the charter pilot's face. "Care to explain?"

"I was scheduled to be the pilot." Gentry Frazier sagged onto a folding chair. "Cashdollar was insistent about taking the old biplane, and I tried to talk him out of it."

"Why?" Wade looked up from his notebook.

"The weather turned so cold. I'm sure I told you I have a written policy where it says we don't take passengers up in an open plane if the temperature is below sixty on the ground. It's much colder up in the air." Gentry's hands trembled as he spread them in the air, palms down. "Here's why I didn't want to go up."

Tony saw the man's swollen knuckles. Arthritis. "So what happened that day?"

"It was so cold. My hands throbbed even with the fur-lined gloves on, and we hadn't even taken off yet. Smith volunteered to fly him. So I thought it would be okay, even though Smith doesn't have more than a private plane license. He's flown the old plane a lot; he's just not certified for charter. If it was discovered, I could lose my business."

"So any accident would not be covered by your insurance?"

Gentry nodded. "Truly I thought he'd be safer with Smith

than with me and my stiff fingers. They took off. Cashdollar had his fishing gear and his thermos. That's normal for him."

"Did he behave in his usual manner?"

"Yeah." Gentry's eyes widened as if he had just remembered something. "Actually, no. He seemed a bit off, you know, confused maybe. It did occur to me that he might have had a little stroke, because he sort of leaned to one side as he walked to the plane. Nothing major though."

"Did you ask him if he was ill?" Tony studied the older man.

"Not exactly, but I did ask if he'd rather go later and his answer was no, let's go."

Wade said, "And then what happened?"

"Smith came back with the airplane an hour or so later. Surprised me. I expected him to stay over and wait for Cashdollar to do his fishing. That's the usual way it goes." Frazier breathed hard, almost panting. "Smith said Cashdollar suddenly freaked out, starting yelling something Smith couldn't hear, and then climbed out onto the wing. And jumped."

"And you didn't call to report it?" Dupont's lips turned down in a frown.

"No. I was shocked and worried, so I took a different plane and flew over the area where Smith said he'd jumped. Smith's description made it easy to spot." Frazier massaged his hands as if they were still cold, then looked from face to face. "I swear, I didn't see Cashdollar anywhere, and I hoped he'd been picked up by someone and taken to the hospital if he was injured. Stranger things have happened, you know. He could have bounced off a tree or landed in a bush. There were acres of trees surrounding a small bald."

"And then, much later than the time you said he jumped, you finally reported it." Tony leaned close. "Why, if you waited this long, when you did call—why lie about the time?"

"Smith was frantic. He kept saying it happened at nine. But I was afraid I'd been seen over here and didn't want to admit I wasn't flying the plane so I fudged the time." Frazier started gasping for air. "I can't lose my business."

Tony's cell phone vibrated in his pocket. The local sheriff. He brushed his finger over the screen to answer. He didn't get the chance to say a word.

"Tony, you'll never guess what we just found." Tony's North Carolina counterpart was laughing. "Good news! We've got the Cashdollar Land Rover."

"Where was it?" Tony couldn't imagine how the thing had managed to stay hidden so long. With traffic cameras and patrols looking everywhere for it. It wasn't exactly a bicycle. "We never saw a sign of it."

"Well, his son told us where he'd picked his dad up, right?"

"Right. But the car wasn't there." Tony had wondered if Carl Lee was mistaken about the parking spot. "And the traffic cameras didn't show the Land Rover going anywhere."

"True. We just located it a bit further from town in a different parking area. That dark green car was way up under some fir tree branches and the weight of the snow had lowered those." The sheriff laughed. "It had its own little hidey-hole."

"Any idea how it got out there?" Tony rubbed his neck. "Carl Lee was very adamant about the location."

"Oh, I have something even better. Something that explains a lot of our questions. Now we think it probably was left just where Cashdollar's son claimed, and when. Our tech is busy with her fingerprint stuff, but there's a new sticker on the windshield, you know, like they put in to show when you need your next oil change."

Tony liked the sound of this. "And?"

"And right there on the front passenger seat is a receipt from the quickie oil change station, dated the day of the flight," the sheriff said. "Most of our search on the camera recordings has been concentrated on the known time of his flight. None of us expected the car to move after he died."

"An oil change?" Tony felt like he'd just been dropped from an airplane himself. "Doesn't sound like something you'd do if you were not planning to return."

"Dupont is on his way to pick you up again. He begged to be assigned to go along with you."

Dupont was smiling when he collected Tony and Wade. "This is the damnedest thing I ever heard of. We're going on a little tour." First he drove to the site where the Land Rover was supposed to have been parked. "We'll start here." He read the number on the odometer and then drove past the front gate of the small airfield, then turned left onto a quiet two-lane road. No traffic at all. Crossing an intersection, he pointed at a traffic camera. "Just after nine in the morning, the Land Rover came through here. It took an unbelievable number of man-hours to find it. Okay now, we're almost there." Before they reached the next intersection, he turned into a drive-up oil and lube business.

They all traipsed inside. Dupont said, "Can we talk to the manager?"

"That's me, sort of. The owner isn't here. I'm Jeremy." The young man squinted at the threesome, all in uniforms. "Y'all need an oil change?"

"No. We need to ask about one recently done here." Tony thought Jeremy didn't look scared. But Tony thought having the three uniforms lined up facing him made him a bit jumpy. Tony pulled out a photo of the Land Rover. "Does this vehicle look familiar?"

"Oh, yeah, a big white dude in a suit brought it in and had the oil changed. I remember 'cause he was wearin' white gloves.

We don't see much of that." Jeremy frowned. "An' he was too busy talking on his cell to look up at me."

Tony couldn't imagine that description would fit anyone besides the butler. "Anything you noticed besides his bad manners?"

"Naw. He paid me and then dumped his trash in the barrel and took off."

"I don't suppose the trash is still here?" Tony thought he'd ask.

"Nossir. It gets emptied every night. There's always lots of fast-food trash. Starts to smell, you know." Jeremy paused, looking curious. "Lookin' for somethin' special?"

Tony felt like he was about to win the lottery. He tried to guess what the killer used. "Maybe a thermos or a travel cup?"

Jeremy looked thoughtful, like he wasn't sure what to say, then softly, "I mighta found somethin' like that."

"I could tell your parole officer you've been very helpful." Sergeant Dupont stepped forward. "Never hurts to have someone put in a good word."

"I ain't done nothin' with it. You know, like washed it. Thought I might give it to my girlfriend." Jeremy reached under the counter and pulled out a white ceramic travel cup with a sip-through lid. "Ain't real pricey, but why toss it?"

Tony gently placed it into an evidence bag and made a few notes. Then he sincerely thanked young Jeremy for his help. An expression of pleased surprise had the young man's mouth agape.

The three men went back to Dupont's vehicle.

"So, from roughly nine in the morning to at least ten, maybe, the butler had the vehicle and a set of keys." Tony checked the list of things found on the body. "He was not using Mr. Cashdollar's keys, though, because they were found among his personal possessions."

"Was that pre-planned, do you think?" Dupont stared at the cup. "Let's see if someone downtown is willing to run a quick analysis to see if there has been something other than coffee and water in this container."

"My thought exactly." Dupont headed his car downtown.

"I've got some very interesting findings from the lab about the travel cup," Dupont said. "They did some quick checks on a couple of things. The full report's not in."

Tony thought Dupont sounded downright giddy. "What's up?" Tony, sitting at a borrowed desk, had been busy trying to run his office in Tennessee over the telephone.

"There are four different people's fingerprints on it. The techs started with people connected with this case. Of course the first ones they identified are our new best friend, Jeremy-the-lube wizard, and Franklin Cashdollar."

"The butler wore gloves. So, maybe the cook." Tony smiled. "And who?"

"Mrs. Laura Dill Cashdollar herself."

"No way." Tony was shocked. Not surprised that she might have wanted her husband dead, but that she actually had touched the cup. Any halfway decent attorney would claim she would naturally have touched her husband's cup as a matter of course and get it dismissed as evidence. "And the contents? Anything?"

"Those tests aren't complete but they have found a lot more ingredients than water and coffee. Some kind of a drug cocktail. Weird stuff mixed together."

Tony said, "I have to call our prosecutor. I doubt our little county can handle a high-profile case like this one. It sounds like a conspiracy."

Tony, Wade, and Dupont sat in a small chamber with mechanic and under-licensed pilot, John Smith. Smith had been offered an attorney, which he rather smugly refused, so cameras and recording devices were busy recording every word and itch and twitch. "First, why don't you tell us all how you did it? We're always interested in a good yarn." Tony smiled benignly, "Just begin at the beginning. How'd he get to the airfield?"

Smith looked surprised. "Had to drive himself out there in that expensive car of his, don't you think?"

"And parked it at the airfield?" Wade looked skeptical.

Smith nodded, but with less confidence. "I mean, wouldn't he? The man was totally obsessed with his car and so whiny about not wanting anyone to scratch it."

Tony half-believed this part of the story because he knew Franklin had a reputation for worrying about scratches. But if he drove to the airstrip, how did the car end up where Carl Lee reported leaving his father and, still more oddly, where the vehicle was found. Loose ends or more lies?

"So, how *did* you plan to kill him?" Tony slipped an antacid from his pocket and popped it into his mouth.

"I knew he'd come back for another fishing day." A smile turned up the corners of Smith's mouth. "People with too much money and no real work to keep them busy are so predictable."

Tony decided John Smith had no filter on his mouth. He thought it, he said it. Tony wrote himself a note. It was not a trait he'd personally want in a co-conspirator. Who would trust this man? The recording equipment would keep track of all details of the interview, but it didn't know what his thoughts were. This note said, "Whines too much."

John Smith looked relaxed, a rarity in this situation. Usually, unless they were too stupid to live anyway, the suspects he'd dealt with had twitched, itched, and wiggled all over the uncomfortable chairs. Occasionally a suspect would spend hours slouched in a position that made Tony's own spine scream just looking at it.

"What was the plan?" Wade tightened his grip on his pen.

"My wife's mother has more aches, pains, and medicines than anyone I've ever seen before." Simple disgust twisted Smith's handsome face. "It was so simple. I just took a couple of pills from each of her jars, you know, and she'd still have enough to keep her happy and I could slip them into Cashdollar's coffee."

"Poison?" Tony asked for clarification.

"No, no, I wanted him alive and conscious. I just didn't want him at his best. Franklin Cashdollar was a fighting machine. He wasn't a young bull anymore, but he stayed fit."

Tony wrote, "coward." He was developing zero empathy for the man. "So you drugged him so it would be easier for you to dump the man, alive but semi-conscious, from an airplane? With no parachute?"

"Yes." Smith hesitated for the first time and looked Tony directly in the eyes. He managed to look aggrieved. "Well, put it like that and it sounds a bit harsh, don't you think?"

What Tony thought was getting increasingly harsh. Having an official laboratory report that there were no drugs in the thermos of coffee, Tony knew this confession was either nothing but a smokescreen, or they still hadn't found everything they needed. Somehow, Smith seemed very sure he could lie about how he killed Franklin and then not be convicted of the crime. Tony was curious about how that would happen. He could play the game for a while longer. "Let's go on. So you drugged Cashdollar and then flew him over to Tennessee and then what?"

"Well, I didn't have to do much. He was really zoned out. I told him to unbuckle his harness, and he did. Then I told him to hang onto his fly rod and he did. So, well, I did a barrel roll with the plane and he fell out."

"How did you know you'd be flying that plane?" Tony understood the switch in pilots had been a last-minute decision.

Smith scratched his ear and focused on the ceiling for a while. "I, uh, well, that is, I said to the boss that I would do it."

Even though it was pretty much what Tony had expected, he sat, frozen in his chair. He believed this part of the confession. Tony thought Smith was extraordinarily calm and seemed rather pleased with himself for making a plan and having it work. The man was a stone-cold killer, at least in his own mind.

Wade said, "This doesn't seem to bother you."

Smith looked up then. "It's not like I worked alone on this. It wasn't my fault. I was just the delivery boy. I did it. I killed Franklin Cashdollar." John Smith said the words but his face showed nothing, not guilt, fear, repentance. "Lock me up. I served under that S.O.B. twenty years ago." Smith glared, the embers of an old grudge still burning bright in his eyes.

"Was he a bad officer?" Tony hadn't loved every officer he'd dealt with, but none had gotten him killed and none had left him with a residue of hatred.

"Militarily, he was all right, I guess. Solid, unimaginative, probably better with his paperwork than with people."

"Did you consider him foolhardy?" Some officers had the reputation, whether deserved or not, of incurring unnecessary losses.

"No. Can't say I have any details. Never got the idea he was prone to tossing his men into a hole. It was his personal life I had an issue with." John Smith's hands balled into fists. "He stole my girlfriend at the time."

Tony's eyes focused on the mechanic's wedding ring. "Did you win her back?"

Smith looked confused for a moment. "Oh, no, I married someone else."

"Children?"

"Sure, we have a couple of kids." Smith caught up with the conversation. "Doesn't mean I can't be mad. She was my girl."

Tony was fascinated in spite of his revulsion. "Who do you consider to be more guilty than yourself?"

"Well, Frazier, for one. He shouldn't have let me fly. Mrs. Cashdollar, for the other." Smith shifted on his uncomfortable chair. "I mean, after all, it wasn't my idea."

There was something so honest about his criminal behavior, Tony believed him. Smith really didn't think he'd done anything particularly illegal or immoral because it wasn't his idea. And lying to protect the guilty? He'd eventually figure out it wasn't a smart decision. Tony assumed Smith was paid well for confessing. But by whom? "Let's take a break, shall we?"

Tony wanted more information. "Now that we have a time frame, let's see what else your camera wizard can find."

CHAPTER TWENTY-FIVE

The camera technician truly seemed like a wizard. His long fingers ran over the keyboard like a hyperactive spider, bringing up various cameras on the route, in a range of dates and times.

"Thank goodness the man drove something easy to pick out of a blurry group of vehicles speeding through a snowstorm." The wizard grinned. "Look at this."

Tony, Wade, and Dupont all leaned closer to the computer screen. The date and time on the recording showed the car was parked, as Carl Lee had said, at the time he'd returned his father to the spot.

"Pause." Tony blinked, focusing on a smudged figure opening the passenger door and putting something inside moments after Carl Lee departed. "Who is that?"

"Too fuzzy." Wade stared. "The coat has some kind of hood, and we've got nothing but the back."

"See here?" The technician touched the screen with his forefinger. "A little later, this guy gets into the car and drives away."

"Where does it go?" Tony stared at the image. "The airstrip or headed for an oil change?"

Wade asked, "And when does it come back?"

"Hopefully I'll be able to let you know the answers to both of your questions. First, I need to find the vehicle again." The wizard tipped his head toward some folding chairs. "Help yourself. There's coffee in the pot."

Like three men at the movie matinee, Tony, Wade, and Dupont sat on their chairs, watching the ever-changing pictures on the screen.

"Okay, we've got a shot of the driver's face." The wizard froze the image on the screen. "Anyone recognize this guy?"

Tony studied it. The picture was not flawless, but it was good enough. "We've met. He's the Cashdollar butler."

"Damn you say?" The tech expert leaned closer. "You mean you've actually got a case where the butler did it?"

"Well, he's driving the car. It looks like it might have only been his job to get the oil changed." Tony wasn't prepared to claim victory. "What's near this intersection?"

"What time is it on the recording?"

"How long before it's returned to the parking space?"

"Take it easy gentlemen." The tech raised his hands in mock surrender. "Sooner or later we'll have a fair idea where, who, and when."

Tony thought the tech had a good point. "Let's leave this to the expert and go see what the butler has to say."

The butler answered the door. He didn't look happy to see them.

"May we come in?" Dupont smiled and indicated the others with him. "You remember our good friends from Tennessee."

"Shall I announce you?" Anderson calmly stepped back to let them enter. "Madam might be busy."

"Let's start our conversation with you." Tony carefully closed the door behind himself. "We've got a few questions about the day Mr. Cashdollar died."

"Yessir?" Anderson stood at attention, his gloved hands clasped at the small of his back.

"You delivered Mr. Cashdollar to the airport?"

"No. I only went to have his car serviced."

"Where did you pick it up?"

"Not far from the airfield. He was very particular about his parking. He had breakfast with his son."

"And? After the oil change? What did you do then?" Tony watched the play of light on his face.

The butler's jaw tensed but he said nothing.

Tony stared at the butler. "Why not park it where it had been?"

Anderson blinked once. Only the movement of his eyelids showed he was alive. "I did."

"We'd like to talk with Mrs. Cashdollar now." Tony wasn't satisfied. The butler's answers filled in some holes and left others. They followed him through the house to a smaller room than the one they'd met in earlier.

The lady of the house was polite, but decidedly less friendly than before as she looked up from her magazine. "Anderson?"

"Madam, you have insistent visitors."

"Yes, there is a whole group of us." Dupont led the way into the room and the three lawmen lined up near the doorway, pulling Anderson inside and closing ranks behind him.

Tony glanced at their surroundings. It was not the huge, uncomfortable room of their previous visits. This evening they had been shown into a much smaller, lighter, and very feminine room. The walls were covered with pale yellow fabric. Tony wouldn't be surprised to learn it was silk. The chairs and chaise lounge were clearly antiques, French was his guess. The elegant fireplace was actually the main heater of the space.

"Yes?" Unlike the room, Mrs. Cashdollar seemed decidedly less welcoming. Cold.

"We've recovered some evidence that your husband was drugged, possibly poisoned, which then led to his death." Tony thought he'd just drop it out there and see if the wife or the butler jumped. "It seems there was a curious mix of coffee and chemicals in his favorite travel cup. Several prescription sleep medications."

The corner of the butler's lips turned down, and his eyes narrowed. He appeared to be seething. Tony thought he recognized the description of the cup.

The widow's face held nothing but disdain.

"Sir," the butler addressed Tony. "She asked me to take the car and have the oil changed and to be sure to throw away all of the trash in the car, including the travel cup."

Was this the truth, or words spoken in spite or vengeance? Tony waited. Wade would have spoken, but Tony shook his head. He wanted to see what happened next.

Laura Cashdollar rose to her feet. "It was a jest, a quip, not a serious offer. I was miffed at my husband. It was his favorite cup. He wouldn't be happy if he lost it." She strode toward the door only to find neither Wade nor Dupont willing to allow her to pass. She turned to walk toward the fireplace.

"Ridiculous." Speaking to her moving back, the butler stayed where he was. "Madam never banters with staff."

Tony pulled handcuffs from his jacket pocket. "Mrs. Cashdollar, I'll guess you got greedy and needed the body for insurance purposes. You'd have gotten away with his murder for hire if you'd left him up on the mountain. You are under arrest. My prosecutor's office is turning the whole thing over to the State of North Carolina. You have the right to remain silent."

Surprising all of them, she did.

Tony was delighted to have handed off the whole Cashdollar case and returned to his own state and his own office. He'd be called to North Carolina to testify at the trial, but he expected there to be years of legal mumbo jumbo. Not his problem. On the afternoon after he returned home, his cell phone rang. Dupont.

"Sheriff, I know you're dying to know this because I was," Dupont said.

"Hello to you too." Tony leaned back in his chair, positive this call wouldn't give him more work to do. "What's up?"

"You ever wonder why that Land Rover kept moving?"

"Absolutely." He did remain curious about the Land Rover's ever-changing parking situation. "Why couldn't the vehicle stay in one place?"

"Our chatty, but not too bright, Mr. Smith has shared with me. Seems the butler put it back where Mr. Cashdollar parked it, but, after she had the butler get the oil change, Mrs. C got nervous. She met Mr. Smith at the car, they moved it, and he shuttled her back and forth and handed over the keys. She did provide, um, a personal service for him before leaving him at his car and driving off. He feels cheated."

Tony started laughing, the two men said their goodbyes, and he hung up the receiver.

Ruth Ann's voice came through the doorway. "Sheriff, the report is in about the skeletons."

Tony lifted his receiver. The phone call came from a Ms. Vera Hunter in the university anthropology department. She got right to the point.

"We've done a cursory examination of your excavation contents. It's a pretty cut and dry case. All of the bones came from four bodies, nothing extra, not much disturbance or signs of animal activity. Given the bone structure and location of the discovery, we're going to say runaway slaves. The skulls showed almost all their teeth missing, even the younger ones, and many of those teeth were found along with traces of mercurous chloride in the surrounding soil." She paused, letting Tony absorb what she was saying. "In short, your people were being treated for cholera, but they died."

"Cholera?" Tony shook his head as if refusing to accept such a diagnosis. "Who has cholera in Tennessee?"

"Had, Sheriff, had. Remember, these people died over a hundred and fifty years ago. Our best guess is they were being treated with *calomel*, which is where the chemical compound would have come from."

Tony fell silent, thinking, condensing her words. "So, you think they were runaway slaves and someone tried to help them, maybe gave them medicine?"

"For all the good it did, yes." Ms. Hunter cleared her throat. "If the people helping them didn't succumb to the disease as well, it was a miracle. In those days cholera medication, if available, was sometimes more harmful than letting the disease run its course. In this case, mercury poisoning."

Tony scribbled a note about mercury. "After all these years, should we be concerned about starting another cholera epidemic by digging them up?"

"No."

It sounded like Ms. Hunter must have shuffled her papers directly into her speaker phone.

"But cholera's nothing to sneeze at. It still exists on the globe and it can kill within a few hours, so let's just say if you develop any symptoms, no matter how minor, get checked out by your doctor."

"Symptoms, like being dead?" Tony's stomach protested the sudden inflow of acid.

Ms. Hunter laughed. "No. Like diarrhea, vomiting, cramps. Don't worry; it's a highly unlikely scenario, but if it happens you'll notice you're not feeling well. Just don't ignore it. Early treatment has an almost perfect record."

"Wonderful news, doctor. Anything else?"

"Do you want your bodies back?"

"Yes. I'm sure our county can arrange to bury those people, in real graves. We don't know where they came from, but they belong in our county now. I'll have Cashdollar's Mortuary contact you."

Tony stared unseeingly at the file. These were not the first old skeletons found in the county. Almost any time someone dug a basement or there was a need to dig a trench, they might encounter old bones or ancient possessions. The bones were always reburied in the cemetery. In the rare case where possessions existed, they became the property of the landowner.

People in the past had simply buried their dead, especially in the far past when disease was rampant, and sometimes they erected no marker. Or a stone or wooden marker had been set once, but years of weather had simply caused them to disappear. Up in the higher hills, and on isolated farms, there might be a family plot, a vaguely organized, moss and lichen covered grouping of stones.

This family would receive a special reburial, in the local cemetery. The headstone would identify them as four souls known only to God.

Theo parked the twins with Maybelle, giving thanks once again for the gentle woman's assistance. Maybelle was quickly becoming acclimated to Silersville and to Kara and Lizzie. And Theo was delighted to have the assistance.

It was time for a change of pace. Theo went to pick up Miyoko. They were headed to Knoxville to reclaim Miyoko's quilt.

The couple responsible for the theft of the priceless quilt had confessed and had thrown themselves on the mercy of everyone—the court, and Miyoko. Because the quilt was undamaged and the couple so apologetic, Miyoko had agreed that six months of community service would be sufficient punishment for the otherwise law-abiding couple.

Theo knew they were lucky—the thieves and herself and the quilt's owner. There had been horrible cases of damaged or quilts stolen and lost forever. Thankfully, this one was not.

Theo looked forward to her first good night's sleep in over a week.

ABOUT THE AUTHOR

Barbara Graham has loved mysteries "forever" and wonders what could be more fun than making up people and killing them off. Legally. She began making up stories in the third grade. Being a "writer" sounds much better than being a "liar" but she considers the two words to be almost interchangeable. Born and mostly raised in the Texas Panhandle, she has lived in Denver, New Orleans, and East Tennessee before moving to Wyoming. Professional mom, ballet teacher, and travel agent are jobs in the past. Her life is filled with family, books, quilts, and a weed-infested garden. Visit her at www.bgmysteries.com